A Hot Dose of Hell

A Tale of Stark Terror

**A Stark Terror Publication
Copyright © 2021 by Steve Stark
All Rights Reserved**

**Cover and art design by
Stark Terror & Mad Dog Marty
Edited by Anonymous**

No part of this book may be reproduced, stored in a retrieval system, or transmitted by any means, electronic, mechanical, photocopying, recording or otherwise without written permission from the author
This is a work of fiction. Names, characters, places and incidents are entirely fictitious or are used fictitiously and any resemblance to actual persons, living or dead, events or locales is purely coincidental.

1

The old dresser with its warped wood and cracked mirror, had been left over from when the building was a hotel. It sat by the tall sash window, which would've provided sufficient light through the day if it weren't boarded up. So would the bare bulb overhead if there were a volt of electricity in the place.

Under the circumstances, a couple of jars stuffed with burning newspaper was the best light source Roxy Weaver could get. Not great, but at least better than those solar-charged lanterns her fellow residents used. They made everything blue. No good for makeup.

Or finding a vein.

Roxy concentrated to still her trembling hand. It maintained just long enough to trace the line of her big eyes with the Maxfactor she'd lifted from Superdrug. She wasn't sure if the shakes were due to nerves or because she needed another hit already. She'd never done this before.

Kenny said it would be easy money for a pretty girl like her and promised he'd stay nearby in case things got out of hand. Aside from the couple of times he'd scored and held out on her, Roxy felt she could probably trust him to do that much. Probably.

If not, she had a switchblade tucked in her bra strap.

Another thing Kenny said was it could sometimes be better just to roll the johns anyway. Every so often you could make a lot more money doing that, provided you chose the right target.

He told her to text him if approached by someone

fitting the bill.

Kenny had a knife too and a harsh scouse accent likely to put the shits up any average Scarmouthians. Those born and bred locals had long ago learned to fear and distrust their northern neighbours. It was a by-product of the town's booming drug trade, combined with its hopelessly scarce work opportunities.

As a rule, there was only one reason for a northerner to visit or move to Scarmouth and this gave rise to a false stereotype which simultaneously rang true. The way a local journalist most infamously put it, "Run into a northerner anywhere else in the country, odds are you won't be meeting a hardened criminal. Run into one in Scarmouth, it's unlikely they're anything but."

Roxy wasn't a Scarmouth native either. Two months ago, she'd moved from neighbouring Trenton after learning of the outreach services and charities in the area.

Turned out most of the help she'd heard about had its funding cut well before she arrived. The rest didn't exist in the first place.

Kenny reckoned it was all just propaganda, designed to herd his and Roxy's ilk out of more affluent counties to somewhere less desirable, somewhere neglected.

Whether that Westminster mob were responsible he hadn't yet decided. The only certainty for him was that it had to be the agenda of *someone* powerful. He took proof of conspiracy from just how far the disinformation had spread, for in their droves they'd arrived at Scarmouth, the derelict, the destitute, out of places as distant as Glasgow.

The migration had begun late November and in

less than two weeks they'd filled up all the beds at the town's sole shelter, half the high street doorways, all the public toilets and the bus station.

This left few places for a lone girl to bed down unharassed and during her first days in Scarmouth Roxy had been driven further and further from the town centre in search of one.

'You ready, Cinderella?'

Roxy paused and used the mirror to look at the thin shape looming in the doorless threshold behind her. If not for his distinctive accent Kenny could be anyone in the dim light, just another anonymous scarecrow silhouette in a building teeming with them.

'Almost,' she murmured.

'Don't wanna miss happy hour,' Kenny said, trying to mask his impatience, aiming for warm. But there was nothing warm about him. Roxy's initial impression that there was had been a mistake, though an understandable one considering the circumstance of their first meeting.

It was Kenny who'd found her sleeping under the pier, just a few degrees from hypothermia. His drug-abused body too frail to properly carry her, he'd simply draped Roxy's arm across his shoulders and dragged her along as best he could, all the way to the disused Victoria cliffside hotel.

The three-storey building stood alone, high up on the coast, overlooking the harbour. Throughout the '80's it'd been a major tourist destination, favourite spot of celebrities whose names didn't mean shit to anyone now.

But with Scarmouth's decline it'd fallen into debt and disrepair before being abandoned to the rats and the elements. In decades to come erosion of the cliff would send the whole thing crashing into the sea.

Until then it belonged to them, the hardcore addicts, those so caught up in the cycle that they'd given up on anything else.

Unlike the charity and council ran hostels there was no curfew here, no behavioural contract, no sanctions. Here was a roof under which a person could freely continue their casual pursuit of self-destruction.

In other words, this was the last stop.

Back in the bare, mould-infested room he claimed his own, Kenny had wrapped Roxy in a sleeping bag with a quart of vodka for company. When she was up to speaking properly, he'd said she could stay for as long as she wanted, an offer which she accepted gratefully.

That night Kenny even shared his skag with her and although it wasn't Roxy's first hit, it may as well have been for how strong it was. The stuff sold in Scarmouth was the purest she'd tasted yet and turned her baby habit into full-blown addiction on the spot.

This new, more intense need saw Roxy's use increase from a cost of thirty quid a day to nearly a hundred. Her shoplifting efforts trebled to support it and those inevitable daytrips to the cells became more unbearable than ever.

By then just three hours without a hit was enough for the sickness to seep in like the rising tide and drag her under, twisting her stomach in knots so tight that if tied by hands it would cause friction burns to the palms.

In Roxy's experience the pigs were rarely all that sympathetic toward junkies, especially thieving junkies. In Scarmouth they proved no different and her delirious convulsions on the cold stone floor went ignored at best, mocked at worst.

After the last time she realised thieving was no longer viable. Her face and tactics had become too well known among shop staff and security guards. It was only too easy to be caught.

That reduced her options to this new low, this last desperate level she thought she'd never sink to, but which now in hindsight seemed utterly inevitable. If you could write a basic plot of your average hooker's life up until the point they fell into the game, Roxy had probably hit every beat along the way.

'You look fuckin' lush,' said Kenny. 'Like somethin' outta a' lad's mag.'

Roxy blinked and assessed her reflection. In the dim light she didn't look far from her prime of nineteen, when she'd fully bloomed and her body could still cope with how she mistreated it. Thick makeup hid those crater-like acne scars, those premature wrinkles, smoothed everything out. She just hoped the streetlights would be so forgiving.

Not for the first time since she remembered the comment overheard from that copper, comparing her face to a bowl of porridge. At the time it'd confirmed a creeping suspicion her looks weren't what they had been. Now it shook her confidence again and at a time when she'd be relying on both assets.

But the longer Roxy dwelt on those words the angrier she became until that outweighed her shame and she sharply stood up from her table, determined and defiant.

She told herself that she was hot, hot enough any man would pay money to have her, no matter what that faggot cop said.

'Fuck it. I'm ready.'

As Roxy strutted toward him Kenny gawped at the amount of skin on show. A flimsy crop top covered the track marks up her arms and showcased her flat, hollow stomach with its pierced navel. Ten inches of miniskirt hovered low enough to prevent a glimpse at her thong, but only just, with slim, milky legs tapering perfectly down into black stiletto pumps. No track marks on those, not yet.

Although the junk had long ago nullified his libido, Kenny watched her like a thirsty dog while she grabbed her jacket off the nail. Then he stepped back into the hallway and half-curtsied in a manner that was only mildly sarcastic.

'M'lady.'

Tinny music trickled down the hall to accompany Roxy's walk, her three-inch heels clicking along the bare boards in time with the muffled beat. They became louder as she descended the rickety stairs to the ground floor, the music fading, and the padding of Kenny's dirty Nikes following close behind.

Pale blue light shone in the hallway below and there was a rustling, scuffing sound caused by something unseen, its activity increasing the further they went. When Roxy arrived at ground level, she instantly recognised the source of that noise, illuminated by the solar-charged lantern it held.

'Hey, Foxy Roxy,' said Slates, pulling a half-toothless grin, and his puffy jacket rustled again as he threw arms up to embrace her.

'Slates,' said Roxy, smiling slightly but snubbing the hug.

She kept walking, not wanting to get the lad's trademark stink on her and as she went by, he used his lantern to give her the full up and down.

'Lookin' *gorgeous*.'

'That's the idea,' said Kenny, coming off the last step behind them, and the unexpected approach sent

Slates hobbling back to the shelter of the doorway, where he mumbled a fearful, 'Alright K.'

Kenny didn't return the greeting. His predatory senses finely tuned for signs of weakness, he immediately noticed the impeded gait and gestured at the dragging leg.

'You still limpin' lad?'

'Yeah,' said Slates, touching his thigh self-consciously. 'But it doesn't hurt anymore,' he added, somewhat defensive.

'That might not be a good thing, lad,' said Kenny, smiling without affection. 'You need to get it looked at, like. I've known a few lads had to get bits amputated, y'know.'

To illustrate the point Kenny's right hand mimed a chopping action against his left arm and he made a cartoon slicing sound to accompany it.

'SHINK.'

Slates screwed up his filthy face.

'I'm fine, mate,' he said. 'You know me. I eat KFC out of bins and I never been sick. Had a habit since my teens and I never OD'd.'

Roxy chuckled and stopped halfway along the hall.

'You're spittin' rhymes there, Slates,' she said, sounding slightly impressed, but not genuinely. It was more like how a kindergarten teacher reacts to a toddler's messy attempts at artwork.

All the same Slates blushed, a state hidden by the uniform light.

'You should see me beatbox,' he said, bringing a hand to his mouth and before he could start Kenny grabbed his wrist.

'I'll beat your box in a minute if you keep holdin' us up, lad.'

Slates cringed, partly embarrassed, partly afraid.

'Soz guys,' he mumbled and with clear disdain Kenny released him to continue along the hall, joining Roxy.

'C'mon Rox.'

From his doorway Slates watched them go while rubbing his sore wrist. Then just before their shadows disappeared into the gloom he called out, 'Catch ya later playa hater.'

Keenly, he waited for any response, his gappy smile fading with each passing instant until it disappeared, only to return broader than ever when he heard a faint yet unmistakably feminine giggle.

'In a while crocodile,' Roxy hollered, a line which made Slates laugh a lot more enthusiastically than it should.

'Shut it, Slates,' someone grumbled from another room. It sounded like Ali, that mean little cockney, and Slates didn't want to upset him any more than he did Kenny.

'Soz mate,' he said, receiving another "Shut up" for the effort as he hobbled back into his own room, that leg itching like crazy.

<u>2</u>

Outside the Victoria Kenny stopped Roxy, his greasy hand clamping her skinny arm.

'Don't get attached to that Slates lad,' he warned, cocking a thumb back at the dilapidated building. 'He won't be around much longer. Know what I mean?'

Roxy glanced to a boarded window and nodded sadly. This wasn't a threat from Kenny, or veiled info suggesting someone meant Slates any harm. It was simply a fact. Anyone doubting it need only look at the lad, at that limp, to know his days were numbered.

'Yeah,' Roxy sighed, and her sad gaze dropped to the floor.

Then she shot him a look full of attitude.

'Wanna get on with it then?'

The wind blew wild across that cliff, threatening to topple the pair as arm in arm they made for lower ground. Down grassy banks they trudged, onto pothole riddled concrete, toward the blanket of neon lights shimmering over the black sea below.

In the distance they could already hear a faint rumble of clashing basslines from the competing bars along the strip. It sounded almost like battlefield artillery or a fireworks display going off, all at once.

'Friday night,' said Kenny. 'Plenty of cash floatin' about.'

'Let's hope so,' said Roxy, who was struggling in those stilettos, her every step unstable, those stick-thin legs awkward, wobbly, reminiscent of a new-born fawn. She couldn't remember the last time she'd had cause to wear heels, probably years ago, and she'd never quite learned how to properly walk in them.

Barker's alley, with its winding slope snaking into the harbour, proved a further challenge and she had to slow to a plod, stretching Kenny's patience to its limit.

'Come on girl,' he said, sharply. 'Hurry it up.'

'I'm not a fuckin' horse, K,' Roxy snapped and Kenny withdrew in spite to swagger ahead, leaving her to struggle on alone.

'Fuck's sake.'

He was waiting, arms folded when she arrived at the bottom and the brief time apart had given him chance to cool his temper. On sight he apologised, blaming his need for a fix, a need Roxy understood all too well since she was already feeling its early signs herself.

'Come on,' she said.

Being winter, Scarmouth's main strip wasn't exactly bustling and there, competition always raged fierce between women of the night. For them, a good spot was essential, somewhere near the right bar to catch the right kind of punter at the right moment, and those holding prized patches guarded them jealously.

In such desperate times fights were prone to break out, fights that women who relied on their looks couldn't afford to have but did anyway. A cut lip or black eye was considered a low price to pay if it meant seeing off a competitor or expanding your territory.

Into this arena young Roxy's presence caused the expected stir, the players recognising fresh competition, and as she gracelessly tottered along the harbourside Kenny shielded her the best he could with his wiry frame.

'Hark at this fekkin' bitch.'

Verbal abuse began right off the bat, coming in

A Hot Dose of Hell

like a rising storm with short, quieter insults gradually building to torrents of shrieked threats.

'Youse cunts wanna get cut or somethin'?'

'*Fuck off ya wee junkie slag*. This is *oor* strip.'

'Yeah, peddle yer crusty minge elsewhere.'

At the memorial fountain the pair relinked arms to hurry past a six-foot amazon in knee-high gladiator boots. Enraged by the intrusion she stalked them to the edge of her patch, an invisible border, issuing the command:

'Keep walkin' while ya still can, skinny bitch.'

Roxy and Kenny did just that, all the way to the end of the strip, where the lights and attractions gave in to miles of unlit road and desolate beach.

'This is it,' said Kenny, breaking away. 'This is the spot.'

Roxy gauged her surroundings with a sceptical squint.

'Who's gonna see me here?'

'Tourists,' said Kenny and he gestured up the coast, to lights on the horizon. 'There's hotels an' b' an' b's all along this road. When they're headin' back in their taxis they'll spot you, like. You won't have any competition here.'

The last was clearly a major factor in Kenny's choice. Desperate as he seemed he was equally keen to stay away from Scarmouth's pros and more importantly, the people who ran most of them.

Roxy couldn't blame him. She'd already heard plenty of rumours about that crew.

'Just put yourself here,' said Kenny and he ushered her to the rear side of a tall sign for Scarmouth sands.

'The road's quiet so you can serve 'em here in their cars or go down to the beach. It's perfect, like.'

Kenny's use of the word "serve" jarred in how

13

professional it sounded, as though this were some legitimate occupation and it gave Roxy pause to wonder just how many other girls he'd talked into the game before her. At least a couple she'd bet.

'An' if we wanna roll 'em,' Kenny went on, 'there's no cctv, no witnesses. Plus, we can cut along the beach for a sly getaway, like. What you reckon? Good thinkin' eh?'

Roxy's sigh steamed in the cold air.

'If you say so.'

'Trust me,' said Kenny. He pointed to a four-foot sea wall. 'I'll be behind there. You can text us if you don't wanna shout, like.'

'Yeah, cheers mate,' said Roxy, not meaning it to sound quite so resentful as it did and she claimed her post near the curb, facing the direction of the harbour, all those shiny lights.

It wasn't long before more lights were coming toward her, then going past. Cars and cabs whizzed up that road at regular intervals, ferrying revellers to and from the pubs and clubs. Every so often lary lads would put down the windows and jeer in that maliciously cheerful way Brits do best. But most ignored Roxy altogether.

She soon started to feel stupid, then angry. This attitude fed into her body language and she paced relentlessly, strutting, showing off her legs, sashaying her tiny ass, advertising herself while simultaneously fighting the cold.

She tried blowing kisses at some cars, cupped her breasts in offering, mimed fellatio at others, all to no avail. What had begun as a sad, desperate act eventually became more a point of pride as the night drew on without a single car stopping, or even slowing.

Closing time at the pubs came and went and traffic dwindled over the following hour. Deflated, Roxy was contemplating the practicalities of burglary when finally, a black Ford with tinted windows slowed to a crawl and pulled up, mounting the curb just metres from where she stood.

Instinct told Roxy this was likely to be police in an unmarked car. With her every fibre she hoped that it wasn't, not because they could really do anything worse than move her along, but because this was the closest she'd come to a job in over two hours standing in the freezing cold.

They'd have a lecture ready for her no doubt, the patronising, insulting kind she'd endured from them oh so many times before. Keen to get that out of the way, she approached the driver's side which emitted a soft hum as the electric window gradually lowered to reveal the kind of face she hadn't expected.

The lone driver was gaunt, runty, with thick spectacles and greasy hair. His expression was startled, deer in headlights, and his manner furtive. He could barely look at her when he said:

'I've never done this before.'

Initially taken aback, Roxy quickly fell into character to give a casual shrug and flash a confident smile.

'Me neither, hun.'

He looked doubtful of that but didn't say. Of course, it seemed like the type of lie a hooker would tell a nervous john, and he was clearly nervous.

His next words stuttered. 'A-are y-you looking to score?'

Roxy gave her best girly giggle.

'I was gonna ask you the same thing, hun.'

'No,' he said, furrowing his brow and he paused

seemingly to gather courage for what he really wanted to say.

'I mean...are you looking for a hit, some err...skag.'

This nerd's use of street lingo surprised Roxy no less than what he was offering, and she gave him a second assessment, intrigued, yet wary.

'Maybe, but I aint got the cash at the moment. Who's askin'?'

'My name? My name's John,' he said, sounding unsure.

'Ha,' Roxy gave a cynical laugh. 'A john called John eh? What's your last name, mate? *Smith*?'

He glanced away, to the road ahead.

'Let's not do last names.'

Roxy's grin faded.

'Alright *John*. How about this then? Are you police?'

'No, no,' John said, far more convincingly than how he'd given his name, and Roxy instantly lowered her guard. She was quite certain they had to admit it if asked directly, otherwise it was "Encatchment" or something like that. She'd seen it on TV.

'So what you sellin' then, John?'

He glanced side to side, as if mindful of prying ears. There was no one around for half a mile, apart from Kenny, waiting in the shadows behind the sea wall.

'Have you ever heard of Krocodil?'

Roxy shook her head.

'It's morphine, really good morphine,' he explained. 'But *this* stuff I've got, this is more like *Tyrannosaurus* and I've got a lot of it I'm looking to sell.'

Roxy's eyes widened at the word "morphine". She was practically drooling.

'How much?' she asked, meaning the average price, but John gave an answer in weight.

'About ten kilos.'

'Shii-it son,' said Roxy, the cogs visibly turning behind her blue eyes, and she couldn't help glancing at the sea wall. She caught herself doing it then leaned in conspiratorially, arm resting on the car roof, body angled to show him her meagre cleavage.

'I might know a few people who'd be up for buyin' some a that - what'd you call it?...*T-Rexstacy*? Whatever. You make a deal an' I get a cut for pointin' you in the right direction. How's that sound?'

'Maybe,' said John, but he shrank back inside the car like a snail retreating into its shell, his gaze settling on the road.

Fearing she'd turned him off then, Roxy pressed harder. 'So, shall we go back to your place then, hun?'

'What for?' said John.

Roxy flashed another smile, licked her teeth, something she thought might look sexy.

'Y' know, so we can seal the deal. You show me the goods an' I'll set you up.'

Still staring straight ahead, grip tightening at the wheel, John swallowed to wet his dry throat.

'I've got them in the back.'

'Oh yeah?' said Roxy, and she slyly drew the phone from her jacket.

Holding it below the window, keys so familiar she didn't need to look, her nimble thumb twitched away while she kept watch on John.

The glowing screen was visible in the driver side mirror, but his gaze remained fixed on the road. If he'd only glanced, he would've seen the message and might've recognised the danger of those abbreviated words.

RL HM
Roll him.

A faint ping chimed in the distance as Kenny received the text. Roxy heard it. John didn't seem to. Then he looked at Roxy.

'You don't believe me, do you?'

'Course I do. Where'd you get the stuff anyway?' she asked, keeping him talking, distracted.

'It's medical grade,' said John. 'A shipment came in by mistake. I don't want to say any more than that if it's alright. I don't want to expose myself.'

Roxy cackled like a loose barmaid.

'Ha, I thought that was *why* you pulled up. I thought you wanted to do a bit more than *expose yourself*, gettit?'

John returned a nervous smile. 'I see.' Then he straightened when Roxy put her hand through the window and stroked his thigh, her unpainted claws working toward the crotch.

'I'm Sally by the way,' she said, thinking it a smart lie.

An inch from genital contact John gently took her hand. His palms were clammy.

'I'm Herma-John.'

'Hermajohn?' Roxy giggled. 'You already told me your name, remember?'

John nodded, seemingly agitated. 'Yes, yes, it's John.'

'Well, *John*,' Roxy said, taking a step back, 'this is Kenny.'

John looked just as Kenny rounded the car. The lanky gimlet-eyed junkie was moving fast in a purposeful manner.

'Alright John,' he said, his voice chirpy yet full of scorn. Then with a speed belying his frailty he

A Hot Dose of Hell

plunged his gangly arm through the open window, snatched a handful of greasy hair and yanked, pulling John's head halfway out to show him the knife.

'What is this?' John whimpered, specs dangling from an ear.

'GET THE FUCK OUT,' shouted Kenny.

'Okay,' said John, showing hands, 'just don't cut me, please.'

The central locking disengaged with a click and Kenny released John's hair to pull the handle on the driver's side door. John kept very still, his head hanging through the window so its inside edge clipped him as the door swung out.

'Soz lad,' Kenny muttered, gripping John's collar.

'It's o-,' John began, the word cut off by Kenny dragging him out, then he flopped to the roadside like a jelly poured onto a plate, trembling thereafter.

'Where's the stuff, John?' said Roxy.

'In the boot, under the flap,' said John, keeping his head down. 'Take it please, just don't hurt me.'

Kenny felt a cruel urge to kick John anyway. He only refrained because Roxy moved so fast to get to the boot.

'What's he got in there, like?'

'A load of gear,' said Roxy, throwing the boot open. 'Said it's so strong they call it T-Rex.'

'Bollocks,' snorted Kenny, glaring down at John. 'This soft cunt? You tellin' me he's a dealer?'

Roxy was busy rummaging in the boot.

'I reckon he's a doctor or somethin'. He said it came in by mistake an' he's sellin' it.'

'Okay,' said Kenny, placing a foot on John's back. 'Is it in there then lad?'

John didn't need to answer. Less than a second later Roxy gasped, 'Shiii-it son,' and Kenny craned his

Stark Terror

neck to see.

'What? You got it?'

'FU-KIN 'ELL,' said Roxy, coming up with a brick of cellophane-wrapped powder in each hand. She tucked one under her chin, freeing her left to produce another brick from the boot, giggles becoming squeaks she was so excited.

'We've hit the fuckin' jackpot, K.'

Kenny's jaw dropped and he immediately forgot about John on the floor. In two strides he was nudging Roxy aside to see for himself.

'Steady on,' she yapped as one brick fell from her grasp and she quickly scooped it back up.

'Could've broke the wrappin' then K.'

Kenny didn't apologise. Arms wide, he leaned over the boot, gripping the edges as if he feared he might otherwise fall in. He couldn't believe what he was seeing. Beneath the turned-up flap of fabric the bricks had been laid out in two rows of five, minus the three Roxy held.

'This is big,' said Kenny and he began stuffing his pockets. 'This is…'

Just one brick was enough to stretch the stitching, meaning he could only conceal four at most. After the first he paused to look at Roxy, who gazed back suddenly afraid, unsure of what he might do next.

This was a big score for two, even bigger if there was no split at all and a thought had occurred - would Kenny go one step further to keep this all for himself?

Her heart jumped when he removed his coat.

'What you doin', K?'

'We're takin' it all,' said Kenny, tying his coat into a makeshift satchel.

'Stuff that in here,' he said, shoving it at Roxy and she obliged, dropping the three bricks in.

At his insistence she took the coat after so he could continue to fill it and they were that caught up in the act, they'd almost completely forgotten about John.

Luckily for them the man was apparently so terrified he hadn't moved a muscle and when they cast eyes back to him, he was still prone on the ground, fingers knitted behind his head, even though they'd never instructed him to do that.

Once it was filled Kenny took the coat satchel from Roxy and feeling a tiny prick of pity, she tottered over to crouch at John's side.

'Soz John,' she said, roughly scuffing his hair.

John flinched at the touch and fell still again. From that point he didn't utter a word of protest, didn't try to bargain or beg, didn't curse or threaten.

'Come on,' said Kenny, pulling her away, then as an afterthought he warned John not to get up for five minutes.

'You've got to count to sixty...*five* times,' said Roxy, nudging Kenny, and they beamed at each other.

This chance meeting had been an amazing stroke of luck for them, such a turn that they could never have predicted. It was like winning the national lottery or inheriting a fortune from a distant relative.

'Result,' cheered Kenny as they stole into the night, giggling like naughty children, elated with their ill-gotten gains.

But had they lingered just a few moments longer, they might've been disturbed to hear that "John" was laughing too.

<u>3</u>

Night shift at the Brokebridge Shopco suited Rhonda Caine. A normal nine hours for twenty percent more pay than the day workers and she didn't even need to deal with customers, well hardly ever. Although there'd be a steady trickle of shoppers coming and going throughout the night, few ever approached for help, meaning she got to focus on the main aspect of her job - getting the stock out.

Most of the time Rhonda wore headphones and could ignore them anyway. Only drunks tended to disturb her then and she didn't have to bother with the niceties on their account. All they ever asked was to be pointed in the direction of the booze aisle and Rhonda would do just that, without escorting them to it or volunteering product information the way Shopco's directors would insist.

The chain's "mystery shoppers" weren't supposed to drink on the job, so she had no fear she'd be caught out on hidden camera failing the brand's "behaviours", if she could even remember what they were.

Like most big companies Shopco used acronyms to help "embed" these mandatory "behaviours" in all their employees. The most frequently mentioned and apparently most crucial was S.G.A.S.S. It'd been posted everywhere, noticeboards, payslips, even the back door of the toilet cubicles. But after three years Rhonda could still only recite the first two abbreviations, S*mile* and *Greet*. The A.S.S part simply failed to stick. Not that it'd trouble her sleep. Very little did.

At ten pm the night shift routine always started

with peripheral tasks, such as waste disposal, basic cleaning and toilet checks. What came next was dictated by another acronym, L.I.C.T.

Look for what needs replenishment. *Inventory* any orders required. *Coordinate* the team. *Tidy* as you go.

For Rhonda, this time resembled a prolonged exercise session as she zipped around, pushing trolleys piled with goods, offloading them at rapid speed.

She actually liked that aspect. It helped keep her body fat down and on breaks she'd often be found working out inside one of the stockroom cages. Until very recently she even had a training buddy on the team, a lad called Mike. But since he joined the marines, she now did it alone.

Steel pipework running the length of the stockroom ceiling didn't seem to serve any present function and was probably a feature of the building's old heating system. It'd been sturdy enough to bear both Rhonda and Mike's weight together as they completed pull-ups side by side, and though she had her pick of the whole length she'd purposely kept to the spot she'd used when training with him.

It was now the only part of the pipe not coated with dust and in certain lights showed an almost perfect print of her hands.

6,7,8

Rhonda was three sets in when Alice entered the room, towing an empty trolley.

Dumpy little Alice looked up at Rhonda hanging off that pipe and watched her struggle through last reps with some degree of admiration. For a time, she'd harboured a cynical suspicion Rhonda only trained here to get close to handsome Mike. But Rhonda's perseverance since his departure proved there were other, not necessarily exclusive, motivations.

'You missing him?' Alice asked, not meaning it to sound quite as bitchy as it came out.

'Who?' Rhonda grunted.

'Mike,' said Alice, rolling her eyes. 'Don't pretend like you don't know.'

Rhonda kept pulling, speaking on the way up as she exhaled. 'We message sometimes.'

From experience Alice knew to leave it there, Rhonda's curt answer told her that was all she was going to get for now, and at a loss for what to say next, she gingerly leapt up, latching on to the pipe directly above.

For a few seconds Alice managed to hang there, feeling the strain on her arms and wrists. She let go the very second it became uncomfortable.

'Whoa, that aches,' she said, shaking her arms out.

'You should start with rows to build up your back strength,' said Rhonda. 'You can't go from nothing to full pull-ups like that.'

'Okay,' Alice nodded as if taking it in, but she had absolutely no intention of following the advice.

'You know, *I* could work out with you,' she said, still rubbing her arms. 'I might go for something different though. Maybe a run. How about that?'

With a gymnast's grace Rhonda dropped from the pipe straight into a set of deep squats.

'I get plenty of cardio here,' she puffed, quads bulging through her Shopco stretch-fabric trousers. 'If I did any more, I'd only lose muscle.'

'Yeah, I know what that's like,' said Alice, gently slapping her own sizeable butt, making it jiggle.

'I wouldn't wanna lose any a' this jelly.'

The joke fell flat, barely earning a snort, and

conversation ran dry once more.

This would've been a good cue to leave. However, Alice wasn't ready just yet. All the night promised was more trolleys, more stock and these little conversational interludes were about the only enjoyable aspect of the job for her, the fact they could pause and have them whenever they wanted without scrutiny from any managers.

Problem for Alice was that most of the night shift workers tended to lean on the antisocial side, with absolutely no interest or skill in small talk, and Rhonda was hardly an exception. If she really wanted to keep it going, Alice realised she'd have to risk provocation and broach a more sensitive subject.

'Hear from your sister yet?'

Up till that point Rhonda had never mentioned the trouble with her sister to Alice, who only knew anything about it because she'd overheard Rhonda telling Mike, in what was clearly intended to be a private moment.

'No,' said Rhonda, a slight edge to her voice, some resentment over Alice knowing her business.

'Have you tried calling her though?'

'She never gave me a number,' said Rhonda, going down, arms out. 'We only spoke through Facebook,' she said, coming back up.

Silence resumed. Even Alice heard the grimness in Rhonda's words, the undercurrent of finality as if already coming to terms with a death yet to be confirmed. It made her regret taking the conversation down this route and she felt an urge to counter with bland optimism, if only for her own sake.

'I'm sure she's okay. I mean, you did say she does this sometimes, right?'

That much was true. Rhonda's sister had a

tendency to cut her off for weeks at a time. Rhonda suspected there was some unresolved animosity around the fact she'd been adopted when her sister hadn't. The occasional cold shoulder seemed to be a way of getting a little payback for having been dealt the shittier hand. But this time was different.

'Roxy's never kept quiet for this long.'

Alice shrugged. 'People are stubborn. Me and my sister fight too. What was it over?'

'I refused to send her any more money.'

The logical question played in Alice's mind. Most people wouldn't ask. Alice wasn't most people.

'Why would you need to send your older sister money?'

Rhonda replied through gritted teeth, 'She struggles.'

'Don't we all. I work two jobs. Can't she do that?'

'She doesn't work at all,' Rhonda huffed, coming up from the last rep and she leant against the cage to stretch her hamstrings.

Unwittingly, she'd allowed herself to be drawn into Alice's trap. The needling questions were provoking knee-jerk answers she wouldn't normally volunteer.

'*That's* why I sent her money, Alice. Help her get back on her feet.'

Alice gave a sceptical look.

'Are you sure it's her and not a scam? My mum's been scammed a few times on Facebook, supposed *investment opportunities* in Africa. Dad has to supervise all her online activity now.'

'Yeah, I'm sure it's her,' Rhonda said, a little insulted. 'We've had a few chats. No scammer would know what she does about our childhood.'

'Fair enough,' said Alice, and she rested a hand on Rhonda's trolley, began idly rowing it, appreciating how smoothly it moved compared to her own.

'You'll probably hear from her soon,' she said, with patronising certainty, 'even if it's just to tap you for cash again.'

Rhonda shook her head, standing up straight. 'Don't know. I'm not waiting for that. Decided to do something about it first.'

'Like what?' said Alice and for the first time in the whole conversation Rhonda met her gaze with a piercing stare.

'I'm gonna find her and bring her here.'

'Then what?'

'Help her get her life back on track.'

'Wow,' said Alice, sounding genuinely impressed, although there was an undercurrent of doubt.

'Just wow. That's really good of you, Rhonda, you know?'

Rhonda wasn't so sure about it being "good" in any unselfish way. Her guilt at being adopted into a marginally better life had more to do with it than any natural generosity and care. Truth was she barely knew her sister. They hadn't actually met in person since their early teens and only messaged occasionally in the last twelve years.

Then two weeks ago Roxy had gone completely offline. Judging by what Rhonda knew that meant one of two things. Either the shelter she was in didn't have internet, or she wasn't even staying in a shelter anymore.

'Can I help?' Alice found herself saying, a reflexive offer, some kind of social-custom Tourettes. In short, she didn't quite mean it. Like when you ask a taxi driver whether they've had a busy night, as if you care.

'I'm going this weekend,' said Rhonda, giving

Alice an easy out - Shopco would never allow two team members the same weekend off on such short notice.

'Where?' said Alice, still curious.

'Scarmouth,' Rhonda said, 'last place listed on Roxy's profile. Homeless people usually know each other, especially in small towns, so she shouldn't be hard to find once I'm there.'

Alice was taken aback by the revelation.

'How do you know she's *homeless*?' she said, whispering the last word as if it were some forbidden term.

'I can see who she's friends with,' Rhonda said, very matter-of-fact. 'Plus, she's let a few things slip about drugs. I put two and two together.'

'Sounds a bit dodgy you know?' said Alice. 'You should be careful around Scarmouth too. Rough town.'

'I know. I'm not going alone.'

'Well, who's going with you?' said Alice, already subconsciously excluding herself even though she hadn't officially retracted her offer.

'There's a group,' Rhonda said. 'They're into charity work. They're going down to Scarmouth because they heard there's a real homeless problem there.'

'Okay cool,' said Alice, who was down with progressive causes, at least superficially. She wore various bands on her arms for the appropriate months, retweeted all the right things.

'Do you know them well?'

Rhonda gave a slight shake of the head, her tightly plaited hair didn't move at all.

'Not met them yet.'

'Shit Rhonda, I know you're hard, but this all sounds well dodgy.'

'There's at least four of them coming. It's fine.'

Alice raised an eyebrow. 'How many *men*?'

'Two maybe,' said Rhonda, twisting side to side, keeping warm for the next set, a simultaneous hint for Alice to leave her to it now. She didn't take it.

'Do you think you can trust them?'

Transitioning from the hammy stretch, Rhonda showcased impressive lats even under her polo shirt. Then she rolled her well-defined deltoids in a purposeful display to support her next statement.

'I can handle a few do-gooders, Alice. What do you think is gonna happen?'

'Anything,' said Alice, wearing a disturbed frown. 'Rape...murder?'

'It's just a shot away,' Rhonda smirked, leaping for the pipe. Her hands made a satisfying slap as they caught it and she started repping again with machine-like pace.

Alice went to leave then changed her mind.

'Look,' she said, 'just promise if anything happens, you'll call me, okay? Doesn't matter what time, I'll drive straight down and get you.'

Slowly, Rhonda lowered herself to catch Alice's gaze and was caught off-guard by its earnestness.

'Cheers Al,' she said, meaning it.

'Don't mention it, *Rhon*,' said Alice, walking off, taking a trolley with her.

7,8-

No sooner had Alice left than the generic alarm chimed on Rhonda's phone, signalling the end of her break. She cursed and dropped from the pipe, a little annoyed at Alice now for having interrupted her flow, forcing her to cut the routine short.

Coming out of the cage she drew her Stanley blade and approached the next pallet. With a swift slash she cut the plastic ties and started piling goods onto the remaining trolley at a pace she hoped might compensate for the lost reps. She stacked that trolley heavy too, much heavier than normal so that she really had to put her bodyweight in to get going. Once she did however, the momentum built fast.

Porthole doors burst open with a bang, pvc strip curtains fluttered and Rhonda hit the shop floor at near reckless speed, rolling straight down the freezer section.

She was halfway along the soft drink aisle when the trolley's rear left wheel emitted a pained squeal and seized up, causing it to veer left in a sharp arc toward a six-foot pyramid of Irn Bru soda.

'Shit, shiiit!' Rhonda hissed, gripping the rubber handlebar tightly, so tightly it burned her calloused palms, and she planted her size 7 Converse, soles squeaking against the resin floor.

With mere inches to spare she pulled using all her might and succeeded in righting the trolley's course just enough that it only grazed the pyramid's outer layer.

The peak wobbled threateningly after, but nothing fell.

Relieved, Rhonda slumped over the handlebar catching her breath.

A voice came from behind, Alice: 'Ooh, is that trolley twelve, Rhon?'

Rhonda checked the faded number on the handlebar.

'Yes it is, Alice. Not the one I was using earlier. *Someone else* must've took that eh?'

Twenty yards down the same aisle, atop a small stepladder, Alice cringed and put a hand over her mouth in mock shock. 'Whoops.'

A Hot Dose of Hell

Rhonda cut a wry smile.

'You bitch, you switched that one with mine, didn't you?'

'Yeah,' Alice said, descending the steps. 'But I really needed that laugh.'

Rhonda cocked a thumb at the Irn Bru pyramid. 'You wouldn't have been laughing if I'd hit that.'

Alice tilted her head, gave a lopsided shrug.

'I would at first, then I *might* regret it.'

'Yeah,' said Rhonda, 'cos you'd be the one cleaning it up with me.'

On that they shared a chuckle while behind them the automatic entrance doors parted and in strode a gaunt, dishevelled man wearing a dirty old puffer jacket.

If the unkempt hair and beard weren't clue enough, the stink he brought with him attested to his derelict status and for one uncomfortable moment he seemed bent on approaching the pair. But then he stopped short at the cold storage, the sandwich section.

In a flash the vagrant pocketed three egg mayos before he turned and made his way back through the still open automatic doors, all without bothering to so much as glance over his shoulder.

'Cheeky bastard,' said Alice. 'Did you clock that?'

'Yep,' said Rhonda and Alice stared at her somewhat incredulous.

'Well don't you think we should *do* something, Rhon?'

'Like what?'

'I don't know, try and stop him?'

Rhonda gave a bored shrug.

'Why? Those are yesterday's sarnies. He's just saved us a job. We'd be throwing them in the bin in a few hours anyway.'

Alice said no more. It seemed fairly obvious from their earlier conversation as to why Rhonda might sympathise with the man and she could appreciate the point of view.

However.

There was something about the way he swiped those sarnies that she found disturbing. It wasn't as if he was playing his attempt at cool, hoping they hadn't seen him do it and trying not to tip them off by acting guilty or suspicious. It was more like he knew full well they'd see him and simply didn't give a shit.

In Alice's view this showed a total lack of regard for not just society's laws, but even its most basic customs, leading her to wonder - were this a man of greater ambition or darker desires at what *would* he pause?

She returned to Rhonda, who was now busy offloading the trolley, apparently untroubled by the incident, and felt grateful she hadn't been taken up on that fickle offer to join her in Scarmouth.

There would be more of those types there, standing between Rhonda and her sister, and no doubt at least a few among them harbouring some darker desires.

4

The stuff certainly wasn't any kind of brown. Kenny could've figured that blindfolded. It felt different, even through the cellophane, denser somehow. His cig-yellowed fingertips were all over the brick in his pocket, weighing, squeezing, stroking while he and Roxy scarpered from the scene of the crime, John's car.

'What's this stuff called again?' he asked, adjusting the makeshift satchel he'd made of his coat. It was heavy to him, heavier than anything he'd had to carry in a long time.

Trotting at his side, just a little out breath, Roxy panted, 'Told ya, bloke called it T-Rex. Reckons it's like Krocodil.'

Mention of the bloke triggered Kenny's nerves. He quickly glanced back, seeing to his relief that the black Ford remained stationary, John too, and yet as he walked on, he couldn't shake the feeling of being followed, of being watched. This wasn't anything new to him, however. Paranoia had been a scourge on his social life, his mental health for as long as he could remember, and experience had taught him it was a feeling usually best ignored.

But just as broken clocks can be right twice a day, so can a paranoid junkie's sense of danger. If only Kenny had looked up, just once, then he would've seen the pair of drones hovering in the sky above, tracking his every step.

'What's Krocodil?' he asked, returning to Roxy. 'Is it like Benzo or Spice or summit?'

'It's morphine, Ken,' she said with a wink, relishing the opportunity to act in-the-know for a change, and she supported the pretence with, 'Can tell you don't go online much.'

'Cheeky bitch,' chuckled Kenny. 'Maybe I'll look it up next time I'm workin' on a project in Starbucks, like.'

A coarse laugh rattled Roxy's throat. She wasn't laughing *with* Kenny.

'What?' said Kenny, frowning.

Roxy grinned. 'Only *projects* you do in Starbucks are the ones coming out yer arse.'

Kenny couldn't help but laugh. He couldn't help throwing a dig back either.

'You use their loos as much as me, ya skank.'

That one earned him a slap, a not-entirely playful slap, on the arm. Harsh truths of their lifestyle included a reliance on the provision of public toilets, something Roxy still found quite shameful at times.

'Steady on, luv,' Kenny cackled. The strike had stung his scrawny arm, yet he'd tolerate the underlying aggression, for now. At present the score was all that mattered and with a flick of his head he beckoned toward the beach.

'We'll go this way and dodge cctv.'

Roxy snorted, 'You reckon ol' John'll call the filth on us? Here, PC plod, these two stole all my illegal drugs. Be a good bloke an' bring 'em back.'

Kenny sucked his few remaining teeth in contempt; this young 'un still had a lot to learn about the life.

'Don't you think those geeks watchin' them cameras in town might wonder what two smackheads are doin' with a bag a swag like this? Pigs'll be on our case soon as we hit the harbour, like.'

'Fair one,' Roxy muttered, and they took the stone steps down toward the shadow-covered sand.

At the bottom she removed her heels to carry them while Kenny led the way, trudging on with his head down. Each of his hurried strides kicked sand back into Roxy's path. She could feel it hitting her bare shins but couldn't see it in the shade of the high sea wall. Only Kenny's outline was visible and the reflective stripes of his coat/swag bag catching moonlight.

'Keep up,' he rasped.

'I'm tryin'.'

For twenty minutes they walked with the sea to their right, crashing and roaring, clawing the coast like a caged animal reaching through the bars of its cell. The thunder of club music, sporadic jeers and laughter of the night scene crowd, told them when they were travelling parallel to the harbour and they continued, clinging close to the shadow of the high coastal wall until it'd all faded behind them.

By the time they arrived at the underside of the pier, where Kenny had first found Roxy, the creeping tide allowed barely a metre width of sand to walk on. If they didn't get off soon, they'd be swimming and following that thread, Roxy realised just how close she had come to drowning that night, if not for Kenny finding her.

This would be a sobering thought for most, but not Roxy who felt a brief chill and nothing more. The concept of her own death always seemed too abstract, too intangible for her to worry on it long, even though her habit tempted the reaper several times a day.

She was tempting him now. In that mile of beach only two sets of steps provided access to the higher street level and those behind her were already unreachable, blocked by rolling waves.

The other set were located only a few hundred

metres past the pier. But with the pace at which the tide was gaining it wouldn't be long before they lay underwater too.

'Come on,' said Kenny and he slipped between two pillars into the pier's underbelly, where the pitch swallowed him completely.

A stride behind Roxy hesitated to follow, bare toes curling at the rough feel of the concrete foundation.

Overhead, the Victorian boardwalk creaked, and a Union Jack fluttered violently in the breeze. That westerly wind didn't trouble those drones, however. They still hovered steadily as if perched on solid ground.

'Kenny wait.'

From the void came an impatient hiss: 'Come on, girl,' prompting Roxy to grit her teeth and pass through. She moved on tiptoe, one hand groping for anything solid to orientate herself and after a few unsteady steps she found the next pillar.

Roxy embraced that cold steel like a lover, barnacles and all. Then she gently swung round, back onto the sand where she could again see Kenny, the flashes of his coat/swag bag.

'Get a fuckin' move on,' he snapped. The temporary lift of adrenaline, of success, had clearly abandoned him and Roxy could tell he was clucking harder than ever, that stuff burning a hole in his pocket.

'Steady on K,' she groaned, feeling it too. 'I'm half your size an' I got no shoes on.'

'I aint carryin ya again, Rox.'

'No one's askin',' said Roxy, doubling pace to join his side and he snatched her wrist.

'MOVE GIRL. We'll be under water in a minute.'

They ran the rest of the way, the black tide closing

A Hot Dose of Hell

fast, almost as though it sensed how close they were to escape. It nipped Roxy's ankle on that first step up to street level, causing gooseflesh to break along her pale legs.

Two steps higher and they were safely out of reach, but she and Kenny continued to jog regardless, putting themselves out of breath by the top.

Arriving there first Kenny crouched low, keeping hidden by the sea wall, and falling in behind Roxy did the same, assuming he'd spotted some form of threat.

'What is it, K?'

His back pressed tight to the wall, Kenny scowled, 'Shhh,' as he slowly inched toward the street.

A car flew past, and he shrank from its headlights, breathing hard.

'Shit,' he whispered, clutching his chest as if a heart attack were imminent.

Roxy curled her lip in disgust.

'What are you freakin' for? It's just boy racers.'

'You don't get it,' said Kenny, shaking the coat/swag bag. 'We're carryin' a lot of weight here.'

'I know we are,' said Roxy. '*I* found it for us, remember?'

'Yeah,' Kenny muttered, and he turned, putting his snarling face right in hers, so close she could feel his breath, his spit as he rasped, 'Don't you think matey's people might be sharkin' for us? What if someone like Scotch Joe catches wind of what we've done? What if that's who he was workin' for like? You don't wanna know what I've heard about them.'

Roxy sneered. 'That stiff? Nah, no way does he have anythin' to do with Scotch Joe, or anyone serious. He was a total fuckin' geek.'

'We still gotta be careful, like. It's no-

Before Kenny could say any more Roxy pulled

away and stood upright, just to spite him. His mood was really grating when she felt they had reason to be happy for once. A nice long nod was on the cards, a jackpot payday too, and Kenny's paranoia was the only thing delaying both.

Angrily he reached for her, but she moved further so that she was standing on the street, looking down at him, smirking like the disobedient teen she'd been almost a decade ago.

'Nothin' to worry about, see?' she said, gesturing with a stiletto in each hand. 'No one knows about this.'

For a moment all they could hear was the sea and, almost on cue, a cricket chirping.

Kenny withheld comment, although his angry face said plenty. It told of irritation, embarrassment and a reluctance to accept that Roxy could be right. In smug satisfaction she watched his frustrated scowl deepen, then saw how it contorted into a look of alarm at the sound of another voice nearby.

'No one knows about what eh?'

Kenny didn't move. He stayed down, bug-eyed gaze trained on Roxy, the only thing visible from his position. That voice had come from somewhere over her left and she pivoted to face it, pulling a bemused sneer.

'Nothin',' she said, cocky as hell. 'What's it to you?'

From the same direction another voice pitched in, this one female, 'What's with the attitude?'

'Somethin' to hide,' said the first, and although much deeper Kenny realised now it was also female.

Two birds he could handle, he thought. All the same he didn't want them seeing what he was carrying, for fear of who they might tell.

'What you up to, little one?' said the second and

A Hot Dose of Hell

Roxy gave a lazy shrug.

'Mind your own.'

The second cackled like a hag. 'Hark at this cheeky bitch. Who do you think you are eh?'

They were moving closer; Kenny could hear their heels clicking on the pavement. Weighing his options, he glanced down the steps and saw how the tide now covered the bottom two. If he went that way, he'd be swimming a mile back to the other steps at risk of losing the stuff in the process. The satchel felt heavy enough as it was, trying to swim with it while fully dressed would be near impossible, plus he couldn't be certain the cellophane was wrapped tight enough to be waterproof.

'Come on who's with you?' he heard the first voice say. 'Who's Anne-Franking it behind the wall?'

'No one,' said Roxy, convincing exactly that many people.

'Bollocks,' the second laughed and Kenny watched Roxy retreat slightly as the sound of the heels grew louder, nearer. He let them come a little further before he finally surrendered and stepped out, wearing the kind of fuck-you glare guaranteed to startle your average party girls.

Only these weren't those kind of girls.

'What the fuck are you starin' at?' went the first, her deep voice perfectly matching her amazonian build. Kenny was surprised he hadn't recognised it from when she'd seen them off her patch earlier. A lot had happened since then though.

'He's tongue-tied,' said the second, who was smaller, more wiry and hard-faced with deeps cracks in her prune-like skin showing through layers of makeup.

'It's cause he aint ever seen such fit birds, Tray.'

Stark Terror

'Ha,' went Tray, the amazon, and she cocked her wide hip, flicked a mannish hand in Roxy's direction. 'Spose you're right, if *that's* anything to go by.'

'Fuck off, skank,' said Roxy, each syllable loaded with pure venom. 'And you, you old bint.'

The outburst provoked nothing but laughter in the two prozzies, harsh, scornful laughter.

Then the amazon's eyes landed on Kenny's swag and she stopped dead.

'What you got there anyway? You been fishin'?'

Kenny self-consciously drew the swag nearer to his body.

'It's fuck all to do with youse.'

That was weak, Kenny knew the second he'd said it, more likely to entice them than anything. In a desperate effort to recover he suddenly stomped toward them, his body language promising violence, wild, clumsy, reckless violence, the kind that sometimes gets people killed, even when it might not be the aggressor's intent.

'Back the fuck up,' he spat.

Unmoved, the prozzies held their ground, forcing a kind of low-threat game of chicken, which ended with Kenny right in the amazon's face. She was so tall in her heels that he had to look up at her, his head only coming to her chin level and it made him seem a little pathetic, more pathetic, this skinny, ragged man dwarfed by this statuesque feminine form.

But he wasn't backing down.

'Move it, bitch.'

'Who you callin' bitch?' said Pruneface, drawing Kenny's focus and in that instant the amazon slyly shifted her weight.

Thick hamstrings rippled under fishnet tights as she loaded a kick, a vicious heel stomp designed to

A Hot Dose of Hell

strip the skin off the receiving shin like banana peel. She'd once dropped an eighteen stone marine that way and Kenny didn't look to be much more than half that. She reckoned it might even snap this junkie's twig leg, but she never got to try because Kenny hopped up first, driving his greasy skull into the soft tissue of her pierced nose.

There was a sound like an egg breaking, then Pruneface let out a panicked monkey screech and the amazon crumbled.

'Come on, Rox,' Kenny barked, glancing back.

He read shock on Roxy's face and mistook it for a result of his own action. He quickly found out it had nothing to do with him and everything to do with the shiv in Pruneface's hand.

That was inside his gut before he knew it, all four inches of stainless steel. Then it was out. Then in. Then out. Then in again.

On the last stab Kenny's free arm flailed at Pruneface and she stumbled back to dodge it, leaving the blade stuck firmly in the side of his abdomen.

'Cunt,' Kenny managed, gargling blood, and he rocked on his heels like a half-cut tree in the breeze, hugging the swag, bleeding all over it.

Roxy dropped her stilettos and rushed up to catch him, coming under his arm the way he'd once held her. She supported his weight, just about, never taking eyes off Pruneface, who only looked to be getting started.

'Just fuck off,' said Roxy and Pruneface sneered. 'Want some as well do ya little one?'

She circled slightly and began to probe the pair, seeing whether Roxy could maintain the distance, assessing how capably they could move in tandem.

Behind her the amazon was already getting up,

face a mask of blood, green eyes glinting with predatory intent. Her appearance distracted Roxy. It was less than a second, still enough that Pruneface was able to make a grab for the swag.

'No,' Roxy cried.

With all her strength and weight Pruneface pulled away but didn't get far. Kenny's death grip held fast, and he bared bloody teeth with the effort.

'Let go,' she ordered, giving another violent yank, yet Kenny held on still.

She did it again and two bricks shook loose, seeming to bounce off the concrete in slow motion.

'Fuuuck,' Pruneface gasped, eyes bugging at the stuff. She quickly lunged for it, immediately forgetting the fight.

'Iz dat wha' ah fink id iz?' said the amazon, honking through her busted nose.

'I think it's skag,' said Pruneface, examining a brick, then she realised it wasn't. Just going by feel she could tell, same way Kenny had, only she never got to say. She was silenced by a flash of steel in the moonlight. It was a wild, arcing swipe that reached her just a fraction after the apex, slashing her cheek all the same.

The amazon cried out something like, 'JADZSH,' and Pruneface fell back onto her buttocks, blood streaming from the wound.

'BACK OFF,' warned Roxy, voice as hard as the steel in her grasp. She aimed it at the amazon next.

'And you, Bigfoot.'

The amazon's hands shot up in surrender.

'Do drubble,' (no trouble) she said.

'Muh fuckin' mouth,' sobbed Pruneface, clutching her mutilated cheek, blood trickling through her fingers. 'Muh face is wrecked.'

A Hot Dose of Hell

A glint in his eye, Kenny gurgled, 'Not as if you was anythin' to look at before, like.' Then he broke into a string of coughed laughs so violent that he began to slip from Roxy, distracting her as she struggled to hold him.

'Shit, take it easy K.'

Right away the amazon saw the opportunity. She zeroed in on the knife handle still protruding from Kenny's side and started to make small, subtle steps toward it, a gradual creep so as not to alarm.

Out of the corner of her eye Roxy noticed and again she aimed the blade at the amazon, who stopped to clear her bleeding nose with a forceful snort.

The big woman kept her head down after in a wordless show of submission, and Roxy returned to Pruneface who remained on the ground, holding her cheek together, those bricks still nestled in her lap.

'Keep 'em,' Roxy said, receiving blank, bewildered looks in return.

'*You what*?' Kenny wheezed.

'Just take 'em,' Roxy said, ignoring him. 'That's all you're gettin' though.'

There was a brief pause and Pruneface slowly brought her knees up, drawing the bricks to her stomach, all the time watching Roxy, wary it was some kind of trick.

'Go on then,' said Roxy, waving the knife, 'jog on.'

'C'mong Jhadzsh,' said the amazon, pulling Pruneface off the ground. Then carrying a brick each, they hurried off to the other side of the road, shortly descending into the underground level of a multi-storey car park.

Once their steps had faded Roxy sighed, feeling a wave of relief, and her trembling hand returned the knife to her bra. Leaving the stilettos behind, she then began to haul Kenny in the opposite direction, but on the third step his head lolled toward hers and he uttered an emphysemic gasp.

'*Rooox,*' he said, spraying her neck with a fine mist of blood.

'What's up, K?'

'*I'm not...alright, Rox.*'

He wasn't wrong. His skin had turned several shades paler than its usual corpse grey and those dark stains were growing on his hoodie. The fabric was really drinking up the blood. Its dripping hem slapped weightily as they moved.

'I know,' said Roxy, 'I know you're hurt. What do you want me to do? Stash the gear an' call an ambulance?'

'*Nah...can't be assed with that.*'

'You can't just leave it, K.'

Kenny looked down at himself, at the knife in his side.

'*Reckon I'm done anyway, Rox.*'

'No, you're not,' Roxy said and she shook her head emphatically. 'Come on. I thought I was done, remember? And you got me through it. It's my turn to sort *you* out now.'

'*Alright...*' said Kenny, eyes rolling, '*you can do us a favour...fix me up a shot of that gear.*'

'I don't think that's a good idea right now. I know you're cluckin', but you need to get looked at first. You've got a fuckin' *shiv* in your side, mate.'

'*Nah,*' Kenny slurred. '*Fuck all that. Just find somewhere, yeah?...please.*'

Roxy couldn't summon the will to argue any more. She'd been done about two lines earlier and was merely going through the motions, performing, the same way someone does when protesting a generosity that they fully intend to accept.

Her own need was getting the better of her and Kenny was making the choice a lot easier than it should've been. Hospital could wait, she told herself. His wounds probably weren't that bad, just seemed worse because he was clucking so hard.

All he really needed was a quiet spot to try this new shit out, take the edge off. Then they'd *both* be in better shape to decide what to do next.

'*Find somewhere*,' Kenny urged.

Thirty metres from where they stood lay a pedestrian subway. Its flickering, failing light offered a beacon Roxy couldn't resist and they shifted course, arriving just as the sky broke.

Gently as she could Roxy set Kenny down against the tunnel wall, falling over in the process as her stick legs finally gave out. His bloodied hands were already fishing in his pockets and shortly produced his kit, wrapped tight in a Tesco bag.

'*Fix up, Rox*,' he begged, blood dripping off his fingers as he held it out toward her. '*C'mon, send us out happy.*'

Roxy accepted the kit and unravelled the bag on her lap. Inside she found three syringe packs, a strip of pins, disposable lighter, bent spoon and a filthy wad of cotton wool. Without delay she set to work mixing the powder with a few drops of rain and soon, held over the lighter's flame, it bubbled down to pure liquid on the end of that spoon.

'*Hurry up.*'

Carefully, Roxy drew the liquid into the syringe through a cotton wool filter, then she brought it toward Kenny. He was waiting, arm bared and tied off with a piece of shoelace, a grateful smile on his bloody lips.

As she handed it over Roxy recalled her first hit, the sense of trepidation at putting some unknown chemical into her body, at not knowing exactly what it might do. It'd never been that way with alcohol, weed, or pills, but this was different, this was heroin. The injection alone had been nerve-racking.

Most people have a rational discomfort around needles, the idea of being pierced by one, and Roxy Weaver was no exception. She'd been so squeamish she'd had to close her eyes and turn away, teeth gritted in anticipation.

A bloke called Shane did the rest. His rough hand held her outstretched arm steady and delivered the first of what would be many track marks in her alabaster skin.

Then once she'd tasted that intense rush, the orgasmic sense of relief and that comforting warmth, Roxy would never be squeamish with needles again.

'*Come on girl...*' Kenny pleaded, impatient, and he snatched from her to jab himself.

Roxy watched Kenny shoot up the way dogs watch people eat. Briefly he stiffened as the gear flooded his system. Then dropping the syringe, he let out a gasp of ecstasy and slumped against the wall, gradually sliding down until his head lightly struck the concrete.

There followed a faint clatter of the prozzie's knife, having somehow worked its way out of him.

'Good yeah?' Roxy said, picking up the spoon, but Kenny didn't respond.

She took that as an affirmative and set about preparing a similar measure of the stuff for herself. Her tolerance was now about the same as Kenny's since their use had become equally frequent.

Matching habits wasn't uncommon among the

Victoria's residents, although it was unfortunate. Pair up a light user with a heavy addict and the result only ever went in one direction - the light user going heavy. There was no such thing as a good influence in their world.

Watching the powder bubbling away, Roxy's mouth went bone dry and her tongue brushed her cracked lips in concentration. Now it was her turn all other concerns faded into insignificance. She no longer noticed the rain, how cold she felt, and spared no thought for the prozzie she'd maimed, or the potential repercussions she might face should they meet again.

She no longer worried about Kenny, bleeding out and likely dying not a few feet away, nor did her mind skip to any more melancholic memories. All that mattered now was the promised rush and relief to come.

So she didn't hear Kenny's gnarled fingers fitfully scratching the concrete, his dirty nails breaking off with brittle clicks like the ticks of a cheap clock.

She didn't notice when the veins he'd once struggled to find rose up all over his body like fat worms, squirming under the skin.

And she certainly didn't see when Kenny's eyelids snapped open to show blue eyes turned completely black from haemorrhage.

Roxy never saw any of it. She was too busy shooting up.

5

Rhonda Caine stood in her bedsit's kitchen eating porridge, laptop on the counter streaming the latest crossfit highlights, competing with the oppressive beat of whatever the Russians upstairs were listening to. It was a little after six pm, not a time when most people were eating breakfast, but this was Rhonda's schedule.

After eating she cleaned up, a brief task when it was breakfast for one. It was always breakfast for one and had been for some months. Not that Rhonda particularly minded. She hadn't met anyone lately worth sharing a meal with, much less anything else.

Just two steps from the kitchen she stood in the lounge/bedroom getting dressed. A slight alcove, behind a curtain was where she kept her limited wardrobe.

Everything has to be limited when you live in a bedsit and Rhonda understood that all too well. Her time in care, where she'd shared a room with up to five other kids, had instilled in her a near obsessive disdain for clutter and provided ideal preparation for bedsit land.

Consequently, her present 100 square ft living space stood as a textbook example of utilitarianism. There was a couch bed, a small table beside it and nothing else. Her laptop doubled as entertainment centre, when the broadband was working, and she had two books she'd picked up from a charity shop which would be going straight back there once she got around to reading them.

At the corner nearest the door, she kept a laundry basket and beside it three pairs of shoes consisting two sets of trainers, one set of pumps, worn twice.

A mirror hung over the defunct fireplace and on the mantle below was where she'd lay out what little cosmetics she wore, right beside a single framed photo of herself and Roxy from when they were children.

It was the sole personal feature in the place. That aside, Sherlock Holmes would be hard-pressed to deduct anything much about this tenant, other than its sex being female, probably.

But Rhonda wouldn't be living in these sparse quarters much longer. This was only a cheap stopgap which had allowed her to save a deposit for a mortgage. Almost six years it'd taken her to gather what she needed, six hard years of moonlighting, stacking shelves, mopping floors, changing bedpans, whatever she could do to make the most as an unqualified worker.

After clawing her way out of poverty, Rhonda had always intended to bring her sister along. But an initial effort of lending money hadn't worked out well. Roxy burned through that five hundred quickly, teaching Rhonda a hard lesson.

She realised Roxy wasn't like her and that her drug use was a far more serious habit than first assumed. To counter it drastic measures were required. What Rhonda needed to do was drag Roxy kicking and screaming out of that world and soon she'd have a place to drag her to.

But not soon enough it seemed.

When Rhonda refused to send any more money, Roxy had gone silent and stayed that way for longer than usual. As kids they'd fought occasionally and as teens there'd been a couple of heated back and forths through Facebook. Although it'd sometimes gotten personal, they'd always made up within a couple of weeks.

Until now.

In her gut Rhonda sensed something was seriously wrong, that her sister was in a downward spiral, and felt she could no longer afford to wait for any house sale to go through before executing her plan.

Worst-case scenarios were all she could think of. In the addict's world overdoses happen at random, infections spread like wildfire and female users can quickly turn to degrading means to support their habit. Degrading and dangerous means.

For the umpteenth time that day alone, Rhonda pushed these thoughts aside. Then she laced her trainers, shut off her laptop, grabbed her sports bag and headed out.

Over the years she'd learned worrying never solved anything, especially when plans were already in motion. She simply had to get on with it, focus on the next step.

Tonight, she would be meeting that charity group for the first time. "Leg-Up" they called themselves, a name so bad it could only be deliberate.

Being as her life revolved around work and gym Rhonda hadn't met many hipsters, but the few she'd encountered were big on improv comedy, nu-folk and looked a hell of a lot like the people in Leg-Up's website banner photo.

A viral news story about them providing high-fashion haircuts for the homeless was what'd first caught her attention. At that point she'd already decided to find Roxy and here was a way she might do it with a bit of support.

Convincing Leg-Up to travel to Scarmouth hadn't been difficult. Scarmouth's homeless situation may

A Hot Dose of Hell

not have made mainstream news, but it was simple enough to find stats on government websites and comments on various social networks.

Rhonda didn't shy from disclosing her own motives either. Her cynical side told her that the added incentive of a good PR story would be hard for any organisation to resist. She could already see the headline "Charity reunites long-lost sisters" and expected someone at Leg-Up would see it too.

Sure enough, they'd got back to her within an hour and planned the trip for the next weekend. Point of contact was a girl called Poppy, who sent another message just as Rhonda locked her front door that evening.

@ the joint.
do u no it?

Rhonda knew the place, although she'd never been inside, only passed it on her walk to work. She messaged back that she'd be there in fifteen, finished locking the door and tried the handle to be certain before moving on.

Down the hall she met Big Greg coming out of the communal bathroom, his hairy gorilla body emerging from a dense haze of steam which trailed off his broad shoulders and balding skull. The towel around his waist seemed so small that it resembled a miniskirt, yet he stood tall and proud as ever. Not that it bothered Rhonda, or that it was meant to.

'Off out?' he grunted.

'Yeah,' said Rhonda, making a conscious effort to ignore the hairy pectorals in her peripheral.

'Was coming to see you first though.'

Greg gave a knowing nod. He didn't need to ask any more. There was only one reason Rhonda would be coming to see him. He switched off the bathroom light.

'Come on,' he said, ambling down the hall, leaving a trail of damp footprints for her to follow.

He stopped five doors down, at his own apartment and she waited outside.

'Be two secs,' he said, closing the door on her, but it was forty-five seconds before he returned, still undressed and shining wet.

'Here,' he said, shoving a small cylindrical package into her hand.

It was wrapped in an envelope, bound by an elastic band, but still made a faint metallic rattle as it was moved, almost as if it wanted to make itself known.

'It's police issue,' said Greg. 'Serial number's been filed off though. Can't be traced.'

Rhonda nodded while assessing the thing. She appreciated how neatly it fit in her grasp and how satisfying the weight felt. She made a slow arc with it, stopping mid-way.

'And it locks out like this?'

'Yep,' said Greg. 'One sharp shake of your arm and it'll pop out. You want it to go back, then you press the end down hard on the ground till you hear a click.'

'Got it.'

He watched her stash it in the sports bag and although he'd been happy enough to take her money, he couldn't resist one last go at their original debate.

'I can still get you CS spray y' know? It's probably a lot better, much easier to use anyway. An' there's less chance a' someone grabbin' it, usin' it against you.'

A steely look glinted in Rhonda's eyes.

'I'd like to see someone try.'

'Fair enough,' said Greg, nodding in respect, and they exchanged a fist bump as Rhonda moved on.

'Just remember,' he added, calling after her. 'You want anythin' else like that you come to me, alright? Don't go buyin' nothin' down the pub or off them *Ruskies* upstairs, yeah?'

Already at the exit to the stairwell Rhonda gave a glance back.

'I know. Cheers Greg,' she said, on her way through.

'Have a good 'un,' she heard him say, the last word smothered by the closing door just as another sound supplanted it.

'-IS SHE? WHO IS SHE?'

What seemed like round two of a heated row was occurring in the stairwell a few floors up, the shrieks reverberating around Rhonda as she spiralled down.

Young Charlie had obviously been cheating again and her girlfriend didn't sound likely to forgive this time.

Either way Rhonda didn't care to hear about it. Drama had never been of any interest to her. She'd seen enough in her twenty-six years to fill a week's worth of Jeremy Kyle shows and quickened pace to avoid hearing much more.

'IT'S NOT WHAT IT LOOKS LIKE.'

Light rainfall welcomed Rhonda outside and she donned her hood before breaking into a fast jog. Having never learned to drive this was her primary mode of transport and yet another contributor to her extraordinary fitness level.

She proceeded through the estate at that rate, all the grim landmarks whizzing by, a burnt-out old Clio mounted on breeze-blocks, the hoop-less basketball post, bottle banks covered with countless graffiti tags.

Her footfall echoed back as she neared the subway underpass, growing louder while she travelled through and fading once she emerged at the other end, alongside a gridlocked train of commuter traffic.

It was all the nine-to-fivers returning home for the day, just as hers was beginning.

Running parallel she continued in the opposite direction, toward the city, soon finding herself in the trendy Buckley district, a hipster haven of vinyl record shops, "ethical" food and clothing stores, tattoo parlours and vegan cafes.

There were buskers lining both sides of the pedestrianised street, each patch roughly ten metres apart. All the usual suspects, the acoustic guitarists, living statues, streetdance troupes and bongo players, were already locked in fierce competition, all vying for the coin of the yuppies dining out.

Strangely, it was a lone beggar who seemed to be pulling the lion's share. A lot of middle to upper-class students were crowding him, waiting their turn for "candid" instagram snaps showing how generous they could be with their parents' money.

The bum was lapping it up and yet Rhonda caught something in his eyes, a glimmer of resentment for his young benefactors. It was just a fraction of a second, but enough to indicate this was as much a performance to him as it was to them.

'Fank yuu so match,' he grovelled, in the type of cockney accent you never hear outside Dickens adaptations. 'Gawd bless ya, guv.'

'I hope that *she,* blesses you too,' was the very deliberate response from a shaven-headed young woman in floral dress and combat boots.

The bum just looked confused.

'Yeah…cheers luv.'

Sixty yards ahead, The Joint's cursive neon sign flickered dimly, suggesting an old dive bar and upon entering Rhonda saw how the shabby interior supported that façade.

The décor was rough, unfinished as if it were the product of an unresolved labour dispute. In the gaps between vintage tin signs, framed newspaper clippings and mounted bicycles, 70's style hex-pattern wallpaper glared through a thin layer of white paint, while radiators, piping and grill vents had all been stripped, rubbed down so that they stuck out like the proverbial thumb.

Mismatched furniture cluttered the bare floor, people sitting on everything from school desks to church pews to bean bags. At the bar, Rhonda eschewed a patched up old stool in favour of standing and found more interest in guessing the weight-bearing capabilities of the pipework overhead than perusing the chalkboard menu.

That drink menu belied The Joint's spit 'n sawdust image. It listed only pricey craft ales and cocktails, and the overwhelmingly well-spoken clientele didn't seem aggressive enough to necessitate the band stage being surrounded by chicken wire fencing. Equally, the all-male band performing behind the mesh looked about as provocative as a sedated kitten.

Singing a slow acoustic cover of "*Do you wanna touch me*", the frontman's anaemic vocal implied a sense of victimhood through its vulnerability, making Rhonda's flesh creep.

'*Beggin' on my knees, baby won't you please, run your fingers through my hair.*'

Such mawkish warbling stood in stark contrast to the aggressive challenge lurking within Joan Jett's snarl of sexual invitation, while completely subverting the original writer's predatory intent.

Assuming that was deliberate would be giving this

quartet of fluffy-bearded waifs far too much credit. For moments later their shift into *"Enter sandman"* made it clear this was how they played everything.

'What can I do you for?' asked a curly-moustached bartender and Rhonda hesitated to reply.

After a beat, he produced a pocket watch on a chain from his waistcoat, a move which was either compulsive habit or blatant hint.

'Water please,' said Rhonda.

'Still, sparklin' or good ol' tap?'

Rhonda thought the bartender's northern-ish accent a little spurious. His delivery came off stilted, like he was having to think before he spoke and the emphasis on "good ol' tap" made her bristle, in that it smelled like a piss-take.

'Tap,' she said, flatly.

'Tap comin' up.'

He served it with ice, a stirrer and a wholly unnecessary miniature umbrella which Rhonda dumped on the bartop before moving on.

She weaved through the oddly arranged furniture, scanning for faces from Leg-Up's website gallery. It was tough to differentiate when so many looked the same and she stopped near the designated vaping area to phone Poppy.

Rhonda's thumb was primed to hit dial when she caught her own name on the air. It'd taken several seconds for it to register, not just because of the music, but because the plummy pronouncement was practically alien to her ear.

'RHAWN-DAA.'

At a table near the back Rhonda could see her standing, waving, big eastern style bangles jangling along a slim arm.

'IT'S ME, POPPY. COME ON OVER.'

A Hot Dose of Hell

As she made her way across the room, Rhonda waded through a smog of sickly-sweet smells, candy floss, doughnut, vanilla ice cream. There was no food, however, only vape smoke emanating off each of the four tables in that section.

Poppy's table hummed mainly of fudge and Rhonda caught a full blast of it upon arrival when one of the males there exhaled a jet of white smoke in her direction.

On reflex she scowled, her laser-glare locked onto him and in turn he gave a gormless, open-mouthed smile. Then he raised the Pokeball-shaped e-cig in a very deliberate fashion, almost like he intended it as a statement, but of what Rhonda had no clue.

'Whassup,' he said.

A quick appraisal told her the bloke wasn't hostile, just awkward. He'd hidden his frail body in the garb of a lumberjack, topping off the incongruence with thick-rimmed specs and a straw trilby which he clearly hoped would be a conversation starter, just like his Pokemon e-cig.

'Alright mate,' she grunted back.

To reclaim the attention Poppy made a dramatic gesture with her hand.

'This is Rhonda everyone,' she said. Then motioning to the other male on her right, 'Rhonda, this is Kibsy, or Kibs for short.'

This Kibs was so similar in look to the lumberjack that they could have been brothers. The extensive sailor tattoos and She-Ra vest beneath his flannel shirt were the only giveaway Rhonda wasn't looking at an exact double.

He even made the same uncanny open-mouthed smile.

'Hey, hey,' he said while Rhonda gave a slight nod,

her lack of enthusiasm obvious.

'And this is Jack,' said Poppy, indicating to a person of indiscriminate sex at her left. This one was also wearing thick-rimmed specs with a baggy black hoodie and had blue hair styled into a quiff Elvis himself would have envied.

Overall, Rhonda thought the fine features and smooth unstubbled skin could only belong to a female, yet this was contradicted by overtly masculine body language and a kind of surly air more befitting a teenage lad.

The mouth and nose, which might have proved the deciders, were covered by a rainbow pattern fashion mask, through which Rhonda received a muffled, 'Hello.'

'And this is Trent,' Poppy said, squeezing the lumberjack's narrow shoulder.

'Hey gurl,' said Trent. 'Welcome to our posse.'

Posse? thought Rhonda, the term conjuring images of rugged old cowboys, vicious bandits, torch-wielding vigilantes, the polar opposite to the group in front of her.

She could already tell they'd be of little help with the plan. Extracting Roxy from her current situation would require some fortitude and a degree of aggression none of them seemed capable of away from a keyboard, if even.

Rhonda could only blame herself though. They'd never claimed to be that and didn't look any different from the photos on the website. She'd just assumed there would be *something* a little bit steely about them, *something* streetwise after their time spent working with homeless addicts, but no. There was not a trace to be found between them, not the slightest hint they'd be able to handle anything more traumatic

A Hot Dose of Hell

than complaining about a wrong order at Starbucks.

'I absolutely *adore* this version,' said Kibs, gently nodding his head to the band while they continued to neuter Metallica's biggest anthem.

'Subversive and touching at the same time,' he said. 'Totally flipping the masculine toxicity of the original into something truly poignant.'

'And heartfelt,' added Trent, to which the others murmured in agreement.

Listening to this drivel Rhonda had to remind herself it was still a lift there and back, extra pairs of eyes to watch for danger, extra hands to dial police if needed. They wouldn't be completely without use.

At least Poppy seemed confident and with good reason. The girl was pretty, tall, athletic, although she didn't work for it, and dressed in a flamboyant bohemian style, all long light materials with intricately detailed patterns. She glimmered with jewellery, much of it from piercings in her caramel skin, and her dark hair was long and luscious, making Rhonda a little self-conscious of her own home-dyed, no frills plait.

'Please,' Poppy purred, 'sit with us Rhonda.'

'Alright,' Rhonda sighed, pulling up a chair.

On the table she noticed a board game, Connect 4, with its yellow and red chips scattered about the "Posse's" drinks. Trent was turning a chip over in his slender fingers and at one point looked set to drop one in the grid when a reprimanding glare from Poppy stayed his hand.

'So we're gathered to discuss our plans for tomorrow,' she said. 'Finalise our arrangements, go through itinerary. Raising awareness is our key aim so we need to document our story in clear photos. Eye-catching images that are easy to take in when scrolling.'

It instantly struck Rhonda how Poppy spoke like a corporate executive, the kind of person she'd encounter for two seconds every six months or so, when her manager gave a tour of the Shopco site.

These people would smile, briefly make eye contact or ignore her altogether. Then later they'd make some naïve, unrealistic recommendation about her job role, based on those two seconds of observation.

Such a position likely awaited Poppy in the future and when the time came this charity of hers would look good on those applications. If not the entire motive behind the venture, Rhonda was doubtful the advantage would've escaped Poppy's notice.

'Trent, you're travel arrangements. Is our ride still confirmed? No last minute changes?'

'It's taken care of, Pops. Edd is picking us up tomorrow.'

'What time?'

'Umm, about nine.'

Poppy's eyes narrowed just a fraction.

'So nine, nine thirty? What time have you arranged?'

'About nine,' Trent said with a shrug. 'You know what Edd's like. He's an anarchist.'

That answer gave Poppy pause, since it presented a dilemma - Would demanding conformity of an anarchist make her a fascist? And while she held an internal debate on the issue, a painfully slow and earnest performance of The Smiths' *"Panic"*, crept over the room.

'Ugh,' went Kibs, giving a soft eye-roll. 'Morrissey is sooo disappointing to me.'

'I know,' said Jack. 'He's like, *literally* a nazi. I feel

like I'm going to have to sell my vinyl of *Meat is Murder* and give the money to BLM.'

Trent groaned his agreement while Rhonda stayed quiet. She didn't get the issue with Morrissey, a gay icon, vegan and animal rights advocate, who she'd expect to be something of a hero for this lot.

But she could finally see the need for the chicken wire now. She realised it would only take a couple of rowdy football fans to wander in and this whiny band would soon find themselves ducking bottles and pint pots.

'Can we stick to the topic, please?' Poppy sighed, returning to the present. On the subject of Edd, she'd arrived at an ideological stalemate, leaving her stressed. It showed in the way she bared her perfect teeth, emphasising the consonants of her next sentence.

'This is important work we're about to do.'

'We know, Pops,' said Jack, 'and we have to be in good spirits to stay inspired.'

'That's right,' Trent agreed, rising from his seat, and he finally plonked that long-held yellow chip into the grid to make three in a row.

He beamed, 'This round on me.'

Poppy shook her head, though she couldn't help but crack a smile.

'Yolo,' she said in surrender and a giddy excitement seemed to infect everyone on the table, bar Rhonda.

Trent received Poppy's permission with another open-mouthed smile. Then, reciting a previous round, he pointed to each member of the posse as he listed their craft ale of choice. The borderline obscene names could easily be misinterpreted as insults to the casual passerby.

Starting with Jack there was, 'Greasy Cock.'

Then Kibs: 'Furry Willow.'

Then Poppy: 'Bishop's Hat,' before Trent's eyes fell to Rhonda and he gave an encouraging smile that was only accidentally patronising.

'I've got work,' said Rhonda.

'What?' blurted Poppy, her lashes fluttering from shock. 'But we were hoping you would share your story. Enlighten us with your truth.'

Having absolutely no desire to go down that road Rhonda took the cue to stand.

'I'd better get going now actually,' she said, slinging her bag onto her shoulder.

'Really?' said Poppy.

Rhonda made a point of checking her phone. 'Yep.'

Truth was she still had half an hour to spare but didn't feel up for spending it with this lot, especially if they were going to pry. Tomorrow she'd have to endure them for the full day and knew she'd need to conserve her tolerance, otherwise she could see herself snapping the way she had with too many people in the past.

'I'll see you all in the morning.' She nodded to Trent. '*Nine-ish* right? Where are we meeting?'

Poppy answered, 'The war monument.'

'Which one?' said Rhonda. 'The line-up or the wall?'

Poppy had to take a moment, translating Rhonda's rough accent, her crude descriptions of those historical landmarks. *Dulaan up? Da wul?*

'The wall,' she said finally, her relief only too obvious, like she'd just found the answer to a quiz question at crunch time.

Rhonda nodded. 'Cool, see you all then. Don't go

too wild tonight.'

'We won't,' said Trent, somewhat proud Rhonda would consider them capable of "wildness", as were Kibs and Jack.

Only Poppy picked up on the hint of sarcasm and she would've been insulted if she weren't so infatuated.

Thirstily, she watched Rhonda walk away until out of sight, when she caught herself gnawing her lip ring. A hot flush came over her then and guiltily she looked around, hoping none of the others had noticed.

'Seems nice,' said Kibs, dropping a red chip to block Trent's last move. 'Very...*authentic*.'

Keen to mark her territory, Poppy was quick with another reprimanding look.

'Don't get any ideas, Kibs. Remember, Rhonda's a vulnerable person going through a trauma, and no woman should be taken advantage of. Ever.'

'I wasn't suggesting anything,' Kibs whined, and he made a point to straighten his She-Ra vest. 'You know how I feel about women.'

Jack pointed a finger in his face.

'That was covert objectification.'

'What?' said Kibs. 'I was commenting on her personality.'

'I could hear it in your voice,' said Jack, keeping the finger aimed. 'You weren't talking about her *personality*.'

Kibs put his hands up as if under arrest.

'I said *seems*. If I was talking about her looks, I would've been more definite, wouldn't I? I mean, her looks are indisputable.'

Jack raised an eyebrow.

'Her looks are *indisputable*?'

'I rest my case,' said Poppy, leaving Kibs in

stunned silence, on the verge of tears and they allowed him to suffer like that for almost a full minute until Poppy saw fit to excuse him.

'Oh Kibs,' she sighed, suppressing a laugh.

'We still have a lot of work to do on you, don't we?'

A broken Kibs merely nodded in submission, eyes cast downward.

'I know. I'm sorry. I'm learning.'

Meanwhile in the face of all this passive-aggressive tension, Trent had frozen, unsure what to do lest he blunder into the crossfire. Chipping in on Poppy's side could be interpreted as chauvinistic. Saying nothing could be viewed as a sign of complicity. He lost either way, but now that there was a break, he seized the chance to escape.

'Sooo, I'll get the drinks,' he said and headed off while the band played on, bending the last notes of *"Panic"* into the opening chords of Chris Isaak's *"Wicked Game"*.

'Tune,' said Poppy, as all around her fellow patrons clicked their fingers in subdued applause.

6

A dirty white transit van hurtled down narrow, hedged country roads, on the back route into Scarmouth. It was the hour before dawn and the driver, Fred McCall, always took this way at night to circumvent police check points, those bored officers awaiting their one in ten seizures of drugs coming from the harbour.

Fred had no such cargo to worry about. However, he was packing an extendible cosh, brass knucks, pepper spray and a three-inch knife disguised as a lighter.

Wiktor Pinkiewicz, the mountain of muscle beside him, had that hunting knife with the knuckle guard.

They'd be facing up to four years each for carrying them alone.

'First blood,' muttered Fred, as the rear wheels spat out an unfortunate badger. Then some wayward branches licked the side panel, forcing him toward the middle of the road where he maintained course for the paintwork's sake.

This time of night he knew the risk of anyone coming the other way was slim to nothing and felt familiar enough with the winding track to comfortably take it at the national speed limit. So comfortably, that his hairy sausage fingers were drumming the wheel in time with Bronski Beat's "*Smalltown Boy*" pumping through the stereo.

'*Cryyyy-ing to your soul,*' Fred howled, painfully attempting to match the singer's falsetto and Wiktor curled a scarred lip in disgust.

'Is shit,' he muttered, hand going for the radio dial.

'HEY,' Fred snapped, 'it's my van, Pinkie. We

listen to that techno wank when we're in your motor, but when we're in *my* van it's classics only.'

'*Classics*,' Pinkie snorted, reluctantly withdrawing his hand. 'This gay shit.'

'Each to their own, Pinkie. You just don't know good tunes cos you wasn't allowed to hear 'em in commie land.'

'Ha, maybe,' said Pinkie, showing teeth but hardly smiling. 'Maybe I grow up hearing this, I become like you.'

'Spose you got off lucky then,' Fred chuckled, his barrel belly pulsing against the steering wheel, and he resumed his song until a steep dip in the road caused him to lose the words.

'Steady,' said Pinkie, with a firmness to mask his creeping nausea. He wasn't soft, but Fred's driving and the twisting roads could inflict motion sickness on a fighter pilot.

'Slow down, eh Fred?'

'No can do,' said Fred, gripping the wheel tight to gun it around a sharp bend.

'Chryste,' said Pinkie.

Something in the back, a tool, came loose, went skidding across the floor while both men leaned against the centrifugal force. Its pull waned once the road straightened, and Fred centred the wheel.

'We're the first response, Pinkie, an' I wanna catch this prick before he gets outta there. Otherwise, we're only gonna have to look for him. An' I don't wanna be knockin' on doors for the next week. Do you?'

Only eight minutes had passed since Fred received the call. It came from one of Castell's brothels, the "budget one", where some john was playing up, playing right up by the sounds. There was a hell of lot of screaming and thumping in the background, loud

A Hot Dose of Hell

enough to drown most of what that prozzie said.

It didn't matter. Fred had got the gist and was already starting the van before the call ended.

'What about guard anyway?' said Pinkie. 'He can't do his job?'

'She said she couldn't find the guard.'

'Probably banging one of the girls then.'

'Perks of the job,' said Fred, just as the road widened and the growth receded, making way for the bright lights of Scarmouth harbour in the distance. They stood out against the black sea and sky, a blanket of colourful neon. From that range a person could appreciate the view. But like Fred's last tinder date, it was far uglier up close.

To Pinkie's grunted approval Fred killed the music there and turned off the main road, embarking on a snaking course through a string of council estates.

Fred knew these streets well from his misspent adolescence, from many small battles fought and mini romances lost. A gang of cider swigging teens at a corner reminded him so much of those innocent days, that he forgave their moody glares on the way past.

'Little cunts,' he chuckled fondly.

The van shortly emerged at the edge of the harbourside, onto a street of formerly desirable luxury apartments, now gone to seed.

The brothel stood at the end of this street. It was a four-storey bloc comprising a dozen apartments, a communal garden and a reception area where a guard was always on duty, twenty-four seven. Although any trouble tended to be minor there was also a burner phone on site holding only Fred's number, to be used in an emergency.

Before tonight, he couldn't remember it ever being used.

At speed, the van pulled into the empty lot, headlights glancing across the faces of a gaggle of skimpily attired women on the porch outside. They looked like groupies awaiting the band, if that band were fronted by Charles Manson and they'd been forced to wait at gunpoint.

A warning light bonged as the passenger door opened and Pinkie's boots touched the ground before the van came to a complete halt. At his approach, the crowd clung ever tighter, while his monstrous shadow grew with every step until it engulfed them all.

'Who called?' he asked, assessing each wary face, and a disarmingly sweet voice answered.

'I did.'

Her dainty hand raised as if speaking in a classroom, this tiny waif separated from the huddle as Pinkie took the first of four steps up the porch to bring his eye level to hers.

'What's occurring?' he asked, the regional phrase sounding odd in his thick Polish accent, and her Arabic-tattooed finger pointed skyward.

'It's kickin' off up there an' we can't find the guard.'

Pinkie followed her aim to gaze up at the lighted windows. When he focused, he could hear a faint thumping coming from one of the higher floors.

'What's up, Pinkie?' said Fred, appearing from behind and he tracked his partner's gaze, failing to notice anything amiss.

'Bird shit on your head or somethin', Pinks? C'mon let's get in there.'

Together the men stomped up the porch stairs and the women scattered like a shoal of fish to pour into the reception, yabbering in various languages, some panicked, some angry.

Before she could join them, Pinkie grabbed the

waif by her arm, reeled her in.

'Which room?'

'Number nine,' she said, a single tear rolling down her cheek. 'Tray's room.'

'What floor?'

'Three.'

She flinched as Pinkie's huge paw came toward her face, but he merely brushed the tear away and released her.

'Get some rest. We handle it.'

The men marched her through to the reception where another prozzie accosted them, a Filipino with a weird hybrid accent, like she'd learned English purely from watching *Eastenders*.

'We aint seen Shaz neither. Reckon she up there too, innit.'

'I know Shaz,' said Fred and he led Pinkie to the stairwell with a flick of his bald head, leaving the women behind at the reception, gibbering like turkeys. Once safely out of earshot he gave Pinkie a nudge.

'Bet this Tray's just on a bender,' he puffed, already short of breath on the first flight.

Pinkie observed him dispassionately.

'You need cardio,' he said. 'And diet.'

'Yeah, alright,' Fred scowled, the ledge of his Neanderthal brow seeming to jut even further. 'You wait till you get to my age, son. That's if the steroids don't give ya a heart attack first.'

Pinkie chuckled mirthlessly.

'Maccie D's will give *you* heart attack first.'

'Ha,' Fred grinned, 'been rubbing off on you 'aven't I?'

'I hope not.'

That thumping noise Pinkie heard outside became

audible from the second floor up. It was a continuous beat as steady as the clicks of a metronome and now Fred could hear it too. At the third floor he took a moment to catch his breath, leaning against the bannister.

'Maybe it's just some rough sex,' he said, sounding hopeful.

Pinkie didn't share his optimism.

'What about guard?'

Fred shrugged, took a deep breath.

'Maybe she's shaggin' the guard.'

'Long time for shagging.'

'Says you,' Fred chuckled, reaching under his gut-roll to cup himself. 'I'm a fuckin' blue-pilled love machine me.'

The expected laughter didn't follow. After a pause Pinkie just snorted and walked away, leaving Fred with a sense he might've touched a nerve, that maybe Pinkie had been having some trouble in that department; a common issue with steroid abusers he'd known.

'I can get ya some if ya like,' said Fred, taking after Pinkie, and he caught up outside a hallway door.

'C'mon Pinks, I'll even do ya a deal.'

'That isn't my problem,' said Pinkie. 'It's the opposite.'

The penny dropped and Fred cringed, 'You mean Anya's pregnant *again*? Fuck's sake man. You never hear of contraception?'

'She's Catholic,' said Pinkie, yanking the handle and the instant the door parted from its seal that banging jumped to thunderous levels, raising the hackles on both their thick necks.

'Whoa,' said Fred.

The noise continued in the same pace while they

A Hot Dose of Hell

made their way down the corridor and when they arrived outside Tray's room there was no further debate as to whether it was a by-product of sex. No sex of any kind sounded like that, not your porn star stallion, nor your *Fifty shades* kink. Each bang fell as heavy and dull as a hammer on brickwork, with a mechanical persistence that didn't miss a beat, right up until the moment Pinkie knocked the door.

Then there was only silence, save Fred's canine panting.

He called out: 'Alright in there, Tray?'

But there was no reply.

They waited a full five seconds.

Still nothing.

'Sod this,' said Fred and he gave Pinkie the nod.

BANG.

From one sharp kick the door flew open onto a room soaked in red light.

Eager as a hound Fred bowled straight in. Almost immediately he tripped on something unseen to fall upon the unmade bed. The sheets were wet on his face, soaking wet, and recoiling from them, he heard Pinkie mutter.

'Chryste.'

With surprising agility Fred rolled off the bed onto his feet to face the room, pulling the cosh fast so that it locked out, ready for use. He saw that he'd tripped over a long female body laying prone near the threshold and was about to say something when the banging resumed.

It was coming from behind the bathroom door.

Calmly, Pinkie stepped over the sprawled legs on his way in and caught a drip from the ceiling on his shaven skull. He wiped it away while glancing up to see that the red bulb overhead was dripping somehow. A leak, he assumed.

Then he noticed that the wetness transferred to his hand carried an unmistakable scent, same as the wetness Fred had found in the bed. It was a distinctly metallic scent both knew only too well, the scent of blood.

'Is she dead?' said Fred, nodding to the woman on the floor.

'Maybe,' said Pinkie. 'Is she Shaz or Tray?'

Fred shook his head, whispered, 'Not Shaz. She's only about five three. That one looks as tall as you.'

'Tray then,' Pinkie said, stepping past her to the bathroom.

'Hey, come out here NOW,' he barked, hammering the door and again, the banging ceased, yet through the quiet moments that followed there appeared no sign of anyone coming out.

It was then Pinkie looked to Fred for the okay to bust in. Only this time the door exploded first, a hail of splinters grazing his face, a spray of blood dousing it.

'Fuuuck,' Fred gasped, an involuntary expression of fearful awe, while Pinkie quickly wiped the blood from his brow to see.

Through the door's busted upper panel, a naked male body now hung prone, twitching fingertips brushing the cig-burned carpet, a steady stream of blood trickling off them.

Neither Fred nor Pinkie could identify the corpse since the entire top of its head was missing. It'd been smashed off rather than cut clean, gory flaps peeling from jagged edges of broken skull, blood pumping from the exposed throat in volcanic fashion. And from the lower jaw the tongue dangled obscenely, reminiscent of the thousands of limp post-coital dicks the room had seen, still wagging slightly, dripping its fluids onto the carpet in long, sticky strands.

Pinkie didn't say another word, just drew his knife. Then there was a flicker of movement between the cracks, and he froze.

After a few moments he could tell that whatever lay beyond the door, whatever did this, was pacing like a caged animal.

'YOU'VE DONE IT NOW, DICKHEAD,' Fred warned. 'BETTER COME OUT BEFORE WE DRAG YOU OUT.'

Still no verbal response came from the other side, only a faint hissing sound.

Cautiously, Pinkie tried the handle. The door was unlocked, so once the latch disengaged it naturally creaked open, swaying outward under the corpse's weight. As it did Pinkie withdrew slightly in wait of any sudden attack and when none followed, he peered around.

The gruesome scene he found was like a flashback to his days working the abattoir floor, with lashings and streaks of blood covering almost every surface, the bone-white fittings and tiles glimmering through in jarring contrast.

Leading with the knife he entered, and his gaze immediately found the top portion of the corpse's head, a hairy pile of mincemeat in the bowl of a broken sink. Just below that a constant spurt of water travelled in an arc from a ruptured pipe, accounting for the hissing sound, and near the end of that arc, tucked tight between a smashed toilet and cracked wall, crouched a small, naked, bloody female form.

Fred used his steel toecaps to push the door wider, accommodating his bulkier frame. Bloody water splashed and porcelain chips crunched underfoot as he joined Pinkie, looking past the Polack's broad shoulder to the woman on the floor.

'Izzat you, Shaz?'

Fred blinked and the woman was on her feet, shrieking like an ape skinned alive. Even facing them he still couldn't tell if it was Shaz. Thick strands of drenched hair hung in front of her veiny, blood-caked face and clung to flat breasts.

Her teeth were the only distinguishable features, molars glinting through a horrific slash along her cheek, giving her a lopsided rictus grin to rival the reaper's own.

Hardened as they were, both Fred and Pinkie stood momentarily fazed by her disturbing appearance.

It proved a critical mistake.

Showing serpentine quickness, she snatched up the cistern lid and swung it directly into Pinkie's chest. Unbelievably the blow lifted the big man clean off his feet, sent him crashing into the soiled tub, the tatty shower curtain falling tidily on top.

He went stiff after, but only unconscious, heavy breaths obvious from the way the curtain still moved over his chest. Fred had that much to be grateful for and little else since there was no way of predicting when his partner might come to. In the meantime, it left him alone to handle this bloody banshee, whoever she was.

At a distance they faced off for several seconds, where Fred noticed that cistern lid in her grasp had been broken in half, leaving it with a rough, jagged edge. After what happened to Pinkie, he didn't much fancy being on the receiving end of it. He also preferred not to hit women where possible, so in an effort to prevent both he first looked to pacify her with talk.

A Hot Dose of Hell

'Steady on, luv,' he said, the cosh drawn to his shoulder, at the ready in case reason failed.

'We aint here to hurt ya.'

Not a flicker of reaction showed on the woman's bloody face. Not the slightest sign she'd even heard what Fred had said. She just stood there watching him with those black eyes, clutching the cistern lid so tightly it lifted several of her bejewelled fingernails.

'That's it, take it easy,' he cooed. Then he spotted it, just below her navel, a familiar tattoo. It was a bird, maybe a dove, and he remembered Shaz telling him how she'd got it to cover a caesarean scar.

'Shaz?' he gasped. 'What 'appened to ya luv?'

He was inching toward her with an open hand for peace when suddenly the cords of her neck pulsed, and she charged with the jagged end of the cistern lid aimed at his midsection. Despite their shared past, their intimacy and his own misguided version of chivalry, Fred didn't hesitate to use the cosh once threatened. He brought it down hard on her lead wrist, spoiling her aim so that the sharp edge missed his gut, grazing his meaty thigh instead.

'CUNT,' he yelped, leg buckling, and he punched her square in the face.

She reeled backward violently, collapsing against the toilet bowl, uprooting it, and a rush of water covered the floor while in the tub Pinkie stirred, throwing the curtain off.

'Bout time,' said Fred, moving to help him. 'Shaz's lost it mate. I 'ad to spark 'er.'

They linked arms for balance and on the way up Pinkie groaned, a stifling pain streaking his chest. Upon standing he set his sights on the woman slumped by the toilet then he stepped out of the tub wearing a look of vindictive determination, making his intent obvious.

'She's done,' said Fred. 'Just leave it.'

But Fred's assumption was wrong for not a moment later Shaz sprang back to her feet. He barely had time to raise the cosh again before he found himself gazing up at the stains on the ceiling, feeling the unforgiving tile at his back.

She'd barged him clean over, as if their weight difference had been reversed, and got right into it with Pinkie, slashing at him with her remaining nails, screeching ferociously.

Although still dazed, Pinkie eventually managed to catch her forearm and, with his other hand, her throat. He held both tightly, strangling those shrieks while her free hand flip-flopped to unnatural angles, slapping limply at him like a dead fish.

Fred's cosh had clearly broken something there and a sharp bone protruding the skin caught Pinkie's brow, splitting it open. He hissed as blood ran into his eye, but didn't let go. Instead, using all his strength he drove her back against the wall, propelling them both clean through the plasterboard and together they crashed to the bedroom floor.

In their wake a cloud of plaster dust billowed up into the air, quickly descending on every surface, coating Fred's clammy skin, his damp clothes. Slowly he turned over to press himself up. He couldn't quite manage it though and had to bring his knees beneath him first.

His head was swimming, bleeding too, and he sat back on his haunches hoping the world would stop spinning soon. Tinnitus hummed through his cauliflower ears as loud as Shaz and Pinkie's noise in the bedroom. He could hear her the most. Not a good sign.

'Hold on Pinks,' he said, moving to stand.

The tub creaked in complaint while he used it for leverage, a deep crack spiderwebbing across. Then by chance he glanced down and caught something shimmering in the light, almost alluringly, a sharp edge gleaming with the promise of brutality.

Eagerly Fred reached in, grabbing Pinkie's knife by its guard. He felt the weight, adjusted grip and went lumbering toward the fresh hole in the wall, toward the sounds of struggle and the hellish red light pouring through.

By now Pinkie had lost the advantage, but was keeping himself safe, just about. He was on his back, legs wrapped around the waist of a thrashing, thrusting Shaz, using his hips to hold her at bay while deflecting her flailing arms with his big open hands. He looked like someone trying to ride a bull from underneath.

On any other day Fred might've quipped about the sexual nature of such a pose, as he'd been known to crack jokes during even the most violent encounters, but not now. This was no time for levity or cockiness.

Through all their jobs together, all those people roughed up, the debt collections, the taxings, he and Pinkie had always held the upper hand, always been in control of the situation. And here, for the first time *they* were the ones in danger.

This adversary was strong, unbelievably strong considering she was around half Pinkie's size, and he'd been known to push twice his own weight in the gym, yet she was somehow overpowering him. Her driving, animalistic thrusts were bringing her closer and closer by the second, her teeth gnashing mere inches from his face with the ferocity of a steel trap.

'FRED,' he bellowed.

Fred wasn't anywhere near as strong as Pinkie and most of his stamina had been spent just climbing the stairs. His head was woozy from concussion and he felt unsteady clambering through the hole in the plasterboard. In his haste he stumbled on the other side, staggered forward, inadvertently driving the knife clean through the back of Shaz's neck.

'Whoops.'

Blood spattered Pinkie's face as the knife tip burst through Shaz's throat. He flinched and cursed some more in his native tongue while she stiffened on top of him, her jaw gaping reflexively to tear her cheek that much further. Bloody bubbles grew from the throat wound in bunches, propelled by an unmistakable death rattle. After the last popped she looked to be dead until suddenly, with an inhuman effort she jerked forward once more, bringing the knife tip poking out of her neck to within millimetres of Pinkie's cheek.

'Kurwa.'

Barely believing his eyes, Fred seized the knife handle with both hands and managed to withdraw it a fraction of a second before the tip reached Pinkie's cornea. The release was so sudden that Fred reeled back, his fall only prevented by the support of the remaining wall which received a fresh T-shaped crevice in return.

'FRED,' Pinkie cried.

Incredibly, Shaz still wasn't quite out of the game, her gnashing teeth now dangerously close to Pinkie's nose, and all the Polack could do was turn his head to buy a few seconds.

'GET HER OFF ME,' he roared, more shaken than Fred had ever heard him and he cried out again just as Fred lunged in. 'GET OFF, BITCH.'

The fat man grabbed a handful of Shaz's soaked hair and yanked using all his weight. It moved her only so far. She was still very much entangled with Pinkie, but at least Fred had her under control, just about.

She pulled against him like a wild stray fighting a dogcatcher's pole, making a gargled scream of frustration, blood bubbling from the wound in her throat with every strained effort. She wasn't getting anywhere, but soon her hair began to part from her scalp with audible snaps. Then her bulging black eyes returned to Pinkie and he saw a manic grin forming on her mangled mouth.

Terror stricken he realised, just as she did, that at any second the hair would break and she'd snap forward like a rubber band, right onto him.

'DO HER MATE,' he barked. 'DO HER NOW.'

A primal, harrowing cry, suited to a nervous breakdown, erupted from Fred's lungs as he plunged the knife deep into the side of Shaz's gut, going right up to the hilt. Repeatedly he stabbed her with rapid, frenzied thrusts, screaming all the while, until that dove tattoo was no more and from its place her steaming insides came oozing out onto Pinkie's lap, soaking through his jeans.

Finally, Shaz went limp, her weight sagging in Fred's grip and a beat later her hair broke, leaving him clutching a handful of strands while her butchered corpse flopped forward onto Pinkie.

Repulsed, Pinkie launched the body off himself, unleashing a stream of Polish obscenities as he scrambled to his feet, shedding the offal from his lap.

'JEDZ GÓWNO, PIEPRZONA SUK-'

The outburst stopped abruptly, and a weary Fred looked across to see Pinkie standing in front of the dressing table, looking down on its surface.

'What is it?'

'You won't believe,' said Pinkie and he turned to show a fat brick of powder in his hand.

'Shit,' Fred gasped. 'Izzat coke?'

'You tell me,' said Pinkie, scanning the dresser, where traces of powder lines were still visible beside a Boots points card and another packet of gear, already open.

Fred shuffled over to join him.

'Whatever it is they done a lot of it,' he said, comparing the open packet to the sealed one.

'No shit.'

The pair spent a few moments in silent contemplation, catching their breath, the only sound the random drips of gore dropping off their clothes and the hissing pipe from the bathroom.

Then something caught Fred's eye, a glimmer of movement in the dresser's mirror, something behind them. He turned and his shoulders sagged, face dropping at the sight. It was the corpse he'd tripped over on the way in, the tall bird, Tray, and she was getting up, slowly.

Pinkie noticed it too.

'You alright, luv?' he asked, but the amazonian didn't respond.

As with Shaz, her hair hung across her face, although it wasn't all bloody and wet, and retained some shape, some sense of having been styled, providing hope she'd be okay. It wasn't until she was fully upright that they got a good look at her and when they did their pulses raced.

Simultaneously both men realised it wasn't the hissing pipe from the bathroom they were hearing. It was her, breathing through the thick froth spilling from her mouth, or what remained of her mouth. The entire upper lip was gone, corroded, showing her upper teeth and gums and above that, a hollow, snotty cavity where a nose should've been.

'Fuck's sake,' said Fred, as she came rushing toward them, screaming like a banshee.

7

The wall of heroes stood six feet tall and twenty feet wide. It was a solid slab of black marble inscribed with hundreds of names, a small acknowledgement for the men of Brokebridge who'd given their lives fighting through world war two.

Dedicated in '51 by Sir Dalton-Moore, this landmark had since remained the site of annual ceremonies and a mandatory destination for any military parade. But more significant than the state's approved reverence was that of the ordinary folk, the locals who could be seen tending to its upkeep in small ways, such as removing litter or educating loitering youths on what it stood for.

They were the unofficial custodians, maintaining the wall for the relatives and descendants who would often travel from miles around and continents afar just to see the names of their heroic kin. To these it was a monument of almost religious importance, a place to reflect and pay tribute.

So it was a jarring and upsetting sight to find a great red swastika emblazoned on its face, a juxtaposition as grotesque and perverse as a piece of dogshit placed atop a child's birthday cake.

Rhonda clocked the symbol from some sixty yards away, when she was still on the hill, squinting against the morning sun. She could see the outlines of bodies gathered around it and a black people carrier parked nearby.

At half that distance she could tell it was the Leg-Up posse and was shortly spotted by Poppy, who stood waving in dramatic fashion, evocative of a shipwreck survivor flagging a passing liner.

'RHAWNDA,' she trilled, to which Rhonda returned a brief, nonchalant wave.

A strange tension pervaded the remaining distance, and the typically flat greeting Rhonda gave on arrival did nothing to dissipate it. In fact, that only made it worse.

'Alright guys,' she said, utterly unaware of how opposed the group were to such liberal use of the term "guys". But it'd once been the topic of a very one-sided meeting with all agreeing to use the more "inclusive" word - *people.*

As the group's leader, Poppy made a mental note to *educate* Rhonda on the matter in another, more private situation. She feared the debate it might provoke could be *triggering* to Jack.

'Whassup Rhonda,' said Trent, while Jack gave a nod and Kibs kept his head down.

They all looked tired, hungover, and were wearing the same clothes from the night before. Everyone except for Poppy, who was bright-eyed and well made up in a completely different combo. Now it was a crop top to display her flat stomach and pierced naval, with paisley print harem pants and a stunningly white pair of Nike trainers.

'Rhawnda,' she beamed, 'you must be so tired after working all night.'

Rhonda gave a half shrug. 'I can get a nap on the way there,' she said, to which an unseen voice objected.

'I aint turnin' my music daan.'

Rhonda looked just as this mystery speaker emerged from the other side of the monument, seeing the tips of the red Mohawk first, hovering above the wall like a reptile's sail before the lizard revealed itself in full.

A pierced scowl dominated his otherwise fine features, the kind of face befitting a model, although his diminutive stature would likely exclude him from the profession. All five foot six of his skinny frame was clad in fashionably distressed black denim, with countless symbols and phrases patched upon the jacket. There was ACAB, Anarchy, Peace, the extinction rebellion hourglass to name but a few.

Rhonda noticed one of these symbols had been tattooed on the punk's left hand, which also held a can of red spray paint.

'Oh Edd,' Poppy sighed, with an almost maternal affection, despite the fact they were roughly the same age. 'That's no way to introduce yourself, hun.'

'Hey, no offence intended,' said Edd, unconsciously slipping into his true Cambridge accent. Then, like some kind of cartoon schizo, he quickly switched back to his Johnny Rotten act.

'I jus' need ma music ta keep me goin'. It's a long drive ta Scarmuff y'know?'

'Yeah, eight hours,' said Rhonda and she looked across at the people carrier, a gleaming VW Caravelle nine-seater, worth three to four times her yearly salary.

'Is that yours Edd? Or did you borrow it from mum?'

Edd smiled yet it didn't touch his eyes.

'Very funny,' he said, switching again. 'Ow abaat you ride in th' boot.'

'Be nice, Edd,' Poppy warned and Rhonda noticed that neither Trent, Jack nor Kibs said anything. They were all busying on their iPhones.

'Edd's our pitbull,' Poppy explained. 'He's loyal, protective and loveable once you get to know him. He just takes a while to warm up to strangers.'

A Hot Dose of Hell

'Uh huh.' Rhonda grunted, her eyes narrowing. Experience told her to just leave it there, get on with the long journey. But she couldn't let it lie.

'Did you paint that swastika, Edd?'

Edd smirked. 'P'raps,' he said, although his deliberate shake of the spray can provided a more definite answer.

'Why?' said Rhonda.

'I'm like, raisin' awareness, innit.'

'Awareness of what?'

'Err, Nazis?' Edd scoffed, gobbing on the floor for good measure. 'They're everywhere y'know. White nationalists are on the rise, hate crime is thru tha fackin' roof. We gotta let people know it's out there, *so they'll do sumfin' abaat it.*'

Unsure if this was a strange joke, some kind of initiation, Rhonda turned in wordless appeal to the rest of the group and found to her surprise they were all regarding her with bewildered frowns, as if she were ignorant of some long-accepted scientific truth, like the existence of gravity.

'It's true, Rhonda,' said Poppy, wearing a sorry-to-break-it-to-you-smile.

'Just look at the hate crime statistics,' Kibs added, gaze never leaving his phone. 'And before you say anything else, maybe educate yourself on history. This is basically a monument to capitalist oppression. If you ask me, they should all be taken down.'

'Bollocks,' Rhonda muttered under her breath.

Edd alone heard and his scowl intensified as he took a step closer, clenched fist by his side implying an impending punch, or at least a desire to throw one.

'Denial is enabling,' he snarled, and Rhonda made a point to meet his wild stare with an even look, showing exactly how unintimidated she was. She felt certain she could take the little punk, but still hoped it wouldn't come to that. He was the designated driver after all.

'Look Edd,' she began, adopting a neutral body language in an effort to cool things. 'If there were so many Nazis about you wouldn't *need* to spray that everywhere, would you? It'd all be right in front of us.'

She cocked a thumb at the offending symbol, so freshly painted its edges were running.

'Funnily enough, I can't even think of the last time I saw a swastika outside TV...till I saw tha-

-You don't know what you're talking about,' Ed snapped. 'You're sleepwalkin' if ya can't see what's goin' on in the West. This is a dark time an' drastic measures are required. If people like you are too blind to see it then people like me 'ave ta rip yer eyelids open an' scream - *LOOK.*'

The group responded to this passionate rant with a round of finger-clicking, some sign of agreement Rhonda guessed, of approval.

'By spraying swastikas?' she shrugged. 'I don't know...Maybe there's a load of Nazis goosesteppin' round your way. But you don't see any where I'm from.'

Edd scuffed his heel and sneered, 'Well, aren't you privileged?'

'What?'

Edd said it again, slower, breaking the word down the way he would to a foreign speaker.

'Aren't. You. Priv-il-eged?'

As an abuse survivor and former ward of the state, Rhonda couldn't disagree more with the posh punk's assumption. Still, she felt no temptation to correct it. Any disclosure of personal hardships always came with a risk she'd be viewed as a victim and she couldn't stand that, all those false looks of sympathy, the condescending hugs, the forced tears.

Nor could she be the type who'd use personal trauma to win points in an argument. That was a "cunt move" she'd say.

Instead, she only snorted in semi-amusement.

'First time anyone's called me that, mate.'

'Oh yeah?' said Edd, his eyes bulging. 'Get used to it, oppressor.'

Poppy clasped her hands together.

'Shall we set off then?' she chirped, desperately trying to alter the mood, the gentle matriarch presiding over a tense family dinner. 'I mean, we've got a long way to go and there's lots to be done. Come on people.'

Obediently the group stirred. Trent, Jack and Kibs started for the Caravelle and a relieved Poppy moved with them, then turned back when she realised neither Rhonda nor Edd had budged.

Edd was still near the wall wearing a cocky sneer, those pipe-cleaner arms folded, yet his confidence waned the longer he gauged the unknown element staring him down.

As much as Rhonda kept icy still and her calm expression gave little away, he began to sense beneath that veneer there lurked not a desire, but a willingness to cause physical harm.

He wasn't far off the mark. Rhonda was angry alright. She'd been thinking about her good friend Mike, decent, hard-working, honest Mike, putting his life on the line overseas, just like the men whose names covered that wall. Desecrating their memorial was unacceptable to her full-stop, no matter what perverse logic you applied, or what cause you claimed. Unfortunately, she could see no way of explaining that to Edd if he didn't understand it already. And as an old sensei used to tell her:

"Where words fail, fists speak volumes."

'Come on guy-*People*,' said Poppy, so flustered she only narrowly avoided uttering the aforementioned wrongspeak. Guiltily, her gaze shifted to Jack, who apparently hadn't noticed the slip. But what Poppy found then was more distressing to her than if it had been heard because she saw how Jack had claimed the front passenger seat, a place which Poppy had earlier marked for herself.

That bitch, she thought.

Behind her, the ongoing standoff between Edd and Rhonda recalled an old western. Edd stood twitchy and intense with bug eyes while Rhonda squinted slightly at him in cool assessment. After a time, she reached into her bag and he visibly flinched, then flushed from embarrassment when she produced only a mere towel.

He flinched again at her approach, but she strode clean past him up to the swastika. Too late he realised what she was up to and before he could complete the word "Don't" she'd already smeared the symbol, rendering it unrecognisable.

'You think that's clever, eh?' said Edd and signalling his intent he shook the spray can, only to freeze at Poppy's hand on his shoulder.

Her touch was light yet restrained him as easily as a man twice his size because he secretly desired it. He almost shuddered with pleasure from the incidental brush of her wrist against his neck.

'Let it go,' she cooed and Edd complied, swaggering off the moment she withdrew.

'Let's roll,' he barked, slapping the Caravelle's

roof. 'Get this show on da fackin' road.'

Rather than join him Poppy stayed behind, watching Rhonda dispose of the towel in a nearby bin and on the way back, she quickly linked arms to walk her to the vehicle.

'Sooo, not the start I was hoping for,' said Poppy, pulling an over-pronounced pout.

'Yeah, me too,' said Rhonda, who only tolerated the touch, just about. 'Your chihuahua has some weird ideas.'

'Chihuahua?' said Poppy, frowning as much as the botox would permit. Then after a beat she broke out laughing.

'Oh, I get it, for pitbull, ha ha...I suppose he is small...But seriously, you'll like Edd when you get to know each other. He once saved me from a far-right hooligan you know.'

Rhonda doubted the truth of both statements yet resisted saying so for the sake of peace.

The engine started as she broke from Poppy to place her bag in the boot, Edd's obnoxious music kicking in simultaneously.

'FUCK THE TORIES,
FUCK THE TORIES,
FUCK THE TORIES.'

The vehicle had four seating compartments. Its cockpit held two luxury seats. The middle section contained two more set back-to-back with another two and in the rear, there was a row of three seats where some had placed their bags.

Rhonda keenly climbed through into this rear area, pulling the pop-up table across behind her to create a barrier. Less than five minutes in and she had her fill of this lot already. A record even for her.

'Are you sure you want to sit back there?' asked

Poppy, shouting over the music. 'I mean, there's plenty of room up here with us.'

Unwilling to shout back, Rhonda simply gave a thumbs up, then pulled her hood over her head, lay back across the seats as Edd pulled off.

'Please yourself,' muttered Poppy.

Being the weekend rush hour wouldn't peak until midday, so it was a smooth run out of the city. From there Edd took the winding A-roads and true to his word he kept the music pumping, right up until the motorway where it was suddenly, jarringly replaced by the wet warblings of Ed Sheeran.

Not that it was at all to her taste, this at least finally allowed Rhonda to snooze in peace, and she only stirred at a repeated chime of metal on metal, accompanied by some very hushed, very panicked chatter.

'Can't believe this.'

'That's not right. They're *so* wrong.'

Rhonda's eyes cracked open and through the gap between the seats she saw Poppy's hand gesticulating furiously, her clashing bangles the source of those metallic chimes.

'-just one salty troll throwing shade,' she was saying. 'Look at the likes. It's four hundred and fifty-two, to six.'

'Uh,' Kibs objected. 'I just refreshed and there's a lot more comments.'

'Well,' said Poppy, putting on a front, but her concern showed in the way her voice went up when she asked, 'and *what* are they saying?'

By contrast Kibsy's tone was flat and grim as a terminal diagnosis. 'It isn't good. They're calling us racist for going to Scarmouth…because it's a mostly *white* area.'

Aghast, Poppy covered her mouth, unable to counter, and in her place, Jack commented, 'I suppose it is a bit awkward that the homeless community isn't more diverse.'

'That's because whites dominate every section of western society,' said Kibs, shaking his pale head with apparent disgust.

'Quick,' Poppy urged, suddenly inspired, 'go on facebook and announce that we're planning to do some work in London next, specifically...*Brixton*. Then, in a few hours, post the link to that fb post on twitter as a reply to the criticism. That way it'll seem like we were *already* planning on going there *before* we read these comments.'

Kibsy's doubt permeated every word of his next question. 'Do you think that'll actually work?'

'Hopefully,' Poppy chirped, nodding in self-agreement. 'And repost a few pics of that homeless *BAME* fellow, what was his name? Y'know, the one who our stylist fixed up. But write some like, generic comment on it as if we're not making a point.'

'Okay Pops.'

Despite his scepticism Kibsy did as told, his thumbs working the iPhone with machine-like speed. He finished composing the text in less than thirty seconds and cleared his throat to read back.

'Okay, check this out…Follow our work in Scarmouth this weekend. Scarmouth is one of the most deprived areas in the country with the highest percentage of homeless persons in the UK. Our next stop is Brixton. Watch this space for updates on how *you* can help. Hashtag homeless, hashtag leg-up, hashtag one love.'

'Brilliant,' said Poppy, with a flamboyant roll of the 'r'. 'Only you need to change the part about how you can help. Go with, *you can help too, click here,* with a link to our donations page.'

'Cool,' said Kibs.

Then it was only the music for a while until he piped up again, more panicked than before.

'Shit. You won't believe this...they're calling cultural appropriation on the BAME person.'

'What?' said Poppy, with Trent's echo arriving a half second later.

'It's his corn rows,' Kibs despaired. 'That's an African hairstyle, but he's *Indian*. They say we're disrespecting the black community while also exploiting a vulnerable person.'

'Oh God,' Poppy gasped, putting the back of her hand against her forehead, like some tormented dame in an old black and white movie.

'I can't...I don't have anything left...Just block them, Kibs. Block them all.'

'Done,' said Kibs. Then in the next breath he cried out, 'NO.'

Poppy dropped her hand.

'What is it now?'

'Now someone else is calling us out, as *misogynists*?'

'WHAT?' Poppy shrieked in confusion. 'But I'm the founder and head, and I'm a woman and Jac-'

She stopped herself from saying any more about Jack, cringing so hard she feared her spine might snap.

'I fail to see how a female-led company could be misogynist,' said Trent, and Kibsy showed him the phone, started scrolling through the photos of their last endeavour. To an outsider, it'd appear more like a portfolio for the stylist they'd used. Just a string of various stages of hair design on several homeless-looking types.

'Y'see,' said Kibs, 'it doesn't seem like we helped any homeless *women*.'

'That's because we didn't *see* any that day,' Poppy stressed, pounding a fist against her seat.

'Yeah, *we* know that,' said Kibs, 'but *they're* saying it's 'cause women's haircuts and treatments like, cost more.'

'Oh yeah,' said Trent, considering the point. 'Women's hair costs loads more to do. I can't believe how much that costs. I was in an open relationship awhile back and for her birthday she wanted a treatment, cut and colour. Even though I split the bill with our other partner it still cost me over a hundred quid.'

This information was met with utter indifference and after a brief consideration Poppy sat back with folded arms, muttered through gritted teeth, 'Just block them as well please, Kibsy.'

'Done.'

In the break that followed Rhonda began to drift again. But the drama didn't end there because Kibs had a concern of his own, something he'd been stewing on for a couple of months. Inspired by the detractors on social media, he thought it a good opportunity to make his play now, while Poppy was weakened, vulnerable.

'You know,' he began, 'maybe this isn't such a bad thing. I mean, maybe we should think about reinventing ourselves, shedding these accounts and starting afresh. I feel like we need to reconsider our name anyway. *Leg-Up* is a bit problematic after all. I mean, it could be read as *ableist*.'

Anger flickered briefly on Poppy's perfect face. So briefly it played like a single incorrect frame inserted into a movie reel.

'Really Kibs? And how is it ableist exactly?'

Kibsy shrugged.

'You know, *Leg*-Up. What about people who don't have legs? What are we saying to them? Are we saying we can't help you cause you like, don't have legs?'

Jack made a thoughtful grunt, 'Well how about *Helping Hand*?'

'No,' said Poppy. 'That sounds like a euphemism. Like something some poor woman's boss probably said to them before a groping attack.'

Kibs raised a finger in objection.

'Leg-Up also has a euphemistic ring,' he said and Poppy's eyes flashed rage at the suggestive way he grinned afterwards.

'You're vile, Kibs.'

'I didn't mean any-' he started, but Poppy wasn't finished.

'You know, just last night this total stranger actually *wolfwhistled* me on my way home. Do you understand? We women live under constant threat every day and jokes like that only embolden abusers, normalising their behaviour.'

'Okay,' Kibs stressed. 'Sorry Pops, seriously.'

'Really Kibs?' said Jack, turning to him. 'After last night, you're *still* not getting it?'

'I'm *sorry*,' Kibs insisted, hanging his head. 'I'm truly sorry.'

'So you should be,' said Jack. 'That was practically a *hate crime* what you just did.'

On that a sombre hush fell over the group and Poppy let it linger until satisfied there would be no further challenge. Then with her authority reasserted, she sat back to calmly declare, 'We're Leg-Up,' a statement met by another round of that weird finger-clicking.

Chatter remained sparse from thereon, finally allowing Rhonda to drift off again for some more hard-earned rest. Her earlier nap had been short and shallow, but this time she fell into a deep, feverish sleep as her body overheated in that cramped, stuffy compartment.

Sweating through her clothes Rhonda dreamed of fire, dreamed of being trapped in a burning building and outside there were people throwing buckets to put it out.

Only the flames weren't going down because the buckets were full of gasoline.

And no one seemed to notice, because they were too busy taking selfies after every throw.

8

An explosion of glass shattered the early morning calm, giving way to a brief, plummeting banshee scream, which climaxed in a sudden, wet crunch followed by a gentle, almost musical, tinkling of glass hail bouncing off the concrete.

Several shards sank into the fallen amazon's flesh, yet she didn't react. She only lay there, broken and twisted like a toy doll flung down the stairs, a pool of blood expanding steadily around her mangled form. To the pair of bald heads crowding the broken window some thirty feet above, the scene was a Rorschach test made flesh.

'She aint movin',' said Fred and he bent, hands on knees, gasping with relief.

'Good,' said Pinkie, apparently satisfied, although he still watched her, wary.

In all his exceptionally violent life he'd never faced such ferocious assailants as the pair of hookers he'd just encountered in this room. The first of them had caught him completely by surprise and although the cuts and scratches she'd inflicted weren't much to talk about, his ribs still hurt, biting every time his massive lungs drew breath.

'Kurwa,' he winced, clutching his side.

When the second attacked Pinkie had been more prepared for the onslaught and as she dove across the bed, claws first like a wild cat, he'd used the momentum to propel her through the sash window. He'd shown no hesitation, no mercy, yet in the aftermath found himself mentally exploring alternative actions, the outcomes they might've produced.

Unlike Pinkie, Fred had already moved on from the moment. As intense and bizarre as it had been, he never dwelt on *anything* for long and was always looking ahead, searching, like a shark.

He crossed the room with a slight limp, leg sore from the cistern attack, not that he'd complain or even acknowledge it, to collect the unopened brick of powder from the dresser.

The opened packet he folded carefully, sealing it with one of the prozzies' hair ties before pocketing that too. Then he was rummaging in the drawers, the wardrobe, flipping the mattress, finding nothing more of note beyond a few unusual sex toys.

'That's the lot,' he concluded, brushing himself down. 'Come on, Pinks. Buck up.'

An irritated Pinkie held his response when he saw that Fred was making a phone call. It would be Glover on the line no doubt. Any incidents needed to be filtered through him before reaching Castell and he had the authority to decide the next course of action.

'We got bad doners at the kebab shop,' said Fred, speaking in code. 'Too much sauce. Made a right mess of the karsie. Needs a good clean and a plumber too.'

During the gap following Fred's explanation, Pinkie tried in vain to listen to the other side of the chat. All he could hear were the gulls outside heralding the coming dawn.

'Right,' said Fred, then he hung up and turned to Pinkie. 'He's sending someone over. We need to sort what we can. They'll do the rest.'

'The women can help,' said Pinkie. 'It will be quicker.'

'Good shout.'

Throughout the incident nearly all the brothel's

resident workers had remained gathered in the lobby. A few were now talking in hushed, conspiratorial tones, some crying, with several of the harder ones looking just a little put out by the disruption, the drama. But drawn by the sound of heavy boots on the stairs, even their jaded eyes widened, for the blood-drenched thugs descending towards them were an alarming sight to behold.

'Right,' Fred scowled, rubbing his filthy knuckles with subliminal menace. 'We need mops, buckets, sponges, bin liners.'

'And bleach,' said Pinkie, flicking another scrap of Shaz's guts off his coat.

'Lots of bleach.'

It took a second to register on their blank faces. Then, as if waking from a trance they began to separate from the huddle. Tears dried quickly, indicating they were more a product of shock than grief and only one among them looked to ask a question. It was stifled by a gunshot-loud clap from Fred.

'C'mon ladies, CHOP, CHOP.'

None protested or showed any resentment, since each of them grasped a general notion of what was at stake here - their home, their livelihood, their freedom. They simply needed direction, and cleaning products.

Thankfully, some years prior Castell had put a premium on hygiene in every brothel, even the "budget" ones, and as such the place was well-stocked with everything required to cover a crime scene.

'Let's go girls,' said the mockney Filipino, her authoritative squawk galvanising the others into a ragged march around the reception desk. An office behind there doubled for a utility room and within moments a team of newly determined women emerged, armed with mops, buckets, bleach spray and marigolds.

The majority were dispatched upstairs with Pinkie, while Fred took the rest outside to tackle the gory pancake formerly known as Tray.

'It's messy,' one warned. She'd happened to be out there smoking when Tray took her fatal fall and witnessed the brutal impact of the landing up close.

'You should see the room,' Fred muttered, ambling on. Then at the porch a worrying thought stopped him in his tracks, and he turned to the nearest prozzie, the waif.

Slyly yet forcefully, Fred snatched her wrist to pluck her from the group and as the others continued past, he reeled her close to his bulky mass, barrel gut nudging her with every subsequent breath.

'There's no johns left in here are there?'

'No,' she said, shaking her fine hair. 'It was a quiet night.'

Fred gave her face a brief assessment, searching for hints of deception. He didn't remotely trust her with that whole butter-wouldn't-melt act, but he'd still avoid asking the other women. Having overlooked that there might be patrons in the building was embarrassingly sloppy, something he'd rather not draw attention to.

'How do you know for definite?' he asked, grip tightening on her tiny wrist, and she shrugged a pale, slight shoulder. The strap of her vest slipping down her arm would've normally drawn Fred's eye to her breasts. Normally. Not at that moment though.

'Everyone was just here,' she said, and Fred looked to say more, but his further questions were delayed when a shrill commotion erupted outside.

'Shit,' he hissed, then with surprising agility for his build, he bounded from the porch steps to land two-footed on the tarmac. A shooting pain through his right leg reminded him why he never moved like that and on the next step his knee buckled slightly, allowing the waif to overtake with small, sprightly strides.

'C'mon,' she urged. 'You've gotta help 'em.'

The chaotic scene ahead centred around Tray's remains, a battle commencing between the prozzies and a squadron of scavenging gulls, looking to claim the corpse for breakfast.

A tall Russian led the prozzie's charge, thrusting a broom like a spear and catching nothing but air. She was backed up by a skeletal Scot swinging an empty bucket while the others kept a distance, hesitant to join in, only offering verbal support.

They had good reason.

Scarmouth's gulls were unlike any found elsewhere in the country. They were over twice the average size and about ten times more aggressive. Rumour had it that steroid-loaded cattle feed contributed to their freakish growth, ever since a video of one fighting a king-sized rat for a pellet went viral.

The rat lost and was eaten first.

Scourge of unwary tourists, who they fearlessly and indiscriminately mugged for food, these monstrous birds unknowingly enjoyed a "protected species" privilege which had allowed them to propagate to plague-like numbers. In force, they'd been known to hospitalise children and pensioners. Individually, they'd been known to carry off guinea pigs, small kittens or, as in one famous case, the odd chihuahua.

Fred couldn't allow them to take anything from Tray, anything which could be dropped, found, reported and processed, potentially leading back here, and to Castell.

Mid-swing he caught the Russian's broom, calmly taking it from her to wade in, and at his intrusion, those gulls let out piercing, angry caws, wings spread like weekend warriors posturing before a drunken scrap. They ducked his first swipes, the broom cutting the air audibly just above their heads, and did so in a seemingly cocky manner which drew involuntary giggles from several of the onlookers.

'Funny is it?' said Fred, swinging harder but those cheeky gulls continued to evade him. Following each miss, they would plunge their beaks into the nearest wound on Tray's corpse and gorge, pulling out again just in time to dodge the broom's next pass.

The sight of these grisly feedings fast silenced the onlookers' mirth while Fred's mounting rage saw his swings double in speed and ferocity. Yet still, he was failing to connect, and it seemed like he never would when out of the blue, he did.

A fat one-legged gull had gotten itself beak-deep in Tray's broken eye socket and was probing deeper, with such determined fervour that it was actually moving her head like some macabre puppet show. Regardless the threat the big man posed, this gull refused to relinquish the prize it'd found there and persisted tugging until the eyeball finally evacuated to the sound of a faint, wet pop.

In triumph the hungry gull emitted an excited coo. However, all had not yet been won. There was further resistance offered by the emerging eyestalks, which prevented the eye from coming away completely, and

Stark Terror

in a sequence dripping with irony that stubborn bundle of nerves served as a gory tether, stalling the bird just long enough for Fred's broom to find its mark.

THWACK.

It was only a glancing shot, but one which stunned the bird so that Fred was able to land a second, a third, a fourth, prompting the other scavengers to flee skyward with warning cries for their kin.

The beating seemed to go on forever. Then with the ninth strike the downed gull finally stopped moving, save its twitching stump leg flicking out.

'It's still-' the waif began, and Fred's big boot stomped the bird flat, earning horrified gasps from a few of the prozzies.

'What?' he snarled, utterly bemused - there had been less reaction to the sight of Tray's corpse. 'What's the problem, eh?'

The question was rhetorical. However, a blonde with dreadlocks saw fit to answer.

'They're a protected species y'know.'

Thinking better of it, Fred suppressed his initial response and leant on the broom to catch his breath, a wry smile shortly breaking across his bloodied cheeks.

'I reckon that's probably the *least* illegal thing I've done today, luv.'

This comment sparked a nervous giggle from one girl, who immediately covered her mouth in fear of dreadlocks' wrath.

Fred noticed and gave her a playful wink in solidarity.

'Right,' he huffed, standing tall. 'We've got about half an hour till the sun comes up. Scrubbers...get scrubbin'.'

The Scot spat a fat greenie onto the tarmac in anger at the slur. 'Prick,' she said, and Fred gave a dry chuckle.

'What no swallow?' Then beckoning to dreadlocks, he barked: 'Bin liners, c'mon. Bring 'em over.'

Dreadlocks shook her head in disgust and shoved the plastic roll at the waif, who accepted without protest, you'd assume because she was so timid, but Fred saw more to it than that.

To him the exchange suggested a degree of responsibility, of blame. The way dreadlocks had handed the roll over practically said: "It's *your* mess," and the waif's dutiful acceptance all but confirmed it.

'Wrap 'em round,' he said, using his bloodied boot to lift Tray's broken leg. 'Cover the whole thing.'

It didn't take long. Three others helped the waif and peer pressure saw dreadlocks make the effort to at least *appear* involved.

Once the body had been mummified in plastic Fred bent to lift and although he could've easily carried it alone, he insisted the waif take the feet.

As he expected she obliged, raising Tray's huge flippers to her waist in a wheelbarrow position, and the corpse farted almost as if in protest, issuing a fine, bloody mist from one of its many wounds.

'It's normal,' said Fred, reading the surprise on the waif. 'Body's all relaxed y'see. Could be worse. I've 'ad one shit on me before now.'

The waif cringed at the sudden cold wetness on her bare legs, knowing that it was Tray's blood. She wanted so badly then to drop the thing and yet, as they headed towards Fred's van, she couldn't help feeling somewhat guilty for how little of the weight she seemed to be bearing.

'Could-' Fred began, his sentence made redundant

when the Russian kindly opened the side door without being asked.

'Cheers luv.'

He walked the corpse in backwards, the growing distance naturally pulling the feet from the waif's grasp, to set it down on an old dust sheet. Her role appearing fulfilled, she went to move on. Then Fred beckoned her inside and she climbed up without hesitation, an act she came to regret when he pulled the door shut after.

'W-what you doin'?'

To her alarm she noticed all manner of tools lay about the van floor. Among them, a shovel, garden shears, a chainsaw, all innocuous in the hands of a working man, but their presence in Fred's van implied sinister purposes beyond the manufacturer's recommended use.

'Now,' Fred began, meaty hands resting on her narrow shoulders, and he dipped his big chin so that his brow loomed toward her, heavy breaths blowing right in her face.

'There's two ways we can do this. Quicker it goes, better it'll be for you.'

The waif visibly trembled, knowing that he'd sniffed her out. Nevertheless, she tried her utmost to maintain a calm, naive exterior.

'Do what? You after a freebie or something?'

Fred gave a hard look and quickly saw her expression twist into a type of tearful gurning usually reserved for hysterical toddlers on their very first boo-boo.

'Alright,' she sobbed. 'It wasn't nothing to do with me though. I was just there an' I didn't hang about when it started.'

Fred's fat, steely fingers dug into her collarbone,

the sharp pain making her squirm.

'When what started exactly? Give us the whole story.'

'Alright, okay, listen,' she said, taking a deep breath to compose herself. 'It was Tray and Shaz. I was in the lobby with Keith the guard when they came back all bloody. Someone done 'em over, some homeless junkies. They slashed Shaz's face and broke Tray's nose. We was worried, but Tray and Shaz had managed to get a load of gear off them skagheads, like a *load* of gear. I reckon it was like...'

She stopped to wipe a tear, sniff back a little snot.

'It was kilos of the stuff.'

Self-consciously Fred shifted his shoulder and felt the weight of the packages in his pockets pull his jacket straight.

'Go on.'

'So Keith made us go upstairs. He said he didn't want the others to see what'd happened cos they'd get upset. But when we got to Tray's room all he wanted to do was talk about the drugs. He said they was worth money and he'd help the girls sell 'em for a cut. They argued about that for a while.'

'Then what?'

'So Shaz was really hurtin'. Her face looked well bad, like her cheek was just hangin' off. She said she was gonna do some of the stuff to take the pain away and Tray said she wanted to do some too, for her busted nose, like.'

'What was the stuff, smack? Coke?'

'I thought it might be coke, but I never saw someone act like that on coke.'

'Like what? Did they go mental?'

'Yeah, Shaz did. She went straight for Keith. She was rippin' all his clothes off like they were gettin' into some rough sex. But then she started hittin' him too, really hittin' him like you wouldn't imagine.'

Fred didn't need to imagine. He'd seen how hard Shaz hit Pinkie with that cistern lid.

'What about Tray?'

'She snorted a load and passed out. Shaz and Keith wound up in the bathroom, sounded like they was still fightin' an' I just left. It was a bad scene an' I didn't want 'em turnin' on me.'

'Then you called us.'

'Yeah, I was runnin' down the hall, an' I could hear it gettin' well out of hand, so I thought I had to do somethin'. We all know to call that number if things go Pete Tong. Never knew whose number it was though.'

'Did Shaz and Tray ever kick off like that before?'

'Nah, I mean they was definitely rough, nothin' like that though. Shaz was messin' Keith right up and he's a BIG bloke. I mean bigger 'n you, hench as fuck.'

Fred remembered the headless male body hanging through the hole in the bathroom door, those massive steroid-pumped arms dangling limply.

'Didn't count for much though, did it?'

'What?' she whimpered, in genuine shock, as if Tray's corpse weren't evidence enough as to how bad things had turned in that room.

'Is he alright though?'

Fred frowned in disbelief. 'No,' he said, and he used his boot to nudge Tray's wrapped corpse. 'I'd say he looks about as healthy as this one. No...worse.'

The sobbing that provoked indicated some kind of friendship had existed between the waif and the guard. Fred felt no sympathy. Seeing the emotional outburst as little more than an inconvenience, he quickly grabbed her face to stifle it.

'Anythin' else you 'aven't told me?'

The waif nodded and Fred relaxed his grasp just as her nose released a stream of snot. It ran onto his glove, but he continued to hold her regardless while she fought through sniffs and sobs to tell the rest.

'Shaz said, *sniff*, the junkies had loads more, *sniff*, but they couldn't, *sniff*, get it off 'em, the shape they was in. *sniff, sniff*. Keith said he was gonna go lookin' for 'em, *sniff*, and tax the rest. *Sniff.* But I 'spose he won't be doin' that now-*oww*.'

The last syllable came out a weak howl as she broke down again and after a few moments Fred released her altogether. She looked so pitiful, like a lost child, that even he felt a brief desire to comfort her. But a rapping on the side of the van held his tongue and an instant later the side door slid open.

It was Pinkie, stood there with two plastic-wrapped bodies stacked across his massive shoulders.

'Hey Mr *Blue Pill*,' he said, a smile barely masking the pain of every breath. 'Now is not the time for romance, eh? Come on we got to clean up.'

Shortly, the duo stood shivering in the brothel car park, stripped to their trunks, arms out in a perversely Christlike fashion. The morning breeze was travelling fast, and both were feeling a little self-conscious of their shrinking bulges before the audience of seasoned women.

Some giggled behind their hands, one couldn't take her eyes off Pinkie's tattooed muscles. But it was dreadlocks who watched them most intently, the hose in her grip trained on Fred's chubby, blood-covered face.

'Get on with it,' he growled. 'If I wanted to take this long, I'd have used your shower for fuck's sa-'

A jet of ice-cold water hit him right in the eyes and

he rocked on his heels but didn't shy away. He leaned into the flow, turning this way and that, rubbing his neck, chest and arms.

'He's good,' said Pinkie. 'Now do me.'

Disappointment showed on dreadlocks' face. She was getting a thrill from torturing Fred and purposely hesitated a few seconds before turning the hose on Pinkie. She spent far less time on him and once he was clean, she aimed the hose at the stain where Tray had hit the ground, blasting her blood into the gutter.

Using the ratty towels provided the men quickly dried off and dressed into coveralls from Fred's van. Fred told the rest of the women to get back inside, lock the doors, close the curtains and not to let anyone in apart from Glover's men.

On the road out he passed a Mondeo that had to be them, a pair of hardfaces with dead eyes in the cockpit. Neither party acknowledged the other, but both recognised their own team.

'Where are we taking these?' said Pinkie, referring to the bodies in the back.

'The moors,' said Fred.

Pinkie's dense brows knitted in disbelief.

'We're *burying* them?' he said, appalled at such a basic, crass method of disposal. Off the top of his head, he could think of at least six other ways to make a corpse disappear that were both more effective and efficient.

'I forget you aint from round 'ere sometimes,' said Fred. 'Y'know there's bodies on the moors people 'ave been looking for gone forty years. An' no one's gonna be lookin' for these three, mate. No one's even gonna miss 'em.'

9

At around the same time Fred McCall was busy battling seagulls, Sebastian, AKA Bazza, Simpkins awoke to find himself in urgent need of a crap. Three days he'd been waiting for that stool to work its way out of him and after half a pack of dulcolax it'd finally arrived.

This should've provided cause to be happy or at least relieved that his heroin-induced constipation had eased, yet Baz was in the grip of sweaty panic because the old Victoria hotel contained no toilets, working or otherwise, nor any sinks he could adapt.

Long ago the place had been gutted, stripped of functioning appliances, including many of its doors. Baz himself had previously made a chunk from what copper piping was left and now bitterly regretted his decision not to spend just a small amount of that cash on a bucket.

'Scabby cunt,' he muttered, cursing himself the way his father so often had. 'Stupid scabby fuckin' cunt,' he said, rising from his blanket-covered pallet.

Once upright a sharp pain in his bowel threatened to fold him, cold sweat breaking all over his hide. On any other day he'd simply use the bushes outside, but so urgent was his need that he feared his arse would let go well before he could make it down there.

Baz knew most of his fellow squatters on the first floor had their own bucket, and he also knew none would be willing to lend. That was a revolting prospect, even for those who would sometimes share needles through laziness.

However, if they happened to be out...

Clutching his gut Baz quickly shuffled down the

hall, scanning each room as he went. He spied Bill and Joey's boots poking out of the shadows, saw the plumpness of Rick, Sam and Ryan's sleeping bags and didn't dare trespass into Kenny's room.

Kenny's girl though, Roxy, was another matter entirely. Her room sat nearest the main stairs and Baz could see the whole of the inside from there without having to risk crossing the threshold. Just a little angling was all it took. A little lean from the bannister and he scoped it out good, finding no sign of Roxy nor Kenny for the moment.

Due to the time of day, Baz guessed Roxy had to be in the cells again, or sleeping in Kenny's room, and he felt sure he could use that bucket, dispose of the mess and return it without anyone being wise.

On tiptoe he slinked inside, bug eyes scanning the gloom, and at first, he feared Roxy didn't own a bucket either. Then he saw how she'd placed it in the darkest, emptiest corner, almost as if it were something to be ashamed of.

Baz moved fast, his jeans, trackies and thermals dropped on the way so that he almost tripped over them. For one terrifying instant he thought he might go before he reached the bucket, that he'd spray his guts all over Roxy's floor and personal belongings, but he made it just in time.

The relief he felt squatting over that plastic rim made the hairs on his neck stand up, sent a shudder of pleasure through his spine.

'Yeah,' he groaned with every staccato burst resonating beneath him and when it was finally done, he had the most intense craving for a cigarette. Idly, he wondered if Roxy had any stashed, then he remembered the danger of his current whereabouts. He had to get out ASAP.

Baz descended the Victoria's main stairs feeling considerably better than he had all week, but no less paranoid than when he'd been sat right in Roxy's room. Now that he'd survived the bowel crisis, fear of being caught was his only concern and with the bucket in hand he jumped at every sound that was not of his own making, cringed over those that were.

At arm's length he carried that fouled container, consciously breathing only through his mouth until he stepped outside into the cool, blue dawn. It'd been raining the night before. Baz only remembered that when he saw puddles in the car park's many potholes, and he was glad for it. He'd need that water to swill out the bucket. Leaves and newspaper alone simply wouldn't cut it this time.

Crossing the lot Baz jolted at the sudden rattle of window boards. He only relaxed slightly when struck by the same breeze causing it. From the west it came, seeming to bully him more the closer he drew to the cliff edge and for fear it might cast his frail frame over, he stopped several feet short to empty the bucket over the sea.

Most of the contents went in the first effort, carried out on the breeze as if fired from a cannon. Baz found it strangely satisfying to watch his waste fly into the horizon and keenly repeated the action. He soon regretted his haste however, as in a nauseating turn the wind changed during the second pitch to blow a fine rain of his own filth back at him.

'Fuck's sake.'

Enraged, Baz slammed the bucket down hard, gurning in disgust. The rotten egg stink invaded his nostrils fast, sending his gag reflex into spasm and he swallowed hard en route to a nearby bush.

In his anger he cut his hand snatching a handful of

leaves which he used to furiously brush himself down, the rough twigs scratching and snagging the fabric of his soiled hoodie. The act didn't achieve much other than that and when he shortly gave up, he became aware of a noise, something previously hidden by his own activity but now impossible to ignore.

The sound was a high mechanical whine, reminding Baz of the air conditioning at the benefits office. He knew it couldn't be anything like that though, as no other buildings stood anywhere near the Victoria and there was no way the old hotel had suddenly grown a working air-con system for itself.

So what was it?

Baz could see nothing in the vicinity, not a vehicle or device of any kind. Still the mysterious sound persisted while he knelt, swilling out the bucket with rainwater and it was only by sheer chance that he eventually happened to glance up and spot its source.

'Fuckin' UFO?' he muttered, confused by the bizarre, alien shape hovering in the sky. To him it initially appeared as a flying spider, but when his eyes focused, he saw it as two straight X's overlapping in opposition.

A drone. He'd seen them before in gift shops, had attempted to steal one a few months prior and got caught. This model was different though, far bigger, sleeker and smooth in its movements, even against the strong wind. All suggested the drone was quite advanced and likely worth a fair bit of money.

Naturally, Baz saw the pound signs. If only he could bring it down somehow or lure it close enough to grab. He quickly became so preoccupied by the goal that he failed to notice something else, footsteps approaching. He only heard just in time to take cover in the bush where he stayed, peering through the leaves.

No matter what, Baz couldn't afford to be seen with the bucket. Word travelled fast in their little community. Secrets were shared freely often out of simple boredom, and although he'd heard the concept spoken about a great deal, loyalty was almost non-existent.

If Baz were spotted by anyone, he knew it would only be a matter of time before Kenny found out and he wanted no part in any drama with that man, not after the last time.

Last time Kenny pulled a knife on him, and Baz was certain it'd only been thanks to Roxy's intervention that he avoided getting marked. When he remembered that he felt a little guilty over how he'd taken her bucket. Out of everyone she might've let him use it if she'd been there to ask.

Roxy was a nice girl. Everyone liked her and they were all jealous of Kenny's ownership of her, not that any would ever dare challenge him.

Speak of the devil - that was exactly who Baz saw approaching. Between the leaves he could see Kenny and Roxy together, walking unsteadily into the car park. They were dragging a weighty bundle with them and right away Baz recognised that gait, "the shuffle" he called it, indicating that both were heavily under the influence, totally out of it, on the nod.

All the same he remained hidden, waiting until they'd passed before he cautiously emerged to follow in their tracks.

For the meantime, Baz forgot about the drone as he still had to replace the bucket. He just wasn't sure how he'd do it safely now that they'd returned. His only hope was that they were so high they wouldn't pay attention to him, or that they'd not remember later even if they did.

All the way to the front entrance he stalked them in silence, and it was here he'd soon make a fatal discovery. In their wake the couple left a heavy trail of wet droplets, which Baz unknowingly trod in, inadvertently collecting whatever it was on the sole of his shoe.

With the first step up to the porch this same shoe squeaked against the tile, a noise as sharp and abrupt as the bleep of a cheap car key fob. The instant it happened Baz ducked fast, taking cover at the side of the steps and for several moments he stayed crouched there, hugging the bucket, holding his breath, praying they hadn't heard.

Like a frightened child Baz closed his eyes, as if that would somehow keep him from being seen. At any moment he expected to hear Kenny curse him out or to feel the sting of the man's fists against his face. But after what seemed an eternity of waiting neither occurred.

Tentatively Baz's eyes cracked open, and he allowed himself to exhale, a staggered, nervous breath as he peered over the top step.

He half expected to face a pair of Nike trainers, Kenny's trainers, and Kenny waiting to kick his head in with them, but the porch stood empty. The only hint it'd been used so recently lay in the smattering of fresh droplets glistening on its tiled surface.

Now that these were right in front of his eyes Baz noticed what they were. Even in the low light he could recognise blood when he saw it.

One of the pair must've been injured he thought, quite severely judging by the frequency and grouping of the stains. He hoped it was Kenny, not just because he liked Roxy better but more selfishly, because Kenny would be much harder to deal with if she wasn't around.

On further thought Baz saw another possibility. Had the blood come from something in the bundle they were dragging? Was it a load of stolen meat perhaps? That seemed a far more likely cause and the assumption set Baz at ease, encouraging him on his way up to the porch.

The first of the morning light now poured through the hotel's door-less entrance, and inside the reception Baz could see more of those stains leading to the staircase. That was as far as the light reached, far as it would go all day in fact. But just on the brink of its range, on the second step, it touched the corner of something else, a large packet that set Baz's heart racing with excitement.

'No way.'

Realising Kenny must've dropped it, Baz hurried over and snatched it up fast before the man noticed and came back.

The packet's weight surprised him. He'd never felt drugs in that quantity before. Always for him it'd come in meagre portions. But this had to be a kilo or more he guessed, and he immediately discarded the bucket to clutch the brick in two hands, rub his unshaved face against it with all the fervour of a cat to catnip.

Whatever the drug inside, it would be Baz's ticket out of here. There was plenty to keep him high for a while and plenty enough to sell. He was wondering whether it'd been cut, and exactly how much more he could make from it if not, when a dreaded voice shattered his fantasies, shit all over his half-formed plans.

'What ya got there Bazza?'

It was Danny.

Of all the people in the hotel it had to be Danny, arguably the second worst person it could be after Kenny himself.

'Go on, gizza look, mate.'

Danny was a tall rake of a man with a vicious streak longer than the M6. When first arriving at the Victoria his long hair and beard gained him the nickname "Jesus", but that was dropped on the second night after he battered his then-girlfriend to within an inch of her life.

There was no nickname after that. He was just Danny, or cunt behind his back.

Looking at Danny, Baz couldn't mask his dismay. The emotion was written all over his face as he slowly lowered the packet from it. He knew there was no point in lying, no way of trying to hide it quickly. The packet was almost double the size of his hand and Danny had clearly seen it.

'It's mine,' Baz said, playing tough. 'I'll give you a taste if you want. A freebie.'

'Nah,' said Danny. 'Where'd *you* get it from?'

'None a' ya business, mate. Look, you wanna fix up or not?'

Danny smirked, holding Baz with a piercing gaze.

'I'm just thinkin' that's not your stuff. I reckon that's someone else's an' I reckon you wanna give it to me, save yourself the bother, case they come lookin' for it. Maybe then I'll let *you* have some.'

'Fuck off Danny,' said Baz, about as weakly as anyone could ever say that.

'Nah,' said Danny and he grabbed for the packet, his hand firmly closing on Baz's.

'C'mon mate,' Baz pleaded, voice breaking. 'Let's

share, eh?'

His grip tightening on Baz's hand, Danny grinned, glimmers of yellow showing through the dark mass of his beard and he drew a sharp sniff.

'Have you shit yourself, Bazza? Christ, there's no need to be that scared. I said I'd let you have some.*'*

Baz said nothing. He just held onto the packet. His hand was hurting a little now, beginning to shake. For him, this situation felt more uncomfortable than painful, but he knew there'd be more pain, real pain if he continued to resist.

Eventually he sighed, 'Cheers Danny,' not meaning it, while making it sound as if he really did, as if it were the most generous thing anyone had ever done for him. Then he surrendered the packet to follow Danny upstairs.

Some was better than none after all.

10

Under the migraine-inducing glare and hum of fluorescent strip lighting, Rhonda stood washing her face at one in a row of seven sinks, the slow-running hot tap trickling away.

A great clock in the service station's lobby had told her it was just after four pm, meaning they'd been on the road for roughly seven hours non-stop until now. From her perspective the long journey seemed brief, since she'd slept through most of it, and she was thankful for that, especially for the reprieve from Poppy and co's inane chatter.

Sometimes it seemed like they were speaking another language, so many phrases she'd never heard, acronyms she couldn't decipher. It was all *Phobe* this and *ist* that. Talk of allies, gender, feminism, patriarchy, oppression, misogyny, empowerment, the far-right.

Everything seemed to be "problematic" or at least "inappropriate" and there was an ongoing, unofficial competition to see who could categorise the most innocuous things under either of these two brackets.

As far as travel games went Rhonda supposed it beat I-Spy for imagination and at one point the bizarre logic used to justify a claim of doorknobs representing "rape culture" almost made her laugh. Almost. If not for the utter conviction of the speaker which made it far more unsettling than amusing. The type of talk belonging in asylum corridors.

'It's an act of penetration don't you see? The latch going into the holder, receiver thing. Think about it, what that says. To travel through a door, IE to get ANYWHERE you are not only turning a blind eye to rape, but you are actually facilitating it by turning the handle. *That* is a subliminal message from the patriarchy designed to make us all complicit with the agenda.'

A toilet flush drew Rhonda's attention. She realised she'd been in a daze for some time, as evident in the near-overflowing sink below. She quickly turned the tap off.

Steam rising from the basin had coated the large mirror above, reducing her reflection to a blurry ghost. For a period in childhood, she'd avoided looking at herself, but that was when the scars were still fresh. In recent years she rarely noticed them, even out of makeup, and would struggle to recall when they'd last made her feel self-conscious.

Only that day was different.

That day the scars seemed more glaring than ever, the first thing to stand out when she wiped a porthole in the steam. Perhaps it was because she had Roxy on her mind. Roxy the unmarked one, the one mother never struck and incidentally, the one no one else wanted.

Ironically, those very scars had saved Rhonda from the perils of growing up in a failing care system. Her foster parents, the Caines, were suckers for damaged things. They owned a mangy old terrier with a bum leg, a one-eyed cat with epilepsy, and loved nothing more than restoring old furniture from the tip to give to local charities.

That was how they first met Rhonda. They'd been donating a set of chairs to the care home she and Roxy stayed in. At the time Rhonda didn't understand why they'd take such interest in her over her more attractive sibling. She didn't yet know about Roxy's record, about that extreme act of violence which would put off any potential adopters, no matter how compassionate, and on a soggy autumn morning the plan was laid out to her by an unfamiliar social worker.

'Fantastic news,' he'd beamed, his demeanour akin to the chummy, cheerfulness of a kids' TV presenter. 'You've been SEL-ECTED.'

Even then Rhonda knew when she was being patronised. It devastated her to learn that she'd be separated from Roxy and although to Rhonda that day seemed to come quicker than the end of summer holidays, Elliot and Florence Caine were forced to navigate reams of red tape before they took her into their home. They had to prove they could support a child, that their intentions were genuine and spent a chunk on solicitors to hurry the process.

It took months of effort, but they were sure this was what they wanted. They were absolutely certain, right up until Rhonda actually arrived. Then a feeling of buyer's remorse gradually set in.

Much like the people who adopt baby tigers, or keep pet crocodiles, the Caines watched in horror as the weak, feral little thing they'd brought home gradually transformed before their eyes into something they considered dangerous.

From day one little Rhonda reacted well to regular, generously portioned meals and quickly grew strong from helping in their workshop. At school she displayed talent in sport, earning some popularity and respect, while at home she presented a serious, organised and slightly aloof character, which jarred with the Caines' hippyish values.

Further to that there was talk of joining the military, the police. But when an aggressive temperament saw Rhonda excluded from cadets, they weren't sure whether to feel relieved or not. True relief only came when at sixteen she left their care to live independently.

'Thanks for having me,' she'd said, more like a plus one exiting a dinner party than a daughter leaving the nest, and in turn they'd each given her perfunctory hugs.

'It was our pleasure.'

'Take care.'

She'd never heard from them since.

'Cunts,' thought Rhonda and she was once again torn from her thoughts by a toilet flush. In the clear patch of mirror, she saw Poppy exit the cubicle behind.

'Freshening up?' said Poppy, approaching the adjacent sink. 'Good idea. We're going to take a lot of pics for *sosh* media.'

Rhonda grunted an affirmative. However, she opted to wear even less makeup than usual. Social media held little value in her eyes and the thought of getting all glammed up to go mixing with derelict addicts seemed *inappropriate* to say the least. All she wanted to do was find her sister. She didn't really care how she looked doing it.

'Got to look on point,' said Poppy, placing her little cosmetics bag atop the soap dispenser, and she set to work with a song on her lips, a whispery rendition of Nirvana's *"Drain you"*. It was the kind of singing which screamed LOOK AT ME disguised as casual and absent-minded. Poppy clearly had some measure of talent, something she no doubt knew and desperately wanted Rhonda to comment on.

'Shot himself didn't he?' said Rhonda, causing Poppy to falter mid-lyric.

'Y-yes, very tragic,' Poppy said, making earnest

eye-contact in the mirror to express what she deemed the appropriate amount of sadness/sympathy for a multi-millionaire rock star three decades dead.

Rhonda nodded in apparent satisfaction. 'Thought so.' Then she exited the bathroom, shortly meeting Trent, Kibs and Jack loitering outside the Starbucks, all holding fresh cups.

Somehow Jack was actually drinking through the fabric of the fashion mask, froth accumulating on its front.

'We've made good time,' said Trent. 'Only ten miles to go.'

The four re-joined Edd outside. Thanks to his angry music the caravelle was easy to locate in the service station's crowded lot.

Edd himself was sat on a short grass bank beside the vehicle, rocking like a demented chimp, his Mohawk now flat and limp. At the group's approach he flicked his head sharply to sweep the hair from his eyes, an act he had to repeat every three to four seconds from then on, like some kind of tic.

'Ready then?' he sneered, getting to his feet. Then flick, 'Where's Poppy?'

'She's coming,' said Rhonda, climbing aboard, yet it was a further twenty minutes before Poppy reappeared, her hair and makeup refreshed, "instagram ready" as she put it.

Thirty-seven minutes on the motorway and they were turning off for Scarmouth. Quite tellingly they were the only vehicle in their lane to do so. From there an ear-poppingly steep hill fed into an unlit tunnel, like some kind of rollercoaster track, and when they emerged on the other side they were met by a sea of vibrant flowers, flanked by the famously incongruous palm trees they'd all seen in the pictures online.

Sprouting on a steep bank just a hundred yards before Scarmouth's border was a twelve-foot-high floral display spelling the town's name. Poppy commented that she found it cute and no one else said anything for another floral display had stolen their attention.

On the hard shoulder, near the end of a faint trail of skidmarks, lay bundles of wilting flowers wrapped in plastic aside an assortment of teddies, some burnt out candles and a couple of home-made placards. Rainfall had rendered the signs' text illegible, all but the name "*Sammy"* scrawled in childish pen.

'How sad,' said Poppy, then a chilling thought darkened her mind. 'Be careful on this road, Edd.'

'Aye, aye,' said Edd, making a cheeky salute and he shortly turned off the main road onto a one-way single lane, following signs for the town centre.

A twisting route took them on a tour of the Scarmouth landmarks, such as the Baroque style town hall, the adjacent courthouse and disused Victorian ballroom. The architecture alone hinted at grander times while the famous "Big Tree", a twenty-foot-tall stump standing sentry at the top of the sloped high street, alluded to a stranger, more ancient history with the Pagan figures and symbols adorning its thick trunk. Among them, a horrific screaming face in the bark caught Rhonda's eye and she lingered on it until the growing distance melted those features into a blur.

Vacant, boarded-up buildings lined both sides of the high street, where only one in three lots were active premises. Those open for business tended to be charity shops, pound shops or chain convenience stores, holding more liquor ads on their windows than anything else.

Pavements were sparse with people, most of them pensioners or single mothers. But gangs of tracksuited teens dominated the space outside the McDonald's and as the caravelle passed by, two shaven-headed youths stepped forward to spout abuse, make obscene gestures at the posh gawkers in their shiny people carrier.

'My god,' Poppy gasped, 'the poverty.'

'I blame Brexit,' Kibs muttered, then he jolted in fright at something striking the back window.

'Little shits,' Edd growled, yet he kept on driving, only stopping a few blocks later to check for damage.

A loading bay outside yet another unoccupied store appeared as good a spot as any and he pulled in without signalling, receiving a horn blast from the van he cut up in the process.

'LEARN TO DRIVE, DICKHEAD.'

The two workmen inside that van were burly, thuggish to Edd's eyes and he didn't dare retaliate or more than glance in their direction. He just turned toward his passengers as the van went by.

'What was it those little shits threw at us?'

'A large coke,' said Rhonda, pointing to the frothy brown residue still trickling down the window.

'Oh,' said Edd, then an electric warning sounded, and he swivelled back to consult the dashboard display.

'Who's left their door open?'

'Poppy?' said Jack, just as Poppy got out.

'Where you goin?' screeched Edd. This was a very hostile area in his view, and he feared he'd be unable to protect the group, *knew* he'd be unable to protect them, if something happened.

'Come on people,' said Poppy, a cheer in her voice as she strode on ahead. 'Over here.'

A Hot Dose of Hell

'Wait Pops,' said Kibs, almost tumbling out after her. 'I'm coming too.'

Reluctantly, the others followed with Rhonda falling third in line and Edd at the back after locking the vehicle. They marched only a short distance, just some twenty yards before Poppy stopped and they all saw what'd captured her interest.

A gaunt, scruffy man was sat cross-legged and barefoot in an empty shop doorway. Laid out in front of him across a strip of cardboard were an array of hand-painted stones. Among the designs were various spiritual symbols and band signs. He also had a bunch of Superhero logos, emojis and Minions for the kids.

'My gosh, how clever,' said Poppy, genuinely charmed.

Kibs stepped next to her and stood hands-on-hips, surveying the range. 'Do you make these all yourself?' he asked, unintentionally patronising.

'Too right I do,' said the bloke, producing a half-finished mandala as proof. 'Where else would I get 'em?' he asked and mid-sentence his focus snapped back to Poppy, although his head did not turn. He simply watched her, side-eyed like a reptile, while she inspected one of his hamsa hand designs.

'How much?' she asked, a smile showcasing those too-perfect teeth Daddy had bought her and in contrast the man bared his own crooked, yellow grin.

'Five pounds each,' he said, a fifty percent mark-up on his usual price. The man knew wealthy suckers when he saw them.

'Five pounds?' Edd snorted, flicking his fringe, 'for an effing stone?'

'It's for the time and effort,' said Poppy.

'And the materials,' said Jack.

The man scratched under his armpit, making a

slightly pained expression. 'I'll do three for twelve,' he said, as if it were a real favour.

'Ohmygod, *sold*,' said Poppy, acting like she'd caught the deal of century, and keeping the hamsa she crouched beside Kibs to select another two.

'You getting a Pokemon?' Trent asked Kibs, who shook his head and showed the Captain Marvel logo already in his hand.

'Gotta go with my queen,' he said. Then to the seller: 'Do you take apple pay?'

The seller looked at him blankly. 'What's that?' and Kibs was about to explain when an angry cry caused him to freeze.

'DON'T GIVE THAT CUNT ANY MONEY!'

All heads turned to another shabby figure lumbering up the street. This one was short, even more gaunt and impeded by a severe limp.

As he came closer, they could tell he was a lot younger than the stone artist, yet in far worse condition. His outgrown hair was greasy and matted, his unshaved face corpse grey and dotted with bulging acne. The baggy clothes hanging off his frail build were tattered and torn, and on his pale hide he carried a suffocating stink, one familiar to Edd, who'd encountered it once before – that time he'd discovered a dead fox on his father's grounds, rotting in the summer sun.

'Fuck off, Slates,' the seller groaned, in a way which implied they'd been through this routine before, but Slates was undeterred and pointed a ragged-nailed finger at the seller.

'He aint even homeless, y'know. He's got a council bedsit round the corner.'

A yin yang stone whizzed by Slates' head. He ducked unnecessarily, well after the fact.

'Shut up, Slates,' the seller warned.

'Is that true?' asked Edd, turning to the seller, who blanked the question and busied himself arranging the stones in tighter rows.

'You're takin' money away from us what need it...*Kaspar*,' said Slates, injecting the last with such contempt it implied insult, yet it was merely the seller's given name.

In turn Kaspar aimed a dead stare at his accuser, dirty hand gripping another yin yang, ready to fling. 'Why don't *you* do somethin' to make some money then...*Robert?*'

At this Slates' eyes widened with righteous anger and his lips drew back to a gappy, manic grin as he addressed the jury.

'See? He's not even denying it. You lot wanna give money to a good cause? You're lookin' at one. 'ere, check out my leg.'

Before anyone could raise a protest Slates unfastened his belt, dropping his jeans and the stained long johns underneath, right down to his ankles.

A shocked Poppy and Jack covered their eyes while the rest instinctively looked away, but they'd already seen that he still had underwear on. It simply took a moment to register. Once it did each of them returned to Slates, curious and wary of what he might do next.

'Here, here, check it,' Slates said. He was gazing down with both hands gripping his upper thigh, pulling the skin taut around a three-inch wound.

Holding it like that he shuffled closer, angling the leg toward the group so they could see, not just the wound but the tiny, milky-white forms writhing and squirming within.

'Fuckin' maggots,' he spat. 'Ya ever seen that

before? C'mon, that's worth a fiver's sympathy at least.'

The group gasped in unison. Then Edd cursed, Kibs covered his eyes and Jack looked away while Poppy's face turned the same colour as the overcast sky.

A few moments later and she puked, fat undigested chunks of Starbucks' vegan falafel onto the pavement.

'Oh Pops,' said Trent, swooping in to hold her as she heaved again. 'That's it, let it out, girl.'

Rhonda sidestepped the spatter and noticed Edd now had his phone trained on Slates, recording a video no doubt destined for the internet. Appalled, she snatched it from him and deleted the recording as she moved toward its maggot-afflicted subject.

'Hey,' Edd cried, but the stone-cold look Rhonda wore, same as at the monument, dissuaded him from further action.

'Look,' Slates repeated, showing his wound, assuming it the reason for Rhonda's approach. 'See 'em wriggle? I can't get 'em out. I tried with one an' half of it's still in there.'

'Pull your kecks up,' said Rhonda, exuding a calm authority Slates had only ever witnessed among experienced Police officers. He didn't expect that and found himself obeying, apologising on reflex.

'Soz like...'

'It's fine,' said Rhonda. 'Look, I'm not interested in your leg mate. But I've got money. So why don't you *tell* me something worth a fiver.'

Confusion streaked Slates' grubby brow while he fastened his belt. 'What d'ya mean? Like a joke? I got a good one about Michael Jackson and Jimmy Savile.'

Rhonda gave a curt shake of her head.

'Do you know a girl called Roxy Weaver?'

On hearing the name Slates immediately lit up.

'Yeah, I know a Roxy,' he said. Then a thought flickered in his eyes. 'Hey, are you family? You look a bit like her.'

Although it should've been cause for joy, Slates' last comment disturbed Rhonda slightly, something suspect about it, and she paused, hearing the quiet apology from Kibs returning the Captain Marvel stone, since he carried no cash to pay for it.

In the reflection of the window behind Slates she saw Trent helping Poppy away and noticed that the others were all leaving too, all bar Edd, who probably only wanted his phone back.

She returned to Slates.

'Do you know where I can find Roxy?'

'Yep,' he chirped, and his dry lips locked tight with just the slightest hint of a smirk. He wasn't going to give it to her that easy.

'Tell me,' said Rhonda.

Slates shook his head, that smirk blooming into another grin, and he made the "gimme" gesture with an outstretched hand.

'Money first.'

'That's not how this works,' said Rhonda.

Slates shrugged. 'Then I aint tellin' ya.'

From his pavement seat Kaspar piped up: 'I'll fuckin' tell ya luv.'

'Go on mate,' said Edd, 'you tell us first and *you* can have the money.'

'Shut up *Kaspar*,' said Slates. 'You don't even know Roxy. He don't even know her.'

In the face of such certainty Kaspar didn't bother to drag the lie out any further. He just sat back wearing a sleazy grin and returned to his stones.

'Tell you what,' said Rhonda, reclaiming Slates'

attention, 'how about you take us to her, then I'll give you a twenty.'

Slates' eyes almost popped out of his head.

'Fuckin' deal.'

'Alright, come on,' said Rhonda, beckoning with a tip of her head toward the caravelle, but Edd blocked their path.

'Wait, he's not comin' in my ride,' he said, adding under his breath, 'he reeks.'

Rhonda didn't dispute that fact. 'But he says he knows where Roxy is.'

Edd gave a callous shrug. 'So?'

There followed another silent staredown, filled with more tension than a fat man's mattress spring. Surprisingly, this time it was Rhonda who broke first to return Edd's phone.

'Here.'

Initially Edd was hesitant to accept it. He fully anticipated a sucker punch coming his way until Rhonda added an earnest, 'Please Edd.'

That approach caught Edd off-guard, and he felt a slab of guilt fall across his chest. On paper he'd signed up to this thing to help people, but in reality, it'd been a bit of a pose, a chance to spend time with Poppy, something to do.

Now faced with a person in need, a person actually asking for his help, the pressure of responsibility, the weight of expectation, were unbearable. He simply couldn't say no - *What would the others think?*

'Okay,' he submitted, throwing hands up, 'but you're paying for the valeting.'

'Fair enough,' said Rhonda and Slates didn't bite or take offence at all.

He had no idea what valeting meant.

<u>11</u>

Static as a resting reptile Wiktor Pinkiewicz sat alone, waiting in Fred's van, not thinking about the sight of shovelled dirt falling onto that hooker's dead face.

Or how it'd looked filling and spilling out of her gaping mouth.

Or the way those frozen, black eyes had seemed to stare at him through gaps in the moorland soil until they were completely buried.

Pinkie wasn't dwelling on any of that. He was thinking about his bonus, the theoretical bonus he expected in return for finding all those drugs. To him ten percent would be acceptable, anything less though…

He scanned his surroundings once more. The view offered little to interest, just a desolate trading estate of mostly unoccupied units and large storage containers.

Fred had entered the unit opposite a half hour earlier. He'd left a CD in the player and the lyrics to Squeeze's "*Up the Junction"* were starting to cut a little near the bone for Pinkie. Like the character in the song, he too had settled down early as result of unintended pregnancy. His wife was now expecting their fourth and he could barely afford their third. A small, weak part of him hoped she might lose this one.

He hated himself for that.

There was a loud mechanical hum and he looked to the unit opposite as its metal shutters slowly retracted, revealing two pairs of feet. One wore Fred's boots. The other, a set of navy-blue Adidas gazelles.

'About time.'

The shutter continued rising and Pinkie adjusted in his seat. Ignoring the discomfort of his cracked ribs, he straightened up to showcase his freakish size, which was the first thing the Adidas-wearer mentioned on approach.

'Got 'nuff headroom thair big man?' he asked, giving a friendly nod. Then to Fred, 'Christ, yer gunee want a bigger van feh this bloke.'

Fred gave a deep-bellied chuckle which stopped as suddenly as it'd started. He was savvy enough to fake a laugh whenever the boss said anything even remotely humorous. He just wasn't a great actor.

'I'm Joe by the wey,' said the boss, offering his hand through the window.

Pinkie shook it while giving the man a thorough assessment. He was of average height, medium build, innocuously dressed in a worn polo shirt and faded jeans, with short-cropped greying hair and clean-shaven face.

He looked just like your average middle-aged, working-class bloke. His features were friendly, almost Dad-like. The only hint at who he really was lay in the lean musculature Pinkie detected under the clothes and a faded battle scar about the brow.

'Ah wantid tae sey cheers for that joab,' Joe said, his grip firm, but not overly so, not like he was trying to make a point, or overcompensating. It was just enough to say: "This is who I am".

Pinkie appreciated that.

'Ah see y' goat stung thair,' said Joe, fixing on Pinkie's cuts. 'Whit Fred told us aboot that gear mus' be spot oan. Canee see many people in their reet mind hovin' a pop at a big guy like yersel' but. An' very few a them wid land anythin' ah bet. Yer into yer MMA an' all that aren't yeh?'

Pinkie gave a slight nod. He was having a hard time keeping up with Joe's accent, a diluted Glaswegian which saw syllables dropped here and there, like loose change in a holey pocket.

'S'what I thoat. Bad stuff, *dangerous* stuff...Look, I gied Fred a monkey as a bonus. S'two fifty each feh yer bother. 'e's gonee tell yeh the rest.'

'Thank you,' said Pinkie, disappointed but trying not to show. Two fifty wasn't much, not even a percentage of what he'd valued those drugs at. The first thing he said to Fred once Joe returned inside the unit was, 'We should've kept the drugs.'

'Nah, they're worthless,' said Fred. 'No one wants shit that turns people psycho. It's all about repeat business the drug trade.'

'Bullshit. They mugged us off.'

'Nah,' said Fred, starting the engine. 'Joe flushed it all right in front of me.'

'He flushed it?' Pinkie echoed, incensed. 'That's worth at least thirty-

-it's not worth fuck all,' Fred barked back and he brought the van around sharply, his dry steering crunching gravel beneath the tyres.

'I told ya, they can't sell shit like that. It'll fuck up all their customers an' bring a load of aggro. They reckon it's a bad batch whatever it is an' I totally get their point. C'mon mate, you saw what it did to those scrubbers.'

When he'd thought about it, Pinkie begrudgingly agreed with the logic. Even still, he wasn't happy and sulked in silence while Fred drove them away from the estate. They were a mile or so down the road before either spoke again and it was Fred who opened his mouth first, shifting back into that default joviality as easily as most people pull on a t-shirt.

'He made us an offer y'know, but I get it if you just want some kip...with your ribs an' that.'

'What offer?' said Pinkie, immediately intrigued, regardless of the pain in his chest the fatigue of a four-hour sleep.

'Joe's offered an extra grand each if we can find the rest of that stuff.'

Pinkie's eyes narrowed.

'If it's worthless why pay us to get it?'

'I just told ya,' Fred huffed, 'they don't want it out there, do they? Imagine that shit gets to half the junkies in this town, it'll be fuckin' carnage. They'll be tearin' civvies to bits in the high street like some bloody zombie movie. An' who do you think the pigs'll come down on? Who do you think they'll blame? Our lot don't have anythin' to do with it, but it could still cause problems, big fuckin' problems. D'ya get it now?'

Pinkie understood, although he hadn't listened to the whole speech. The zombie part struck a chord, sent him elsewhere in his head and his gaze stretched into the distance, the glazed, thousand-yard stare of someone revisiting a trauma. He didn't disclose the memory, but after a full minute's silence a single word tripped off his cut lip.

'Krocodil.'

'You what mate?' Fred snarled, his first instinct to assume it was some Polish insult.

'Your newspapers call it zombie drug,' said Pinkie. 'In Gdansk we call it Krocodil. It makes people look like that, like those hookers did.'

Fred's temper quickly cooled. He could recall a dramatic headline in *The Gazette*, "ZOMBIE NATION", accompanied by gruesome mugshots of junkies afflicted with extreme gangrene, going down

A Hot Dose of Hell

to the bone.

Worst of them was some poor girl who'd lost most of her scalp and part of her cheek.

'You reckon that's what the stuff is, Pinks?'

'No,' said Pinkie. 'The zombies *look* like those hookers did, but they don't act like that. They act like...just junkies, not like animals...like rabid...'

'Yeah, I know what ya mean,' said Fred, 'reminded me of my dog.'

'What?' Pinkie was suddenly intrigued. 'I didn't know you have dog. Where do you keep it?'

'*Used* to have one,' Fred explained. 'A big Rottie when I was about seven or eight. Back then my grandparents still had a little farm an' we used to go up there every weekend, let him run about the fields. Then one day he got bit by a badger or fox or somethin', went rabid, broke into the chicken coop, tore up everythin', proper rampage.'

'You saw it?'

'I saw it. All those chickens squawking an' shit...I just remember walkin' in, feathers everywhere, floatin' in the air like it was snowin'. Then I noticed some of those feathers were red and there was a lot more red the further I went in.'

'You kept going?'

'Yeah. I came round a corner an' there was my dog, this big rottie, probably about the same size as me at that point...maybe bigger. He had a chicken by the neck an' he was just shakin' it an' shakin' it, feathers an' bloody froth goin' everywhere. I felt wet on my face an' thought I'd started crying. You cry all the time when you're that age don't ya? Cry cos ya didn't get the toy you wanted. Cry cos you fell off your bike. Cry cos you're fuckin' tired. But it was blood on my cheek an' I must've made a noise then, cos he dropped that chicken and just looked at me, looked right at me.'

'He recognise you.'

'Nah, that wasn't it,' said Fred, a wry smile on his lips which died long before it touched his eyes. 'That wasn't it at all, mate. He just looked at me like another thing, like the way he looked at those chickens. There wasn't nothin' goin' on in them eyes, mate. They were like fake eyes, like doll's eyes y'know, just black and shiny. Thing that got me with that hooker Shaz, was she had that same fuckin' look. I mean, I must've shagged that bird a dozen times last year, an' I know she's a pro, sees a lot of blokes. But we spent a bit of time as well, an' when she saw me earlier it was like-'

-What happened to the dog?' said Pinkie.

'Granddad came in an' stabbed it with a pitchfork. Just fuckin' pinned it to the floor and held it, thrashin' about on the end of those spikes till it bled out. Took fuckin' ages. You should've heard the noise man, that yelpin' whine. Had to cover my ears.'

Pinkie took a moment to absorb that, then asked, 'What was dog's name?'

'Rex,' said Fred and he snorted at the irony. Such a generic, innocent name, but one also shared with the most fearsome of the great reptiles - The Tyrannosaurus.

'Alright,' said Pinkie, 'how can we get hold of the rest of that gear?'

'What?' Fred wore a quizzical smirk. 'That little story inspire you, did it?'

'A thousand pounds inspires me, mate. I have mouths to feed. So, how can we get the rest of that gear eh?'

Fred was fully smiling now. 'The old-fashioned

way, Pinks. That little prozzie told me Shaz took it off a couple a' smackheads. We find them, we find the gear, or what's left of it anyway. Now chances are those two are homeless, which means they're only gonna be in some doorway on the strip or at the old hotel.'

'What old hotel?'

'The Victoria. Used to be a top hotel when I was a kid. Then it went bust about twenty years ago. Been empty ever since. Everyone knows it's infested with smackheads, but no one cares long as they're out of sight.'

To Pinkie that seemed the most logical place to start. If anyone had used that stuff on the street they'd be arrested or dead already. Only place they might go unheard would be an old squat like that.

'Alright, let's go. But we're tooling up, yes?'

'Fuck yeah, I aint takin' chances with anyone on that stuff.'

'We can go to my lockup,' said Pinkie. He needed to re-arm. They'd ditched their other weapons back on the moors, far from the grave sites.

'No need, mate,' said Fred. 'I've got plenty of stuff we can use in the back.'

'Like what?'

'You'll see. There'll be something to tickle your fancy, promise ya.'

'If you say so,' Pinkie muttered, folding arms, then immediately unfolding them to relieve the pressure on his injured ribs.

Fred clocked him doing this.

'You'll need to take somethin' though. Can't have you flinchin' if we come up against more like Shaz and Tray.'

His fat hand went into his coat and promptly

dumped a cellophane-wrapped bundle of assorted meds right onto Pinkie's lap.

'Help yourself.'

Two tramadol later and Pinkie felt good, the ribs no longer troubling at all. To counter any sluggishness, he dropped a dose of MDMA on top, which soon saw him bopping his head and punching the roof in time with The Stranglers' *"Let me down easy"* on the stereo.

Much to Fred's amusement, Pinkie began to hum along as they entered Scarmouth and when they passed the famous "Big tree" at the top of the high street he was actually singing the chorus.

'Let me down eeesaay,
LET ME DOWN EEESAAY.'

Pinkie seemed almost oblivious to what he was doing, as if this were an involuntary response, some kind of drug-induced trance. He was only snapped out of it by a near miss from a people carrier crossing their lane, and he abandoned the song then to support Fred in cursing its reckless driver.

'LEARN TO DRIVE DICKHEAD!' went Fred.

'Yeah, STUPID CUNT!' Pinkie bellowed, yet he feared it may have been wasted effort, for Fred had continued to drive and by the time he'd uttered the second syllable of "STUPID" they were already onto a tight, potholed road curving behind a string of shops.

There graffiti covered the rear of every building, with efforts ranging from crude tags to a ten-foot Theresa May fellating a penis-shaped EU flag. An obscenely muscular devil grinned at them from the last building in that row and its great red face hovered in Fred's rear view all the way to the harbour.

Scores of chairs and tables sat unattended outside

A Hot Dose of Hell

the strip's numerous bars and cafes, while wilting palm trees swayed in the wind whipping across the grey sea and a mob of seagulls battled furiously beneath a billboard still showing the sun-bleached ghost of Jimmy Carr from his 2017 tour.

At the roadside, a train of taxis waited for no one and beyond them, just after the turn he needed to take, Fred glimpsed a panda car lying in wait, its occupants no doubt itching for something to do.

On sight Fred killed the music and slowed to the exact speed limit. Pinkie noticed and quickly clipped the seat belt he'd so far eschewed for the sake of his ribs. There should've been nothing to fear, since the van no longer carried any trace of the grisly cargo they'd smuggled to the moors, but it was always best practise to avoid attention from the law.

Like an OAP, Fred signalled eight seconds in advance, smoothly made the turn and cruised past, the two constables in the panda never paying them a moment's notice. All the same, Fred maintained speed past a string of tourist gift shops and cafes and at the end of the strip a steep, winding hill carried the van away from the harbour, out along the coast.

Atop that hill the once-glamorous hotel Victoria loomed like some old, haunted house, like Dracula's castle, a near ruin, its decay visible from hundreds of yards away. The old building spanned three floors and looked a similar design to the budget brothel they'd attended that morning - another product of the post-war boom gone to pot, though not so dramatically as here.

At a glance the first, most noticeable detail was the collapsed chimney against the grey sky. A portion of its structure still stood impotently while all around it, parts of the roof's skeleton glared through gaps in the slate.

Glimpses of the old lettering were visible beneath a sheet of ivy sprouting from ground to gutter. Growth covered the entirety of that side, as though it were in the process of devouring the building and any betting man would have trouble guessing what would claim it first between that and the thick patches of moss sprouting across the facade.

Long reeds dangled several feet from the guttering with some stretching past the boarded top floor windows. Every window was boarded up, yet there was no door or barrier on the entrance. It stood wide open, inviting anyone to venture in.

'What a shithole,' said Pinkie.

'Wasn't always,' said Fred, killing the engine to coast silently into the lot. 'You know, I heard Michael Barrymore used to stay here sometimes.'

Once it cleared the gate-less gate posts, a wide U-turn set the van facing outward for a quick getaway and Fred parked up across the faded lines of two spaces.

Pinkie frowned. 'Who's Michael Barrymore?'

Fred cut a smirk.

'Let's just say he's someone you never wanna go for a swim with.'

Pinkie's frown deepened. 'Don't get it.'

'Of course,' Fred tutted. 'You probably don't even know who *Drew* Barrymore is do ya?'

'Who?' Pinkie shook his head. 'I don't know either of those blokes, mate.'

'Like I thought,' said Fred, getting out. 'Don't worry about it, Pinks.'

They regrouped at the back of the van. Fred pulled both doors wide and climbed in. He sat on his knees in the middle, passing tools from one side to other, laying them out for Pinkie to choose.

'Why do you keep all this in your van?' said Pinkie, feeling the weight of a claw hammer.

'I'm a workman,' said Fred. 'That's my cover anyway. But I can do some odd jobs, a bit of paintin', landscapin'.' Point is, I can drive about all hours with this gear and no copper's gonna be bothered if he pulls me over an' finds it. *You* might get a caution for carrying a baseball bat in your boot, but I can have all this, and no one minds.'

Pinkie set the hammer aside and considered the chainsaw. 'I see your point,' he said. Then he set that down as his gaze fell to something else.

Half-buried under various other tools, this item lay glimmering with the promise of devastation. Pinkie's great arm swept the others aside and he grasped its handle with two hands, slowly raising it aloft.

It was a 20lb sledgehammer. But in Pinkie's grip it was a warhammer, the kind of thing his ancestors had used to bludgeon invading Roman soldiers, to smash the shields comprising their fearsome testudos.

Fred had donned a headtorch. 'Suits you sir,' he said, knowing Pinkie would fail to grasp yet another pop culture reference and Pinkie ignored it altogether.

'Not just a weapon,' he said, lowering the sledge. 'We could use to knock down some doors.'

'I like your thinking,' said Fred. 'Are you sure that'll be any use with your ribs though? Gonna put 'em under stress when you use it.'

Without warning Pinkie performed a practice swing, a wide diagonal arc, the type of swing that would destroy bone, crack concrete and dent steel were it to connect. He controlled it easily, making the hammer seem much lighter than it was, and pulled it back in to rest against his broad shoulder.

'Can't feel them now,' he shrugged.

'You're buzzin' eh?' Fred chuckled, snatching up a hatchet which he handled and twirled expertly, earning an impressed nod from Pinkie before he holstered it in a loop on the hip of his coveralls like an old west gunfighter.

'You've done that before.'

Fred beamed with pride. 'Pub axe throwing champ 2018. My picture's behind the bar in my local boozer.'

Pinkie snorted, 'That's because you're barred.' And Fred cracked up, his big belly laughs shattering the eerie silence, ringing out through the hollow building nearby, where deep within its bowels shadowy figures stirred in response.

'Smart arse when you're pilled-up eh Pinks?'

'Yeah,' Pinkie nodded, seeming amused by himself, then his expression turned grave. 'Maybe we should get job done before I come down.'

Fred nodded in agreement. 'Alright, let's rock 'n roll,' he said, and they started for the entrance.

In tandem they took the porch steps where Fred pointed out some faded bloodstains. They didn't linger over them, but at the threshold they held back and stood gazing into the dense shadow past the foyer.

Both were wary of what might be skulking under cover of that shadow. No doubt there would be a few ruthless characters amongst the pathetic ones and perhaps there would be more like those prostitutes, more rabid dogs. Only this time Fred and Pinkie would be ready for them. This time they'd strike first, ask questions later.

'Good thing I brought this, eh?' said Fred, flicking on his head torch. 'Thought you'd take the piss.'

Pinkie gave Fred a playful nudge. 'You are miner as well? I didn't know you were Jack of old trades.'

'It's Jack of *all* trades,' said Fred, scanning the foyer, and finding the coast clear he led them inside.

The moment they crossed the threshold both men felt the temperature drop. It was like the difference between shallow and deep water.

They were in the deep now, treading across some yawning abyss with all manner of unseen threats lurking below.

'Which way?' said Pinkie.

'Here,' said Fred, passing through a doorway at their left. It fed into a large room and as he scanned side to side his headtorch caught a glint off an old brass sign, reading "Black Tie Only".

'Damn,' he muttered, 'left mine at home.'

They proceeded past a toppled podium, boots crunching grit with every step on the bare concrete. Fred kept his head down like a bloodhound, scanning the foreground for potential hazards. Finding none he looked up and what he saw then gave him pause.

In three rows stood an array of tents, at least thirty in total.

'Anybody home?' said Pinkie.

'Don't think so,' said Fred.

All the same he gave each one a cursory glance on the way, shining the torch through to find only scattered trash, empty sleeping bags.

Near the last his toe clipped an empty can of special brew, sending it tumbling noisily into the darkness and he followed its trajectory with his beam, seeing it come to an end against a rickety old spiral staircase.

The hollow clank of the can off those metal stairs was amplified by the structure and travelled upwards to the higher floors which shortly returned another sound - a low and wavering moan of despair.

'*Someone's* home,' said Pinkie.

Fred walked over, shining his headtorch up. The beam reached the bannister of the next floor and he could tell that the stairs went further than that but couldn't see any activity.

'Let's introduce ourselves, eh?'

Before proceeding Pinkie grabbed the rusted rail, gave it a firm shake. The staircase let out an unnerving squeal and shuddered for several seconds after.

'You first, mate.'

Fred huffed, 'It's a fire escape. Should be sturdy enough.'

'Yeah,' said Pinkie, sarcastic. 'Well on you go.'

The pair exchanged looks, holding a brief standoff. Then after a few beats Fred gave a disgruntled snort and began the climb, the staircase creaking, screeching with every shift in weight.

These sounds intensified once Pinkie started to follow, and the racket seemed to antagonise the distinctly human moaning above.

Soon they realised that voice was coming from somewhere on the second floor, so they continued up in search of its owner, their weapons gripped tight.

Both men were secretly dreading what they might find up there, but would never admit it, not even to themselves.

12

The smell inside Edd's caravelle was unbearable, even with the windows, all of them, fully open. It was a rancid cocktail of sweat, booze and piss, like the bins out the back of any pub combined with the most neglected public toilet.

In the front seat Poppy pinched her nose discreetly and at the wheel Edd wore a sneer of disgust. On the next row Kibs had his head angled out the window like a dog, while Rhonda suffered silently next to Jack, who could have been retching under that mask for all anyone knew.

On the rear-facing seat behind them, Trent kept his head down, desperately avoiding eye contact with the smell's owner, sat opposite.

Slates' gaze felt unsettling, and he had a habit of holding it for too long, leering right through any subject as if they were just another inanimate thing.

'Where am I going?' said Edd, to no reply. Then he raised his voice, projecting it toward the back, 'WHERE AM I GOING?'

Slates leant forward, his dirty face appearing in the gap between Jack and Rhonda's headrests. As he spoke his foul breath blew warm on the back of Jack's shaved neck, who shrank into the seat, repulsed, pulling that mask a little higher.

'Turn right 'ere, mate. Then go straight to the 'arbour.'

The great devil smiled down on the vehicle the same as it had Fred McCall's van not long before and Theresa May still had that penis-flag in her mouth.

At the harbour all the cafe seating remained empty. The seagulls' battle raged on, now spilling into human passers-by. But the panda car had moved off.

'Right here,' said Slates, a little later than was helpful so that Edd had to brake and yank the wheel sharply to make the turn.

'More warning next time, mate,' he said.

'Whatever,' Slates mumbled. Then even quieter, 'Not my fault stupid cunt can't drive.'

Had the panda still been waiting there the officers would've certainly stopped Edd for erratic driving. They would've looked the vehicle over and they would've taken Slates, who was wanted for a public disturbance earlier in the day.

But as usual, luck was not on Slates' side, for a night in the cells would've been far preferable to what he would experience over the hour to come.

'Cute shops,' said Jack, tapping the window at the string of grockle shops, and Trent suggested they stop by there after.

'I'd love a browse. Bet they've got some kitschy merch.'

Slates was set to disclose that he'd been banned from these shops when out of the blue Poppy asked, 'Hey Slates, can't you just like...have them removed?'

'What?' said Slates and he once again pushed his face through the gap between headrests to bring it level with Rhonda and Jack.

'What's that luv? Move what? What you on about?'

A row between them Poppy refused to turn around, preferring to watch Slates through the rear view. It gave the illusion of greater distance.

'The *maggots*,' she said, and she seemed almost annoyed by Slates' affliction, as if it in any way inconvenienced *her*. 'Can't you just have them removed?'

'Where can I do that then?' said Slates. 'I got

kicked outta' hospital, didn't I?'

'Why did they kick you out?' asked Trent, pursing his lips thoughtfully, and after a tense pause Slates sat back to face him once again.

'Kicked off 'bout the wait, didn't I?' said Slates, glowering at the memory, but directing it at Trent almost as if he were to blame. 'I mean, I'm sat there four hours straight with fuckin' maggots in my leg, then along comes this spoilt little kid with this *tiny* cough who goes straight through. Fuckin' prejudice I tell ya. So I kicked off an' security slung me out.'

'That kid must've had something more serious,' said Rhonda and Slates waved off the notion as if it were a fly, which incidentally is what those maggots would eventually become.

'Nah, she was fine. Just a cough I reckon.'

He leaned forward again. 'Hey, straight up here.'

Giving a slight nod of appreciation for the notice this time, Edd obliged and continued onto a steep hill where he was forced to drop a gear.

The caravelle climbed higher above the sea to their right and yet the choppy surf still licked the roadside barrier, sending spatters of its froth to pelt the vehicle's side. Here the wind increased with the incline and feeling the chill Poppy hugged herself, fingers brushing gooseflesh.

Right away Edd took the hint to raise his window, but Kibsy's remained down, his head still outside. He'd happily endure the sting of cold wind whipping his ears over breathing Slates' offensive odour and didn't care whether his fellow passengers felt the same.

Out of all of them Rhonda was the only one unaffected, her body used to working around freezers all night. She had a question for Slates and unclipped her belt so that she could face him, read his reaction to it.

'When was the last time you saw Roxy?'

'Saw her go out last night.'

'Is she alright? Where was she going?'

'Out...' said Slates, his gaze dropping, and he offered a slight shrug. 'You know how it is...gotta survive.'

Rhonda caught the gist without Slates needing to spell it out and was the only one to do so, going by the non-reactions around her. She could be glad of that at least. Despite all their talk of compassion, Leg-Up were a judgemental bunch in her view, and had they cottoned on she felt they would secretly ridicule Roxy, not that she could really blame them.

For any of their group to sink low enough to even consider prostitution they would need to crash through at least ten financial safety nets first. They would almost have to *try* to reach such a low. How could they understand, let alone empathise?

'Did she look okay?'

'Yeah, she always does,' said Slates. 'Kenny was with her like always too. That's her fella by the way. Can't even say hello to Rox without him givin' you evils.'

Jack piped up, 'Another possessive chauvinist,' and Trent tutted in support.

'That's the least of it,' said Slates, not really knowing what the word "chauvinist" meant, only discerning that it was negative by Jack's tone. 'The bloke's a psycho as well.'

In silence, Rhonda sat back considering this information. The introduction of Kenny presented a new problem. If it turned out Roxy was truly attached to the man, how could she convince her to leave him behind?

Then again, why would she need to go through Roxy? Rhonda figured any man so weak he'd willingly pimp out his partner could probably be bought or frightened off with relative ease. On that thought she went into the bag on her lap, fingers finding the cosh she'd bought from Big Greg, closing on it.

One way or another she'd convince Kenny to let Roxy go.

'There it is,' Slates cried, his pointing hand shooting through the gap by Rhonda's head. 'The old Vic.'

'I see it,' said Edd, as the angle of the road increased, forcing him to drop another gear. Under his breath he muttered, 'Not like anyone could miss it.'

The landmark had been visible for some time before Slates said anything and it was Kibs who'd spotted it first from his unobstructed view out the window, yet he'd remained conspicuously silent.

Shortly, Kibs returned inside and sat back as a queasiness seeped into his gut, a creeping dread chilled his blood. A long-forgotten incident was bubbling in the back of his mind. Something which had occurred inside a similar derelict structure, one of his father's renovation projects, he assumed.

The memory was vague, amounting to the chalky feel of dust on his skin and the echo of whimpering. All Kibs knew beyond that was that he was afraid, although the erection throbbing in his jeans told a different story.

Like a movie montage more images began to occur to him, flashes of skin, a scattering of bright clothing. Then there was a voice, and he almost remembered a face to match, but it was all torn away when the vehicle suddenly swerved.

'Ohmygod,' Poppy gasped.

Seemingly out of nowhere Fred McCall's transit van had appeared. It was sat partially blocking the entrance to the Victoria's car park, on any day an unexpected position, impossible to see coming up the hill until it was almost too late.

Luckily Edd's manoeuvre came just in time so that only his wing mirror clipped the side panel and he cursed in response while the very sight of the van hurled Slates into a panic.

'Oh shit! It's a raid! It's a fuckin' raid!'

'It's not police,' said Rhonda. 'That's a trade van.'

'Oh yeah? So what's it doin' here eh?'

'Maybe someone's buying the place,' offered Kibs.

'Better not be,' Slates growled, as if he'd have any influence on the matter.

'Over there,' said Poppy, pointing, and at her instruction Edd brought the vehicle to a gentle stop inside a faded parking space near the hotel entrance.

'Easier to offload the stuff here,' she explained, awarding him a stroke on the shoulder.

'Good driving,' she added, causing him to flush with pride then he flinched a little when Rhonda leaned forward and gave his headrest a gentle tap.

'Cheers Edd,' she said, meaning it.

As much as she'd disagreed with him that day, Rhonda appreciated that he'd driven for eight hours without complaint, much complaint. In addition to that he'd allowed Slates along, allowed that filthy wretch a seat inside his expensive vehicle.

Rhonda couldn't honestly say she would've done the same in his position.

'You're welcome, losers,' said Edd, affection in his tone, and he gave Rhonda a shy smile via the rear

A Hot Dose of Hell

view. Over time they might've come to some understanding, found a little common ground, only the events of the night to come would permanently prevent any chance of that.

'Let's get in there, peeps,' said Poppy, prompting them all to disembark.

Edd was last out and after first checking the wing mirror he stood stretching, leaning on the vehicle door. Then while the others went around to the boot, he stood surveying the Victoria's dilapidated structure, its rot and disrepair.

On the second floor one of the window boards dangled precariously in the breeze, which poured in noisily through the door-less entrance to create the illusion of a great mouth sucking breath.

Edd stubbornly ignored the chill crawling up his spine, the warning signals his senses were giving him and quipped, 'Hope my tetanus shot is in date.'

No one laughed. Trent simply opened the trunk. Inside, beneath some of their personal luggage were cases of toiletries, toothbrushes, soap, razorblades and deodorant, intended as giveaways for the homeless. He and Kibs had gathered a trolley-load the previous week, but Poppy said it was too much to take on this one trip.

Trent disagreed at the time and looking at what they'd brought he still didn't think it was right. By his calculation they only had enough for thirty people to get one of each item. Hardly worth the trip.

'Getting dark,' said Kibs, and it was dimming rapidly. A heavy greyness had already settled over everything. Reflections on the caravelle's shiny surface were gone, evaporated.

'So we'd better get started,' said Poppy. Then she turned to Kibs, lowering her voice: 'Don't worry, the dark will enhance the photos we're going to take. It'll like, really highlight the grimness of these people's lived experience.'

'Oi,' said Slates and due to the timing Poppy feared she'd offended him with her last comment. She fumbled for an apology but held off giving one when Slates turned and semi-swaggered over to the cliff side of the hotel. He returned seconds later, carrying a solar-charged lantern, an excited skip in his limp.

'Let there be light,' he said proudly.

Edd snorted, unimpressed, and drew his iPhone, lighting its torch feature.

The pride melted from Slates' expression as he saw the rest of their party's phones lighting up one by one.

'Trent, get your phone out as well,' Poppy said, her bangles jangling with a typically theatrical gesture. 'We want lots of pictures. We need to show everyone what it's like here, what we're dealing with.'

Trent made a pained expression. 'Don't you want me to bring this stuff? I can't do both.'

'Leave the stuff for now,' said Poppy. 'We'll assess the place first and then bring people out one by one to give them the aid packages. That way we'll be able to get the best shots and ensure that things stay-'

'Oi,' went Slates, 'you aint 'avin' my picture 'less you pay me.'

'Wow,' Poppy sighed, rapidly blinking as she processed the outburst. 'Is it really all about money with you? You know that we're trying to raise awareness of *your* situation here, right?'

Slates cackled like a blocked drain.

'Last I checked I can't eat *awareness*, can't drink it, can't shoot it up, so what good's it to me?'

'More people will want to help,' said Trent. 'The government might step in. It's about time they

A Hot Dose of Hell

acknowledged the results of their spending cuts.'

'Government?' Slates jeered, cracking a grin so broad it would've shown his back teeth if he still had any. 'And what will those cunts do? Put me in supported livin'? Been there, done that. What else can they do? Put me on Methadone? I'm on it now an' I'm still shootin' skag. C'mon what you got, eh? What could your *government* do for me?'

Neither Trent, Edd, Jack, Kibs or Rhonda had anything to counter Slates' nihilism since it was coming from experience none of them knew much about. Being the group's leader, all eyes went to Poppy who, at a loss for any practical answer, merely spoke louder to compensate.

'I don't know...they could...just...*help*.'

'Yeah, but how?' Slates asked, leering, and for a moment he looked set to square up to her when Edd stepped in between.

'Just back off, mate,' he said with an unintimidating flick of his hair. 'We're here to like, help you out. Don't give Poppy a hard time, okay?'

Stepping back, Slates raised hands in submission. 'Alright, whatever you say, Skrillex. Look, I don't give a shit what you lot think long as I get paid.'

'You get paid when we find Roxy,' Rhonda said, zipping her hoodie, then she tucked her right into its front pocket, feeling the retractable cosh underneath for assurance. While the others had been distracted, she'd clipped the weapon's pouch to the front belt loops of her jeans, keeping it concealed yet easy to be drawn when needed.

'Now let's get on with it.'

'She's right,' said Poppy, reclaiming her thunder. 'Let's *go* people.'

In loose formation the group approached the

entrance and they filtered through the wide doorway two abreast, blissfully unaware of the dried bloodstains they walked upon. Slates went first, limping past what had been the reception desk toward a staircase, with Rhonda keeping close behind.

A two-metre gap stretched between them and the Leg-Up posse, who were proceeding much slower, with greater caution and in a tight huddle. Bare, dusty floorboards creaked and groaned beneath them while darkness solidified the deeper they went, the combined light of their iPhones only reaching a few feet ahead.

At the stairs Slates paused, his foot on the first.

'We're goin' up,' he said and Edd trained his iPhone on the man's face, it seeming worse somehow then, uglier. Lit that way the junkie resembled something from an old horror movie, the black and white stuff his grandmother sometimes watched in the afternoon, Fredric March as Mr Hyde.

''urry up,' Slates beckoned, that chimpish grin fading. 'What ya waitin' for?'

From her jeans' back pocket Rhonda took out her phone and stepped right in line, but Leg-Up held back, their path blocked by Edd at the front who was studying Slates with a sceptical eye. For him there was something untoward about this sudden eagerness and stuck-on smile. The junkie seemed far too keen to herd them upstairs.

'We should check down here first,' said Edd, a slight edge to his tone which he hoped Poppy would catch. He stared at her deeply throughout, almost willing his thoughts into her brain and after a few beats her eyes widened a fraction, giving the impression it'd worked.

'O-kay,' she said and Edd visibly sighed with

relief, shoulders relaxing, although as Poppy spoke on it became clear she hadn't a clue what he'd been trying to tell her.

'Sooo what if Rhonda finds her sister? We'll miss that wonderful moment.'

'Sister?' said Slates, beaming at Rhonda, and he made a dip-snap in celebration like Ali G.

'Fuckin' knew it.'

Rhonda ignored him, but again her hand went to the cosh under her hoodie.

'I'll go with them,' Trent offered, speaking up from the back, and slowly the group parted, allowing him to come forward.

Edd used the shuffle as cover to give Poppy a quick squeeze on the arm. She frowned with annoyance, looked at him, then reading his face finally realised something was up.

Normally she'd be stubborn and dismissive of any opinion outside her own. But here, in this place, this hostile, alien territory, she trusted Edd to recognise dangers she might otherwise miss herself.

'Oh...okay then, Trent,' she said, unsure, glancing back to Edd for confirmation. 'We'll come up after we've explored down *here*?'

Edd gave the subtlest possible nod and Poppy said it again, this time with absolute certainty.

'We'll come up after we've checked down here. Anyone you meet along the way, let them know who we are, the work we're doing. Plus make sure to get some good pics.'

'Will do,' said Trent, taking after Rhonda and Slates.

From the foot of the staircase Edd watched the trio climb. It was strange to think how once upon a time those same stairs had held up elegant ladies in glamorous ball gowns and powerful men in sharp tuxedos.

Now they were walked by a very different sort, a sort Edd didn't really understand, but was beginning to fear the more he did. He could also sense Poppy and the others watching him, no doubt judging him, and the instant he thought Slates was safely out of earshot he spoke to justify himself, explaining his concerns.

'I wanted us to stay down here,' he whispered, 'near the door.'

Poppy tilted her head to the side the way dogs sometimes do. 'But why?'

'I don't trust him,' said Edd.

No one rushed to say otherwise.

'But what like, could he really do?' Jack whispered. 'Like, he can barely walk. I feel like you're being a bit *prejudiced* there, Edd. Not a good look y'know.'

Again, Edd flicked his hair, a scowl breaking across his unlined brow. 'What about his mates, Jack? Did you think about that? He could have six blokes waiting to ambush us. I mean, he was super keen to get us here, don't you think?'

'So you let Rhonda and Trent go?' said Jack. '*Really*?'

Edd shrugged. '*She* wouldn't listen. And I didn't like, personally let Trent go. I mean, *I didn't tell 'im ta do it or anythin.*'

'You can't be-

Poppy intervened before the argument could escalate, putting a hand in Jack's face to command attention.

'Look, let's not be so quick to *judge* Slates,' she said, apparently feeling warmer to the man now that his stench was out of range. It was a classic case of

having one's cake and eating it. Poppy felt quite content to accept the protection of Edd's instincts, while assuming the moral high ground for herself.

Never mind the corporate world, Westminster beckoned.

'Slates is like, a victim,' she said. 'You heard him. He's got no hope or faith in anything. Literally *everyone* has failed him...don't you think so Kibs?'

An uninvolved Kibs was staring absently into the depths of an empty, unlit room, his hand moving slightly in his pocket, fondling something. It took a second prompt from Poppy to break the spell then he withdrew the hand, a shifty look on his face.

'Right, right,' he said, sensing that his agreement was expected, as it so often was.

'There,' said Poppy, satisfied, and she lowered her hand from Jack's view.

A brief hush followed, each member of the group retreating inside their own thoughts. Gradually their ears attuned to this quietness and shortly detected that the hallway was not entirely as silent as first seemed.

Overhead they could hear footfall, staggered and singular, indicating it did not belong to Rhonda's party. At least one other person was up there alone, wandering aimlessly, in circles.

Outside, a strong breeze bullied the bushes, that loose window board slapped against the hotel exterior and Edd instinctively held his breath as they all noticed another sound close by, a brushing, shuffling, erratic yet persistent.

'It's coming from there,' he said, pointing at a room past the stairs.

'Okay, let's go introduce ourselves,' said Poppy and she looked to Edd. 'Lead the way.'

Edd cringed, not really wanting to move, but he

proceeded regardless. With every step his boots seemed loud as slammed doors, the jangle of his various pins and chains sharp as breaking glass. Although he expected to encounter someone, he cursed these sounds for they'd already stolen any opportunity he may have had to turn back, to change his mind.

This other would almost certainly know he was coming now, and any retreat would only draw them out through curiosity, territoriality.

He'd be facing them either way.

'We're with you,' Poppy stage whispered from the back, her hands on Kibs' shoulders, his hands on Jack's as they formed a kind of conga line.

In lazy sync the trio tiptoed down the hall, the light from Jack's iPhone bridging the gap between them and Edd, who stopped outside the room, back pressed to the wall like cops on TV. After a few short breaths to steel himself, he craned his neck around the door frame, peered inside.

The room sat partially lit, last embers of daylight bleeding through cracks in the boarded windows, highlighting swirling dust motes in the air. At first glance it seemed to be completely vacant and bare, but then a flurry of activity drew Edd's focus to a darkened corner where he saw something twitch.

Now much closer, the noise it made was kind of crunchy, artificial, plastic.

With another flicker of activity an edge of the material touched the light and Edd saw that it was just a sheet of tarpaulin fluttering in the wind. He pocketed his iPhone and with restored swagger crossed the room toward it.

'What is that?' said Poppy.

She, Kibs and Jack remained near the door,

watching while Edd threw the sheet aside and all screamed at the thing he unwittingly released, as it shot from beneath the tarp, came flying toward them.

Kibs ducked, pulling the others down with him so that the object passed clean overhead. The sounds it made were more obvious then as it went flapping and cooing down the hall.

'Just a pigeon,' said Jack.

Relieved giggles broke out all round but quickly died at the start of a heavy stride coming from the blackness of the adjacent room.

It was getting louder, the walker heading right toward them. Then suddenly the pace quickened to a furious rush as a tall, imposing figure burst from the shadows to take Edd by the throat.

13

No one moved. Not Poppy, not Jack, not Kibs. All froze in the face of this sudden assault.

His throat gurgling horribly, Edd clawed the attacker's hands in attempt to pry them from around his neck. But they were just too strong. In turn the grip only tightened to where Edd's bulging eyes streamed from the pressure, his head going light.

What strength Edd possessed fast abandoned him then, oxygen-starved arms dropping to hang limply about his sides, skinny legs threatening to buckle. He could do little more than blink at the foul spittle spraying his face as a rough voice hissed...

'That...was my *fuckin' dinner*, cunt.'

From Edd's view the shadows behind the tall man were growing, spreading, until they were swarming his vision like a billion ants.

This is it, he thought, already surrendering in contradiction of so much past talk, of all the angry lyrics he'd so often quoted, and his bladder promptly evacuated, contents dribbling through the painstakingly deliberate tears in those designer jeans.

Poppy wailed, 'WE'RE SORRY,' and the tall man's grip slackened slightly; he hadn't considered the others, hadn't really been fully aware of them until that moment.

A sidelong glance found where they stood cowering, and on a second's thought he carelessly released Edd, letting him crash to the floor.

'Who the fuck are you lot?' said the tall man, turning square. 'What're you doin' 'ere?'

No one answered. Poppy and Kibs could only gasp in horror as Jack broke away, rushing directly at the

A Hot Dose of Hell

tall man. Anticipating a fight, he clenched his tattooed fist, but then Jack stopped short, dropping down to tend to Edd, unwittingly kneeling in his urine.

Poppy squeaked through her bejewelled fingers, 'Is he alright?'

'I don't know,' said Jack, cradling the punk's head. 'I think he's breathing. I don't know.'

Flat on his back Edd lay shell-shocked and rigid, staring up at the ceiling, watching those shadow ants gradually evaporate. He didn't seem able to move and for a long, excruciating minute his respiration was a strangled wheeze, like a draught through an old house, until finally he broke into a string of coughs, spluttered the words:

'Okay...I'm okay.'

The relief was palpable. A single tear absorbed into Jack's facemask. Kibs bent hands-on-knees as if to puke and Poppy clutched her chest dramatically, her overplayed sigh skirting unintentionally close to a sexual moan.

'Hey,' the tall man barked, eyes darting between all four strangers. 'I said, who the fuck are ya?'

'We're called Leg-Up,' Poppy said, standing tall and speaking with a firm confidence she didn't quite feel at that moment. 'We're a recognised charity group.'

'Some fuckin' charity,' the tall man grunted. 'You just cost me my dinner.'

Poppy's lip curled; her vegan sensibilities appalled. 'The *pigeon*?'

'Aye,' he said, as if it were a stupid question and on reflex Poppy regurgitated a line she always served up to meat-eaters.

'Vegetables are much more sustainable you know.'

Poppy regretted it the moment it came out, for she

Stark Terror

saw how the tall man bristled, fists clenching with the promise of further violence.

'Fuck's that got to do with anythin'?...'ere, you lot just lost my dinner. So what you gonna do about it eh? How you gonna pay me back?'

'Pay you back?' Poppy shrieked in outrage, her plumminess showing through even more than usual. 'You mean...for the pigeon?'

The tall man rubbed his rough hands with menace, a sound like sandpaper on wood.

'That's right princess. What you got?'

Watching those big hands, a creeping sense of vulnerability saw Poppy withhold her answer. Instead, she moved behind Kibs, who couldn't have looked more uncomfortable if he were attempting the splits across a bed of nails.

'We have supplies outside,' he offered. 'Deodorant, toiletries, skincare products. Things you might need.'

'Don't need none 'a that shite,' the tall man said, contrary to his shabby appearance. 'I just want some grub. What else y'got? Money?'

From behind Kibs Poppy gave a firm, 'No.' And Jack looked up from stroking Edd's head.

'Who carries cash these days?'

The tall man frowned. 'Me...when I've got some.'

'Right, well *we* don't,' said Poppy.

'I always pay by card,' Kibs explained, voice going up an octave as if he'd just hit puberty.

'And I only use apple pay,' said Jack.

The tall man's eyes flashed rage. 'You mean you toffs don't have anythin' on ya? Bollocks,' he snorted, and his predatory gaze surveyed each of them, eventually settling on Poppy's wrist, on her bangles, gleaming in the light every time she moved.

'Alright, what about that bling there?'

A Hot Dose of Hell

'My Buccellati?' said Poppy, horrified, and she drew an arm across herself to clasp a particular bangle. Amongst her own kind such a reaction would normally invoke sympathy, respect, an understanding of the item's personal significance.

Here, she'd only convinced the man it was something worth taking.

'Yeah, I'll 'ave that one,' he said, a slow grin breaking to reveal teeth so black they first appeared missing.

'No,' Edd protested, sitting up, and for his effort he received a penalty kick to the ribs which laid him straight back down.

'Ohmygod,' said Poppy, somehow managing to sound disingenuous even though she felt truly appalled.

'Is that really necessary?' she asked and in spite the tall man primed another kick, but he relented when Jack selflessly fell upon Edd to shield him.

'I wouldn't hit a bird,' said the tall man, and no one felt compelled to correct him on Jack's gender status. 'But you better give us that bling or I'm gonna kick the shit outta this punk.'

'What about my iPhone?' said Poppy, offering the device. 'You can have *that* instead, okay? My bangle was a gift from my mother...she died btdubs.'

Unmoved by the revelation, the tall man simply shook his scraggy head.

'Nah. Mate of mine got caught with an iPhone. They got trackers in 'em or somethin'. I'll take the bling thanks.'

'And what if I say no?' said Poppy, a hint of defiance in her tone to show this was more than a hypothetical. 'What will you do? Beat us *all* up?'

The tall man pondered that for a second. Then with

a sick smirk tugging his slack mouth, he rolled up a coat sleeve to reveal a nasty trail of track marks spanning the length of his forearm. Even in the dim light the purple and green bruises showed on that cadaverous hide, looking as though a lava lamp had been frozen beneath the skin.

'You know I've got HIV?' he said, and as the room looked on aghast, he proceeded to pick at one of the many scabs there, quickly drawing a thin trickle of bloody pus which he collected on the tip of his index finger.

'So give us that bling now,' he said, pointing the bloodied finger like a gun. 'Or I'll come over there an' shove this down yer fuckin' throat.'

'Oh God.'

Kibs immediately recoiled at the threat and pushed back against Poppy behind him.

'Just give it to him, Pops....please.'

'What?' cried Poppy, horrified. 'My Buccellati for a bloody pigeon? *Seriously?*'

'I'll buy you another myself,' Kibs snapped. 'Just give it to him before this gets any worse. I really don't want to get HIV.'

Poppy opened her mouth to object and was stifled by Kibs grabbing her arm, set on removing the bangle himself. So rough was he that her wrist suffered a scratch in the process. Then without word of apology he pitched her treasured item across the room, into the tall man's clutches.

'KIBS!' Poppy gasped, nursing the wrist. 'I can't believe you just did that.'

The tall man waggled his new prize tauntingly.

'Cheers *Kibs*,' he said, cruel laughter in his voice as he stepped back to merge with the shadows once more. His footsteps faded shortly while others

A Hot Dose of Hell

sounded above, loosening dust from the ceiling which rained lightly onto Jack and Edd.

'Rhonda?' said Poppy, glancing upward. 'Trent?'

Everyone else looked up in wary anticipation, but there was no further activity, not a single sound before a tearful Jack softly confessed, 'I want to go home, Pops. You're not paying me enough for this.'

Kibsy's face dropped.

'What? You're being *paid*?'

He wheeled on Poppy, eyes wide with indignation. 'Why aren't I being paid?'

For a second Poppy wore a look like she'd been caught with her hand in the cookie jar. She recovered quickly though, bolstered by her anger over the bangle.

'You *volunteered* remember? That's like, literally the definition of volunteer, that you *don't* get paid. So are you saying you won't help people unless you're being paid? Is that it Kibsy?'

'No, I just-

'What about Edd?' said Jack. 'We should probably take him to the hospital or something.'

'I'm fine,' said Edd, shakily getting up and Jack started to help him.

'Careful Edd, the floor's wet.'

'I'm alright,' Edd muttered, shirking the touch. Then he furiously brushed down his jacket, his jeans, not commenting on the wetness of his palm after, or acknowledging the puddle under his boots.

'Are you sure?' said Kibs, purposely loading his tone with scepticism. 'You could have a concussion. We can take you to-

There was an abrupt clomp as Poppy angrily stamped her foot for attention.

'We're not going *anywhere*,' she said. 'We've come

all the way here and I won't let this fail just because of some wretched *pigeon man*. Come on. Let's go find some people like, actually *deserving* of our help.'

'I'm with you,' said Edd, nodding at Poppy. He had something to prove now, pride to regain from his humiliation by the tall man. At that point there was little she could've asked of him that he wouldn't at least attempt.

'I don't think it's a good idea,' said Jack.

Kibs concurred and Poppy wheeled on him, pointing an accusatory finger.

'*You* owe me a Buccellati. The least you can do is follow this through.'

'But-' Kibs began, to which a furious Edd lunged forward, grabbing him by the collar.

'You're comin' with us, Kibs,' he snarled, unashamedly transferring his anger about the tall man onto the much safer, weaker target. 'And you're gonna buy Poppy another bracelet, right?'

'I said I would, didn't I?' Kibs whined, squirming in his clothes. 'I'll buy her whatever she wants. Whatever.'

'You'd better,' Edd snarled. 'Or I'll be comin' for ya.'

'Okay, okay. Swear down, Edd...seriously. I swear down.'

'Please Edd,' said Jack, in a calming tone, and though he was relishing his display of dominance, Edd obliged the unspoken request, shortly releasing Kibs with a firm shove.

Off balance, Kibs stumbled back against the wall, where Poppy gave him a look of appraisal, from head to toe and back. Utter disgust covered her face by the time she returned to his.

'Call yourself an ally of women, Kibsy?'

A Hot Dose of Hell

Kibs gave an exaggerated shrug.

'Actually, if you think about it, I like, probably saved us all from getting HIV.'

To this Poppy's scowl relaxed slightly, her lips hinting a smirk. 'HIV isn't *that* easy to catch, Kibsy. Where do you like, get your knowledge? The uhh...eighties? You do know it's not just *gay men* who get infected don't you?'

Edd sneered, 'Homophobe.'

'But I never said that,' Kibs whined. 'That's totes unfair. You can't call me a homophobe unless I said it. Come on, I go to PRIDE every year. I've literally *kissed* men before.'

Poppy narrowed her eyes at him.

'Yeah, well who knows what you like, *really* think. For a so-called male-feminist you were very quick to hand my bracelet over.'

'I would've done that to a man if I had to. Actually, it would've been like, misogyny if I di-

The topic could've been argued for hours if not for the timely intervention of a gruff voice booming down the hall. 'SHUT UP YOU CUNTS,' it bellowed, immediately killing the chatter.

Edd, Kibs, Poppy and Jack, were all leery of another assault and there was a pause lasting several moments before any of them dared speak again. When they eventually did it was at a far lower volume; the conspiratorial hush of scolded children slowly rising to resentful grumbles.

'I didn't know it would be like this,' said Jack. 'I thought they'd be, y'know...grateful.'

'You'd think,' Edd huffed and again Jack looked to Poppy with pleading eyes.

'Can we just go please, Pops? This is triggering my anxiety.'

Poppy gave a curt shake of the head.

'What about Trent and Rhonda?'

'I'll round them up,' Edd offered. 'You lot can wait outside.'

'No,' said Poppy and for once she allowed herself to be candid. 'Let's do what we came here to do. Let's get some good pubs for the brand. There's bound to be *someone* here who'll be happy for some free stuff. We just have to like, *locate* them. If Trent finds Rhonda's sister, then he'll get some good pics of that and we won't require a lot more. Maybe a few snaps of at least one other person. Then we can *bounce*, okay?'

Nobody registered surprise over this mercenary tone. It was as if they'd each secretly known publicity was the goal all along.

Kibs simply nodded in agreement while Edd took out his iPhone, switched the torch back on.

'Let's do it.'

All eyes then fell to Jack, who was almost impossible to read behind that mask.

'Fine. Photos then we go. I'm not hanging around here any longer than I need to, okay Pops?'

'Fair,' said Poppy, her teeth shining unnaturally under the torchlight and she smiled like the cat that got the cream when Edd bumped Kibs with his shoulder.

'You first, mate. You've got some making up to do.'

__14__

In single file, Kibs, Jack, Poppy and Edd proceeded down the narrow hall, passing through a heavy fire door which slowly closed itself behind them like some sort of trap. It was much darker on the other side of that door and although Kibs was trying to play cool, the frantic movements of his iPhone torch betrayed the act.

He jumped at everything, vague shadows, drips of condensation, the groans of the building shifting with the dropping temperature, while Jack and Poppy walked a few steps behind, holding hands for comfort.

'I wonder how Trent's getting on?' said Jack.

'We'll catch him in a mo,' said Poppy and she gave Jack's hand a gentle parting squeeze.

'I feel like it'll all be fine now, y'know? I feel we just had an unlucky start.'

Unnoticed at the back Edd was now lagging, stumbling, his head still woozy from the strangulation. Just to keep from falling he had to lean against a wall for balance, ancient paint flaking onto his jacket as he went.

They soon arrived at a staircase, and he took a rest there on the second step without bothering to inform the others, who continued into a large room. A dusty placard on the wall outside identified it as the hotel's dance hall and they could hear a faint sound of vigorous movement coming from within, almost enough to imply it might serve that function still, for someone.

'Hello?' Kibs hollered, detesting the nervous tremor in his voice. 'Anyone there?'

Their iPhones held high, Poppy and Jack trailed him closely, each step revealing only more of the dusty boards under their feet. The cobwebbed ceiling hung high above the range of their torch beams, those crusty walls stood too far apart, and soft echoes of their movements made the room feel cavernous, empty, aside from a small blue lantern winking like a beacon in the distance.

Kibs called out again: 'Anyone here?'

No answer came, but Kibs noticed how the lantern lay side up on the floor, rocking in a way which suggested it had very recently been toppled, or dropped.

He went over, intent on picking it up.

'Wait,' Poppy whispered, tugging his sleeve and Kibs froze, seeing what had alarmed her so.

There were two shadowy figures entwined upon the floor, just below the stage. Both appeared fully clothed, yet they were thrusting as if in the throes of heavy passion, wet, squishy sounds only adding to that sense.

'Gross,' said Poppy.

But Kibs didn't think so. The image, the noises instantly transported him back to one long-forgotten summer afternoon, something his brain had been teasing ever since he laid eyes on this place.

At last, he could picture the girl. Inga. The foreign student who'd brought him that weird-tasting candy from her homeland. It was among several gifts she gave his family as thanks for housing her that summer.

'Tusen tack,' she'd said.

From the start Kibs had liked Inga, liked her a lot. He remembered the time she took him to the fairground and that she'd gladly kick a ball round the yard with him whenever she was out there having a smoke.

But above all, he remembered how she'd looked lying on the stone floor of that derelict church house, her slight, pale form squirming beneath his elder brother's porcine bulk, fighting against it.

Kibs remembered her screams, her tears, her pleas for help.

And he remembered how he held her arms down.

Through all the years since Kibs hadn't paid that incident a second thought. It'd been buried somewhere deep in his subconscious, a state supported by Inga's sudden departure, her name never to be mentioned in the household again.

Now reliving it all, he felt some measure of shame, of fear, along with the most intense arousal, enough to take him to the very brink of orgasm, if not for what happened next.

'Totes disgusting,' said Poppy.

'What is it?' said Jack, picking up the lantern, and the fresh light cast on the scene revealed it was something other than sex taking place at their feet, something else entirely.

'RUN,' Poppy cried, shoving past a wide-eyed Kibs, who bolted in turn.

'GUYS WAIT,' went Jack, ditching the lantern to follow suit, just as the two figures on the floor broke from their embrace.

One sprang to its feet and came charging. In its wake the other remained on the ground inert, a steady flow of blood trickling from empty eye sockets, spine glaring through a wound in its neck.

There was blood everywhere, showing black against the blue light of Jack's hastily discarded lantern.

'Kibs WAI-' Jack screeched, the last of that cry smothered by filthy, wet hands, then silenced forever with a sickening snap.

Kibs never looked back. Not when he heard Jack's body flop to the ground or that rapid footfall gaining behind. He darted through the door and into the hall fast as his legs could take him.

'UP HERE! COME ON.'

Poppy was scrambling for the stairs, encouraged by Edd who was already halfway up. He hadn't seen what pursued them yet. If he had, he wouldn't have waited.

'MOVE IT.'

Kibs bounded for the second step, but his progress was stalled mid-air by a snag at his collar, then reversed altogether with a violent yank. He fell badly. Whiplash effect bounced his head like a ball, shedding his specs, to leave him squirming on the floor, much like the way Inga had.

'Please,' he said, hands out in defence and between splayed fingers he saw the assailant's face loom into his myopic view.

'Oh God,' Kibs choked, for it was a horrendous sight.

Leering beneath strands of stringy hair those evil eyes were bulging black with blood, like two ripe plums. The nose was flat, streaked with unnaturally thick veins, and bleeding into an unkempt beard, through which a purple tongue worked thirstily across a ragged line of yellow teeth.

Right away Kibs knew this was not someone he could reason with. Unlike the tall man from earlier this face showed no emotion, just pure animal intent, the intent to harm anything crossing its eyeline. He appealed all the same and was no less distraught at its

A Hot Dose of Hell

failure as he felt a sudden sharp pain, like a hundred needles pricking at his scalp.

The black-eyed savage had taken ahold of Kibsy's hair with both hands and used that purchase to cast him face-first onto the steps. The impact stole the breath from Kibsy's lungs, leaving him gasping like a landed trout, eyes wide in surprise, gazing up at the blurry outlines of his friends on the stairs above.

'Get up, Kibs,' urged Poppy, who'd now reached the halfway point where Edd previously stood.

Edd himself was higher still, near the top. Kibs could just make out the shine off those Doc Martens. He reached for them, as if to drag Edd down with him, and felt a lance of pain shoot through his spine as the ceiling came rolling into view.

Then it was the edge of the step hurtling toward his face, again.

And again.

And again.

Relentlessly, the savage dashed Kibsy's head off the unforgiving wood, like a thirsty ape trying to crack a coconut. Poppy covered her mouth in horror then screamed through her fingers when a squirt of blood struck her face and she fell back upon the stairs just as Kibsy's skull exploded in a dark red gush.

Terror-stricken she hesitated to move from that spot, only jolting at an unexpected touch from behind.

'COME ON,' Edd barked, hooking her armpits to lift and Poppy assisted, pushing with her legs while the killer gradually tilted his head to set that coal-black gaze upon her.

'QUICK,' she urged, suddenly galvanised by a glimpse of the killer's first moves in pursuit. He was fast and inhumanly agile, scrambling up on all fours in the fashion of some ravenous beast.

'GO, GO,' Edd chanted, taking her hand in his and together they rushed up the stairs, him pulling her along.

But on the eighth step from the top Poppy noticed a snag at her pants' leg. At the next she felt a wet clamp tight around her ankle, the pinch of jagged fingernails at her Achilles.

Immediately she stopped running to plant herself, priming for explosive movement. Then using all her might she pulled and as he fell back past her, into their pursuer, the look of shock on Edd's face was almost equalled by her own.

'NOOOO...'

The sacrifice paid off for Poppy. Her ankle was freed, yet she didn't move on right away. Instead, she wasted a further two seconds watching the pair tumbling down together in an arachnoid tangle of limbs.

Once the darkness swallowed them, she hurried to the top, sealing the fire door behind. But to her dismay she found no lock to keep them out, nor anything nearby which could serve as a barricade.

If that black-eyed maniac had survived the fall, he could easily walk right up, pull the door at any moment and knowing she didn't have the strength to resist, Poppy abandoned her grip on the handle to seek refuge elsewhere.

At quick pace she tiptoed through the shadows, passing through a succession of connected, door-less rooms, most empty, some scattered with sleeping bags and tents.

On entering the fifth she immediately pressed herself against the adjacent wall, hoping anyone rushing through after her would neglect to look back.

For what seemed an eternity then she listened out

for the maniac's approach, hearing nothing more threatening than a persistent draft and an intermittent drip.

Drip.

Drip.

When she'd recovered her senses, Poppy used this reprieve to seek help. She went into her pocket for the iPhone and praised God upon finding it there.

Having watched far too much American TV her first impulse was to dial 911. But she caught herself early enough to prevent the call going through and quickly dialled the correct 999.

Once she could see it was transmitting, she brought the iPhone to her ear and in the process, illuminated the silent figure standing directly behind her.

His hands smothered her scream.

15

The dusty old stairs creaked and squealed under the varying weights of Slates, Rhonda and Trent as they ascended to the first floor.

At the rear Trent briefly paused for a wistful glance back at his comrades, the Leg-Up posse below. Although he hadn't said and was doing a good job of playing nonchalant, he held slim hope at least one might decide to accompany him upstairs.

But they weren't even looking in his direction anymore. They were all huddled close in conspiratorial chatter and he felt a pang of jealousy at being left out, a pang which evaporated the very instant he noticed Rhonda's butt ahead of him at eye level.

It was an impressive sight to say the least, the type of butt he'd never seen outside athletics on TV, muscular yet shapely. Continuing up, he shortly became aware of just how long he'd been staring and flushed in fear she might've noticed. Luckily for him her focus was elsewhere.

Rhonda didn't trust Slates.

It wasn't only because of his shifty demeanour, his sweaty eagerness to get them here. It was the fact he said she looked like Roxy; a comparison few had ever made.

From an early age Rhonda recognised that she and Roxy shared little to no similarities and always assumed this was largely due to having different fathers, though neither girl knew their respective father to say for sure.

Rhonda's dark hair, olive-skin, strong bone structure and athletic build were in direct contrast to

Roxy, who was small, blonde and fine-featured with a striking alabaster complexion.

Playing devil's advocate, Rhonda speculated they might at the very least share some mannerisms, since that can sometimes make people seem alike even when their looks don't match. At school she'd known two very different-looking boys who were often confused for one another, purely because of how similarly they acted, spoke and carried themselves. It was possible Slates had made that same error with her and Roxy.

Or he might've just been talking shit.

Rhonda felt more inclined to believe the latter, but she'd play along since this was the only lead in her search so far. If Roxy wasn't here and this was a ruse for a robbery or something else, she could justifiably beat some info out of this junkie when he showed his hand. He'd at least be able to tell her where others stayed, point her toward someone else who might know Roxy, and in preparation for that outcome she popped the button on the cosh pouch, folded the flap back for a quick draw.

'Not far now,' said Slates, glancing back, his tone and timing suggesting he knew, as if he somehow sensed her thoughts.

'Right,' said Rhonda, never taking her eyes off him until they reached the top where she began scanning for additional threats.

The light from Trent's iPhone behind her cast ominous shadows down the corridor ahead, some appearing like looming figures separate from their party. As they rounded a corner one startled Rhonda and she quickly shone her pocket torch on it, revealing only a stain on the mildewed wall.

'A'mirin' our décor?' said Slates, giving a phlegmy

rattle of a laugh to prove his humorous intent. Unreciprocated, it died fast while another sound came into focus, a steady rhythmic tap on the wood floor.

'Someone's knocking?' said Trent, then a fat drop of water onto his head caused him to look upward.

There was a chunk missing out of the ceiling. A gaping two-foot hole revealing a strip of pipework and a view into the room above.

'Just a leak,' said Slates. 'We got a few. Know any plumbers?'

This was clearly a joke, but one which gave Trent pause. He could honestly say he'd never met a plumber in his entire life, however there may have been some who attended the same dojo. Trent understood Jujitsu attracted largely working-class types, but he'd trained privately, one to one, paying a rate of forty pounds an hour to ensure he'd avoid such people.

The thought of their rough hands touching him, the fear they might take liberties with his body, that they would not show the restraint of a paid instructor made it money well spent in his eyes.

'Up here,' said Slates, pausing outside a door-less room. 'This is Roxy's.'

Cautiously, while trying not to make it seem so, Rhonda stepped up and entered first at Slates' behest. She slyly drew the cosh as she went, but refrained from locking it out, preserving the element of surprise for a more useful moment.

The room inside lay pitch dark and she flashed her torch around for occupants, finding only an old dresser near the boarded window. The beam reflected off the dresser's cracked mirror to the floor and a sleeping bag draped over wood pallets.

A large rucksack sat beside them and a smaller

sports bag; a close match for one which Roxy had carried in a recent facebook photo, the very last photo she'd posted in fact.

Discreetly, Rhonda re-holstered the cosh to delve into the bag, searching for proof, anything which might confirm it as her sister's. She fast grew impatient using just one hand to rummage and beckoned Trent in so she could share his light while pocketing her own phone.

'Careful,' Slates warned, 'might be sharps in there.'

Trent turned with a quizzical look, 'Sharks?' and Slates pulled a bemused sneer.

'No, *sharps* mate. Y'know pins? Needles?'

He mimed injecting drugs into his arm, something he'd soon be desperate to do again. It'd been hours since his last hit.

'Oh, for drugs?' said Trent, giving a soft eye-roll at his own naivete.

'Well they aint for knittin',' said Slates, returning to Rhonda who flipped the bag upside down, emptying it out onto the floor.

Slates' warning proved well founded. Among the items scattered before Rhonda there were indeed sharps a plenty, although they remained sealed in their packaging. The used pins were all safely stowed in a little plastic container so heavily stuffed it didn't even rattle.

Nevertheless, Rhonda took great care when unravelling the extra small t-shirt, the paraphernalia had been wrapped in, and her heart raced when she saw the faded print of its design.

"Paradise fields 2015" read the front. A list of obscure band names covered the back.

'Fuck.'

'What is it?' said Trent.

Sallowhill's Paradise Fields was a low-budget local event Rhonda had never known of outside a few old pictures on Roxy's facebook page. The odds of finding another 2015 attendee in here of all places was slim to none. This had to be Roxy's.

Staring into the design as if doing so might unlock further secrets, Rhonda wistfully brushed a finger over the lettering and was struck by a memory of bike races from back when they were still living with mum.

Any time they'd raced around the estate Roxy always outran Rhonda, not because she was faster or more able, but because she possessed an innate fearlessness allowing her to take risks Rhonda would never attempt. The many hazards marring their route, such as dumped couches, stolen trolleys, potholes, were actually an advantage to Roxy, things which could be jumped, while the more careful Rhonda always lost time avoiding them.

Only once had Roxy ever failed to win. That was when a near miss from a passing car resulted in a spill, a bump and a skinned knee for the more daring sister. But that race was a no contest because Rhonda had stopped to help, and she never forgot what Roxy said to her after.

'You should've gone for it Rhonnie. You could've won that time.'

Even now it shocked Rhonda how that was the very first thing on her sister's mind. Not the pain, the embarrassment, any reflection on the close call. Roxy just seemed baffled by Rhonda's decision to stop, as if that never would've occurred to her.

But to do anything else was unthinkable to Rhonda. She could never imagine riding off while her sister lay sprawled on the road, no matter what prize

A Hot Dose of Hell

was at stake.

This highlighted just one of the ways in which they differed, and she wondered then if her sister had ever learned the value in helping others. Judging by current surroundings, Rhonda assumed the answer was either *too late* or *not at all*.

'This is Roxy's,' she said, holding the t-shirt in her fist.

'No way,' said Trent, while Slates pulled an indignant frown.

'Told ya...now can I get paid or what like?'

Trent turned his torch on Slates, who shielded his eyes with an irritated snarl.

'Not until I see her,' said Rhonda.

'Fuck's sake,' Slates grumbled and he limped toward her, reaching out demandingly. 'I done my part. C'mon, cough up.'

Not liking this change in attitude, not liking it one bit, Rhonda dropped the t-shirt and reflexively drew the cosh, extending it with a snap of her arm. The sharp sound of metal cylinders locking into place caused Slates to flinch and fall back immediately. He'd been on the receiving end of one of those at least twice before and hoped to live the rest of his life without experiencing that pain again.

'Alright, alright, steady on luv,' he said, backing against the wall, holding the lantern as a flimsy shield. 'There's no need to be like that. Maybe she's in Kenny's room.'

That gave Rhonda pause, yet she kept the cosh raised.

'I thought you said Kenny was her boyfriend? Why doesn't she room with him?'

Warily Slates lowered the lantern. Then he shrugged and held the pose as if he were trying to shrink into himself, a tortoise lacking a shell for cover.

'Well, maybe that's a bit too much of a commitment,' he offered. 'Or maybe they jus' like to have their own rooms. How should I fuckin' know? They can use as many rooms as they want. It's not like anyone's gonna complain to the *manager*, is it like?'

Rhonda didn't respond verbally. Her grip audibly tightening on the weapon said enough.

'He might have a point,' murmured Trent, now loitering uncomfortably by the door. 'It is a big place. Roxy might even be out.'

Rhonda considered that while keeping her gaze trained on Slates.

'Show me Kenny's room,' she said, giving a slight flick of her head as permission to move.

'Alright,' said Slates, clearly relieved, and he backed out of the room, almost tripping over Trent's Moncler sneakers.

'This way,' he panted as he proceeded to limp down the hall in double-time. 'C'mon.'

Rhonda and Trent followed and although they could very easily catch up to the hobbled junkie they deliberately trailed at a distance of metres. All the while Rhonda remained alert with the cosh at her shoulder as Trent lit the way from behind, several feet behind.

'Trent, keep it steady,' she whispered. 'I need to see what's coming.'

'Don't think I can,' said a shaken Trent, prompting Rhonda to use her phone's torch once again.

Up ahead, Slates proceeded to beatbox, providing a soundtrack to match his gait until both came to an abrupt stop, right in the middle of the hall.

'No fuckin' way,' he said, looking down at the floor.

'What's-' Rhonda began, then on her next step she felt something crunch softly underfoot, like sand.

Trent felt it too and lowered the torch beam to reveal trails of dusty whiteish footprints criss-crossing the corridor ahead.

'Well, at least *someone* else is here,' he said, aiming for dry humour with a sitcom delivery.

'Yeah,' said Rhonda, grimly, 'but where are they now?'

Their torches scanned the floor for a clear answer. But the amount of partial shoe-grip impressions and the way so many overlapped, made it impossible to gauge the number of persons they belonged to, or any one's most recent direction of travel. For all they could tell the tracks might've been made by six different people, or sixty.

'No fuckin' way,' Slates gasped again and he dropped on his knees to inspect the suspicious dust, quickly confirming his unspoken theory that it wasn't dust at all.

'This is gear,' he said excitedly, bringing a pinch to his face. 'This is gear,' he repeated. Then he snorted a little.

'Christ's sake,' Rhonda huffed as Slates reacted to the narcotic rush flooding his system. It was an ugly picture the way those bloodshot eyes bulged, the way the cords stood out on his scrawny neck and how he arched back in orgasmic ecstasy, gasping with pleasure.

From that moment Rhonda knew he wouldn't be helping anymore. He had no need when the means to fulfil his only pleasure, his only ambition, sprinkled the floor in abundance, free for the taking.

'Keep moving,' she said to Trent, and they stepped over Slates' skinny legs. 'Come on, we'll find Roxy ourselves.'

On down the corridor they followed the thickening powder trail, with Rhonda becoming increasingly concerned by just how much of the stuff lay spread about.

One night at Shopco, Alice had spilled a bag of sugar and that'd been messy, but not like this. This was more like someone had spilled *ten* bags of sugar, a staggeringly high quantity of drugs for anyone who wasn't Pablo Escobar.

Like the sugar, Rhonda noticed how the substance glimmered under torchlight and she could see a fine layer covering nearly every square inch of the floor to the end of the hall. Places where it'd piled up against the skirting reminded her of ant-killer powder, something the Caines had reluctantly used to combat an infestation one summer.

Those quasi-hippies were appalled by young Rhonda's interest in the poison's results, seeing vindictiveness where there was only curiosity. Rhonda genuinely took no pleasure in watching the ants die. The way they lost all sense of direction, the way they fell out of line from their hive army to wander in circles was kind of sad, as sad as it was disturbing when they eventually succumbed to that final squirming fit on their backs.

Trent called down to Slates, 'Which room's Kenny's?' and received no reply.

Slates looked like one of those ants now. He was laying supine, stiffening limbs up in the air, mouth wide in a silent scream.

That wasn't how they showed heroin in the movies. There it was a calming, euphoric anaesthetic. But then

A Hot Dose of Hell

who said this stuff was heroin? It could've been anything, like those dodgy "Legal highs" that were all over the news a couple of years back, products like *Benzo Fury* and *Devil's Weed*.

These were psychoactive drugs which had been sold freely on the high street under the guise of plant food by exploiting a bizarre legal loophole. They were designed to mimic the effects of illegal highs such as cocaine and speed and in some cases were said to have been far more potent than the genuine article.

Spice, the most well-known among them, was notorious for inducing an incoherent, uncoordinated, zombie-like state, which to any passer-by would invoke pity or laughter, depending on their disposition.

Even now youtube is awash with tragic videos of Spice users, all privately filmed by everyday folk on the streets of poor suburbs and council estates, many cheekily synced to songs like Michael Jackson's "*Thriller*" or Chumbawumba's "*Tubthumping*".

A fear she'd one day see her sister go viral for shuffling around to the tune of Afroman's "*Because I Got High*", was just another factor leading Rhonda here, now, to this godforsaken place.

But was she too late? Had Roxy already stooped to lower lows or succumbed to worse fates?

With her eyes on the powdered ground, Rhonda had become so caught up in these thoughts that she failed to notice the shadowy figures lurking in her peripheral. They were just beyond the threshold of several rooms she passed, not moving, just waiting it seemed.

Silently, these statues observed her for several moments until one large figure lurched out from the inky blackness of the far end to block her path ahead. But it wasn't the movement that finally caught her attention. It was his heavy, rancid breaths.

16

For Trent, a single glimpse of that man was enough to tell this was no humbled little vagrant stood before Rhonda. Not with that drooling, manic grin, those shiny black eyeballs. Everything about him screamed danger, from his imposing stance to his bloodstained clothing to the prison tattoos on his face, and Trent quietly fled with no warning for Rhonda, left behind.

Heading back toward the stairs Trent stalled when Slates suddenly came around. The little junkie sat up sharply, then popped to his feet in explosive yet awkward fashion, like a marionette in novice hands.

Trent didn't want anything to do with that either and quietly slipped into the nearest room. He was just a step in when he heard sounds of violence from the hall behind, but thought of going back, of helping Rhonda never occurred to him. He just crept on through the empty room to another corridor at the other side.

Wind howled, battering the boarded windows as he ran left, passing door after door after door. Near the far end shadows suddenly seemed to shift, a shape parting from them, and in fear he quickly ducked into another room. It occurred to him then that the iPhone's torch could telegraph his whereabouts, so he quickly switched it off, cloaking himself in darkness.

Navigating through that wasn't easy. Trent had to rely on touch to maintain course from there on. As his hands groped the rotten walls, they shed flaky paint onto the wood floor and at one point his heel clipped a protruding nail, almost causing him to trip.

The very next step saw Trent cringe at the sticky cling of cobweb on his cheek. Then he froze at the

Stark Terror

unwelcome tickle of something exploring his neck.

Spiders, bugs in general, had always made his flesh creep and he shrank into a corner while he worked to locate it.

There Trent stayed when he caught the sound of someone's approach. Suddenly a curious spider was the least of his concerns and while the sound drew closer, he instinctively made himself small, curling into a ball, pulling his coat overhead. His hope was that a cursory glance of the room might miss him tucked away back there. Anything more though and he'd be found for sure.

Peering out through the neck of his coat, Trent saw the figure enter the room and he shut his eyes tight like a kid watching a horror movie. With a gutful of dread, he heard every step magnified, to him the sound of a giant stalking its prey, and he held his breath while it crossed to somewhere frighteningly close.

Then to his horror, it stopped.

Whoever it was must have seen him and was now considering their next move. Trent began doing the same, his adrenaline on overdrive, every breath under that coat a rush of white noise like the roaring tide battering the coast a hundred feet below.

First impulse was to run, but what if the person attacked him then? Standing upright Trent was as vulnerable as anyone else, whereas the ground was Jujitsu territory. There he at least stood a chance.

From his current position Trent thought of how easily he could adopt the guard to protect himself. The guard is a seemingly passive way of holding out an opponent while on your back and can lead to various submission holds. If nothing else, Trent felt he could ride out an attack from that position, then escape once his assailant grew tired.

But when he finally forced his eyes open again, he found with overwhelming relief that it was not some zombified junkie standing over him. It was Poppy, gorgeous Poppy, his secret crush, his employer, and she hadn't even noticed him there. She was too preoccupied with her phone, its screen emitting a soft glow, which he feared might soon draw attention to them both.

Careful not to startle her, Trent quietly stood and drew breath to gently whisper. But she suddenly turned the phone toward herself and when the light fell upon him, she was panicked by the unexpected presence.

Although he'd never dream of touching her uninvited before, not even a hug or pat on the shoulder, the very instant the scream left her throat Trent found his hands were already covering her mouth.

'SHHH,' he hissed, 'it's me, it's me.'

He saw recognition gradually override the terror in her eyes and felt her jaw relax. Smiling then, he withdrew his hands to whisper an apology she'd never hear, for it was stifled by sound of a rapid approach, culminating in a collision which floored them both.

Like skittles the pair fell away from each other, Poppy landing ungraciously on her backside, her phone spinning out of reach.

A furious rustle of fabric, the grunts and gasps of a struggle were emanating from the pitch at her left. Someone else was in there with Trent, someone like the black-eyed man who'd killed the others.

'No,' she heard Trent say and she dove for her phone to shed light on the scene, revealing a tangled mess of limbs, dark clothing and shaggy hair.

Trent lay squirming on his back beneath another man, his legs wrapped around this stranger's waist as if they were lovers. Arms were swinging and flailing, difficult to tell whose was whose, until miraculously Trent seized upon one of his attacker's, trapping the elbow joint against his thigh.

I've got him, Trent thought, buzzing with excitement. All that training had paid off, Jujitsu had saved him. This shaggy man had barely managed to land a few glancing shots and now Trent had him, he had him locked in with an armbar. As his instructor would say:

Guaranteed tap out.

But the shaggy man didn't seem aware of just how compromised he was and persevered with the struggle. To make it clearer for him Trent applied some pressure, enough that he expected to earn a yelp. However, the shaggy man didn't yelp. He didn't flinch. He didn't even seem remotely uncomfortable, only seething, a frenzied animal temporarily ensnared.

'You better calm down,' Trent warned. 'I could break it.'

He gazed up at the shaggy man's face as he said this, and realised words weren't going to help. Those shiny black eyes were unmoved, and those rotten teeth were bared not in anguish but rage, primed to sink into his flesh at first opportunity. Again, Trent felt those wiry muscles flex against his grip and knew the shaggy man was bracing for some kind of move. As a deterrent he cranked the pressure, stretching that elbow to breaking point, to where he'd be screaming himself if positions were reversed.

It had no effect at all, and in a near superhuman display of strength the shaggy man used that trapped

A Hot Dose of Hell

arm to hoist Trent into the air, all the way overhead.

'HELP,' Trent cried, hugging that arm like a monkey on a branch. 'Help me Pops. I don't know how long I can hold him.'

Poppy didn't budge. A life of privilege, of being pampered to, pandered to, had made a spectator of her in times of crisis. She was still anticipating someone else would come rescue her the way Edd had on the stairs, the way someone always had, before it dawned on her that there was no one else to come.

All the others were dead.

She quickly tried to dial police again, but the cracked phone screen had trouble detecting touch and was staying locked on her wallpaper image, a duckface selfie at the Burj Khalifa. She dropped it in fright as the shaggy man slammed Trent onto the floor and was surprised to see her friend maintain his hold on that arm after such a heavy impact.

Trent had barely managed it though and only narrowly escaped losing consciousness when the back of his head struck that floor. He knew he might not be that lucky on the next go, so when the shaggy man braced to lift once more Trent jerked hard, producing a brittle snap as the compromised arm splintered then broke.

Being a self-proclaimed pacifist Trent would never normally resort to such a debilitating measure. However, he quickly found there was no cause for guilt and no time to rest, for the shaggy man remained unaffected, undeterred, even when further struggle drew the bone's broken end through the skin.

'Oh gawd,' Poppy heaved.

A shower of dark blood came spurting from the wound, its flow diverted in odd directions by the protruding bone. In a few seconds it soaked through

Trent's clothes, splashing his face, and then somehow, despite the state of that arm, the shaggy man proceeded to lift him again.

Going back up Trent clung on for dear life, unaware of how frayed that broken arm was becoming. An unmistakable crunch soon told him, and he yelped as the limb disconnected at the elbow to drop him from four feet in the air.

Trent landed with a thud and in a daze, he lay there after, still clutching the detached limb, while the shaggy man spared a moment to notice the injury.

Blood was now gushing freely out of the stump's frayed end, its rate of flow so fast and steady that Trent felt certain the man would collapse at any second, yet he somehow remained standing, almost casually regarding the exposed shard of bone.

For a brief instance, the monstrous adversary seemed as though he might be neutralised, caught in a kind of trance. That was when an involuntary whimper from Poppy brought him back around.

Before Trent could do anything, before Poppy could even scream, the shaggy man turned and plunged that bone deep into one of her pretty brown eyes. Blood squirted from the socket as the jagged point pierced her brain and she shuddered fitfully, bangles going like a tambourine.

As though she weighed nothing the shaggy man raised Poppy aloft on the end of that shard, her legs doing a lazy Riverdance. Then with a callous flick of his stump he cast her corpse aside, focus returning to his original foe.

Shock had drained all the fight from Trent's body.

The jagged bone entering his neck drained the blood.

17

Rhonda stopped just a few metres from where the tattooed man stood in the doorway. He said nothing and moved no further, yet through his silence and blank, black-eyed stare he radiated malevolence.

In anticipation of his next move, she planted her feet, grip tightening on the cosh. Behind her she heard Trent's retreat and knew she was facing this on her own, whatever it was, a robbery, an assault.

The tattooed man's teeth, what few he had, glinted in the torchlight and Rhonda lowered the beam, catching the torso of another body standing just within the door to his right. She became aware of others around her then, perhaps several at her back. They weren't advancing or making any noise, but she knew they were there, the hackles of her neck telling her so.

'I'm just looking for someone,' she said, taking a slow step back, and a floorboard creaked, signalling the tattooed man's charge.

As he came, she quickly raised her torch again to dazzle him. He shied from the glare, making an irritated hiss, taking his gaze off her for just a second. In the next instant the cosh flashed before his black eyes.

CRACK!

Rhonda didn't linger to see the effect of her strike. She immediately turned to flee, blindly charging into yet more danger when what seemed like a forest of arms sprang out around her. These pale, gangly, track-marked limbs snagged at Rhonda's clothes, her skin with ragged nails and in turn she started to hack away at any she couldn't avoid, furiously beating a path.

But these assailants were relentless. Their clawing, groping hands dogged Rhonda all the way down the corridor. It seemed every time she struck one another sprouted up to take its place and as they swamped her, tearing the hoodie from her back, she faltered, dropping down to one knee, where she smashed her phone into an oncoming face, accidentally killing the light.

'Shit.'

In the sudden darkness Rhonda felt surrounded, yet her enemies were disorientated, tripping over each other, lashing out amongst themselves while she remained low, crawling fast. Through all the confusion she glimpsed the blue light of Slates' lantern and knew she must be getting near to the stairs. The stairs weren't far from the front door, and it was just a short downhill run from there into town, into the safety of civilisation.

If she could just make it to that door.

Gritting her teeth, Rhonda came up swinging and bravely battled on through the gloom. She hacked and hacked, shedding the remaining scraps of her hoodie as she passed into the blue end of the hall. She was soon making headway, regaining momentum.

Then things took a turn.

At the apex of a backswing a hand caught Rhonda's cosh, caught it firm, and the weapon slipped from her grasp so that she lashed out empty-handed, hitting nothing but air. Her heart plummeted at the realisation, a sense of doom, of hopelessness suddenly looming over like the shadow of a great tsunami, yet still she refused to surrender.

The next hand to grab her received a deep bite in retaliation. Another had two of its fingers snapped like a wishbone and she pressed on in this savage fashion until only a trio of hostiles barred the path ahead.

These three came in staggered formation, lumbering toward Rhonda with arms outstretched. She spat to rid the taste of blood from her mouth, then deftly eluded the first like a pro football player rushing the field. The limp coils of the second fell away at a swift forearm and she pivoted off to drive a flying knee directly into the face of the third.

The stairs weren't far at all now, but to her dismay Rhonda realised there was no way she'd get down, for the disturbance had drawn more attention and another wave of black-eyed zombies was scrambling up.

Meanwhile, those at her back were still gaining and contrary to logical expectation not one of their number had been disabled by her assaults. They'd been injured, even disfigured, yet in every case their falls had been temporary, brief delays which had only caused them to cede position in the pursuit, not drop out.

Backlit by the beam of Slates' discarded torch their swarm appeared like one terrible, multi-limbed mass, like some giant centipede from hell, and caught between these two packs Rhonda's outlook seemed grim.

She wouldn't make it easy for them. She'd resist until her final breath and with that in mind she thought to stop running, preserve her energy for the inevitable fight. However, it was just as she prepared to do this that she glimpsed a crack of light through the boards above and remembered the hole in the ceiling she'd soon be passing under.

Know any plumbers? Slates had asked, the words replaying in her head as she pictured the exposed pipework. She'd briefly flashed her torch on it at the time, inadvertently burning the image into her mind's eye, and could now visualise jumping up, using those pipes to climb into the room above.

It would be risky, yet there seemed no other option and she was fully committed to that path, dashing at full pelt, when a further complication sprang to mind. Vertical leaps and horizontal leaps are two different things, requiring very different approaches. Horizontal leaps are performed following a sprint for forward propulsion, whereas vertical leaps require a less linear approach, meaning a sacrifice of speed she could ill afford.

The choice that left her was far from simple: Keep going at current pace and risk overshooting, or drop a gear and risk being grabbed even before the jump.

That wasn't much choice at all, certainly not the type of decision anyone wants to make in the ticks of a second. But then at the last instant Rhonda saw an alternative and with no more time to assess its potential risks, or change her mind, she leaped directly toward the adjacent wall.

To her pursuers this must have seemed a mistake or kamikaze move, but in the split second where the ball of her foot met brickwork Rhonda pushed off it to alter direction, while also adding height to her leap.

Straight up she flew, reaching for the pipes overhead as a swiping hand grazed her trailing leg. Still in the air she stretched and stretched and for one brief, heart-breaking moment her fingertips brushed cold metal, failing to secure purchase.

I'm done, she thought, feeling the tug of gravity in her stomach, when suddenly her right hand clamped onto something solid, something metal, the way it'd so often gripped the pipework in Shopco's storeroom.

A Hot Dose of Hell

'YES,' Rhonda gasped, every muscle in that arm straining to halt the momentum, to bear the weight swinging back. Then she stretched up her left to seize on a join and with a grunt of effort managed to heave herself up through the hole, narrowly escaping the sea of grabbing hands below.

'KURWA,' someone growled and as she emerged Rhonda looked up at a huge man in coveralls standing over her. He was holding a great sledgehammer which he drew back behind his shoulder, the shadow passing ominously over Rhonda's face giving a clear sign as to where that steel head would fall.

Breathless from exertion and with her body still only halfway through the hole, Rhonda's first impulse was to put a hand out in defence. She didn't believe for a second that would protect her from such a weapon, but the gesture might give the man pause, a chance to see she was not his enemy.

Judging by the unchanged look on the brute's face it didn't work. There was not a flicker of recognition in those wild eyes. Then Rhonda saw his big arms flex under the fabric and all she could do was wince in anticipation.

'STOP,' she heard another say and she felt herself dragged into the room by someone with tremendous strength.

It was this second man who held her, a stocky, bald gorilla with the face of a cherub, if that cherub had been through two tours in Iraq.

'You alright, luv?' he said, squatting down, his headtorch blinding.

Rhonda struggled to give an affirmative between gasps, and she raised a bloody hand to shield her eyes. That hand trembled so much she made a fist to still it. Then she glanced to the larger one, seeing that he'd lowered the hammer.

'You were lucky, girl.'

Of that Rhonda had no doubt. This man would've pulverised her had the cherub not intervened and she was about to ask who they were, what they were doing here, when a snarling, spitting black-eyed head breached the hole in the floor right beside her.

It was Slates' head.

'*That's* one,' said the cherub while the bodybuilder was already in motion. He swung the hammer fast, catching Slates' narrow shoulder and something under the skin made a sick pork crackling sound, yet Slates persisted, wriggling through the hole like some malignant worm, or like the very maggots infesting his leg.

'AGAIN,' barked the cherub.

This time the hammer end connected flush with Slate's skull, and he plummeted out of sight, landing with a crash on the first floor, a light plume of dust billowing up in the aftermath.

The cherub cackled coarsely.

'Reminds me of fuckin' *Whack-a-mole* down the arcades,' he said, receiving a bemused look from the bodybuilder.

'Whackermal?'

The cherub shook his head in dismay, went to Rhonda: 'Bloody foreigner, never knows what I'm talkin' about.'

He forced a chuckle after, to make it clear he was being humorous, and Rhonda showed no reaction. She looked to the bodybuilder, catching an intense stare.

'What you doing here, girl?'

Before Rhonda could answer another bloodied head bobbed up through the hole in the floor.

No. It was the same head as just a moment ago, Slates' head, only his cranium had collapsed like a deflated ball, altering the shape of his face so that the brow wore a permanent frown and the nose had turned up into a piggish snout. Popcorn sounds occurred at his neck as he swivelled toward Rhonda, and she saw that one of his eyes had come unhoused. Like a piece of ripe fruit, it dangled by nerve stalks against a fuzzy cheek, almost slipping into his gaping mouth when he loosed a harrowing simian screech.

'Christ's sake,' went the cherub and Slates' working eye shot him a glare fit to chill the blood of a serial killer.

In turn the cherub snarled, 'Who the fuck are *you* lookin' at?' almost as if this were some standard barroom confrontation, then the hammer struck again, pounding Slates back down through the hole.

'Cheers Pinkie,' said the cherub.

'No names,' said the bodybuilder, tipping his head at Rhonda.

The cherub screwed his fat face up, asked, 'Who's she gonna tell?'

The bodybuilder just glared at him.

'You'd better watch that hole,' said Rhonda, getting to her feet. 'He only had one working leg and if *he* can get up here, any of 'em can.'

'See?' The cherub grinned at his partner. 'She's alright. I'm Fred by the way, luv.'

He offered a handshake but stopped when he spotted another head breaching the hole in the floor.

'Cheeky cunt,' he said, stomping it back down.

When he was finished Rhonda asked, 'What's going on here? What happened?'

'What's it look like?' said Pinkie, as if the answer were obvious.

'You're bleedin', luv,' said Fred, his thumb brushing his lip and Rhonda wiped her mouth with the back of her hand, inspecting it after.

'It's not my blood.'

In light of that reveal Fred's face said it all. He spoke regardless.

'You wanna be careful. Some of that lot are likely to have HIV, hepatitis, stuff like that. You should get yourself checked by your GP, soon as.'

'Uh-huh.' Rhonda gave a slight nod, not wanting to let on how much the information troubled her. At the time she hadn't considered the unseen risks of biting that hand. Now reflecting on it she felt a little queasy, a surge of cold sweat seeping through her clothes.

Unlike Slates, that last black-eyes wasn't trying for the hole again. No others were either and the room fell eerily quiet. After a while Fred inched toward the edge, craning his tree stump neck to shine the headtorch down through.

'Careful,' said Pinkie.

'When am I not?' said Fred, leaning further, and waiting below he found the black-eyed mob glaring back up at him, their rotten mouths wide in anticipation, like hungry zoo animals at feeding time. They were clearly seething, yet apparently deterred from further climbs for the moment. Perhaps not quite as mindless as he'd assumed.

'We was lucky we missed 'em on the way up. I reckon there's about twenty or more.'

'Twenty,' Pinkie echoed grimly. 'Two was bad enough. How many could be in here?'

Fred shrugged. 'Fuck knows, you saw all them tents. Just be ready to swing at anyone who comes our way.'

'Wait,' said Rhonda. 'I'm with some people.'

'Who?' said Pinkie, his eyes ablaze with angry suspicion and Rhonda put a hand up for calm.

'Just some charity workers,' she explained. 'Bunch of hipsters. No one *you* should be scared of. Just don't hurt them by mistake, alright?'

Fred nodded to the hole. 'You reckon they could survive a run-in with that lot down there?'

The following pause was pregnant with doubt.

'Trent might've got away,' said Rhonda. 'He ran soon as they showed up.'

'Shit,' said Fred, turning to Pinkie. 'He'll call the pigs.'

'Is that a bad thing?' said Rhonda. 'The police would help us.'

Fred looked at her as if she'd just proclaimed the earth as flat.

'We should get out,' said Pinkie, 'forget about job.'

Fred scowled. 'An' chuck away our bonus?'

'This isn't worth a grand,' said Pinkie. 'I don't-

Rhonda butted in: 'Wait, you still didn't tell me, what's going on here?'

'It's a bad batch,' said Fred, punctuating the sentence with a grating snort as he dragged a noseful of phlegm into his mouth, and he spat through the hole, hitting one of the black-eyes square on the cheek. It was a great shot, the kind he'd normally celebrate, yet the black-eyes' non-reaction nullified the act, leaving him dissatisfied and disturbed.

Curious, Rhonda stepped up to have a look for herself and as she peered down what she saw stole her breath, set her heart to double-time. This wasn't just the grotesque sight of the black-eyes themselves. It was the recognition of one of their number.

Roxy.

There she stood among the throbbing crowd, her little face so gaunt it was virtually a skull, her big eyes black and shiny as buttons and a look within them of complete and utter absence.

To Rhonda that slack-jawed expression recalled the brain injury victims she'd once cared for. It was only a temp job, maternity cover, but in that short time she'd noticed how even the most severely damaged patients retained flickers of personality, emotion, whereas she could see nothing like that in Roxy now. Whoever her sister had been was long gone and what remained was just a bloodthirsty husk, a creature unworthy of sympathy, only repulsion and fear.

'They'll get to us somehow,' said Pinkie, standing beside her. 'They don't give up.'

A single tear streaking the dried blood on her cheek, Rhonda looked at him. 'How do you know?'

Pinkie pointed to his face. The cuts from Shaz were still raw.

'Personal experience.'

'Right,' said Rhonda and she drew a harsh sniff, almost as if annoyed by her own grief. Then she wiped the tear on her wrist, refusing to shed another. Crying was a luxury she'd have to deny herself with danger still so close.

'Who are you two anyway?'

Fred offered a playful wink. 'We're just a pair of good Samaritans, luv. Don't mind us alright?'

'Good Samaritans?' Rhonda sneered. 'Yeah right. What's your game here?'

'Seriously,' said Fred, giving her his best "not-guilty" face. 'We aint here to do any 'arm. We only wanna find the rest a' that stuff they've been takin' an' get rid of it.'

'More like sell it,' said Rhonda.

'No one's sellin' that shite, luv,' said Fred. 'No good for return business, is it?'

'Whatever,' Rhonda shrugged, stepping away from the hole. 'Look I really don't care. I only wanted to find my sister...Now I just want to get out of here.'

'Well good luck to ya then,' said Fred, turning away. Then as an afterthought he asked, 'What about your sister?'

Rhonda pointed to the mob below.

'*There's* my sister.'

Fred followed her aim and gently shook his head, sucking the air through his teeth like a mechanic assessing a write-off.

He returned to Rhonda.

'Not anymore, luv. Soz to break this to ya, but she's on a bad trip and she aint comin' back. There's no sobering up off this gear.'

Rhonda took a long slow breath. He'd confirmed what she already knew.

'Sorry for you,' said Pinkie and Rhonda shot him a look.

'You know there's loads of that stuff on the floor down there?' she said. 'Like loads.'

'You what?' Pinkie growled, turning on Fred. 'You said we should look up here.'

'I heard that noise,' said Fred, casually drawing the hatchet from his coveralls. 'An' it's lucky I did otherwise we'd be wadin' through that lot. You fancy doin' that?'

Pinkie cocked a thumb at Rhonda.

'*She* did it.'

'Yeah,' said Fred, 'an' probably caught AIDS along the way...no offence luv.'

'Prick,' muttered Rhonda and Fred accepted it with

a shrug.

His subsequent comment, 'Fair enough,' was drowned beneath a rumble of movement as the mob below suddenly scattered.

'We should move,' said Pinkie.

No one disagreed.

18

In the emptiness of that hollowed-out hotel the direction of the black-eyes' stampede was impossible to determine by sound, since everything echoed. But the unlikely trio of Rhonda, Fred and Pinkie ran regardless, unsure whether they were moving toward or away from the mob, just running for the nearest way out.

Being the quickest Rhonda led the way down the second-floor corridor, while the heavier men trailed with their weapons in hand, big boots thundering along the bare boards. They sounded like giants. All around them moonlight broke through cracks between the covered windows, through holes in the rotted ceiling and walls, revealing sections of what lay ahead.

'Which way?' said Rhonda, seeing a junction coming up.

'Keep goin...' Fred puffed. 'Left at the end.'

He was directing them back to the spiral staircase. That structure was rickety and rusted, but if clear it would take them all the way down to the dining hall on the ground floor. A room which had been utterly vacant just a short while earlier.

'HEADS,' Fred bellowed.

Rhonda saw it just in time to duck. The tall man's hand caught nothing but air and his overreach put him off balance. As she passed, turning left, she drilled him with a forearm to the sternum, knocking him back.

When he rebounded from the wall Fred's hatchet took his jaw clean off.

Blood splashed the floor, just after the jawbone

and something metallic, a bracelet went rolling. The tall man recoiled in shock, his freshly exposed tongue probing the air obscenely, eyes bulging. To his surprise Fred saw then that they were not black like the others but white, normal.

'Oh shit,' he cringed, lowering the hatchet. 'Soz mate.'

In response the man could only make unintelligible croaks, blood bubbling and squirting from his exposed gullet, bloodshot eyes showing every ounce of pain. Fred stayed with them, his face a mask of excruciating guilt, but they looked past him and widened in fear at what they saw coming down the hall.

'MOVE,' Pinkie roared.

At full pelt he came charging and bumped Fred aside to slam the hammer's end straight into what remained of the tall man's face, obliterating it against the brickwork in an explosion of gore.

'Christ,' said Fred, shielding himself from the chunky splatter. 'Shit, Pinkie. He wasn't one a' them.'

Pinkie stood over the felled corpse seeming wholly unconcerned, watching the last spurts of blood erupt from its stump neck. He'd been soaked himself, all down his arms, his chest, his face which he turned toward Fred.

'Oh well,' he shrugged, and Fred frowned in disbelief. Then gradually his chubby features started to crack until he could hold it no longer and burst out laughing.

'You silly cunt.'

This levity was short-lived however, for just a moment later Rhonda came rushing back toward them.

'GO BACK,' she cried, panic on her face and a

pack of black-eyes in pursuit.

A shirtless, skeletal wretch was right on her tail. The rest were moving in a cluster some sixty metres behind, hissing and spitting all the way. They sounded like a sack of angry snakes.

'GO,' Rhonda shouted, confused as to why Fred and Pinkie were still just standing there. 'MOVE.'

Fred simply gave Pinkie a nudge.

'Scuse,' he said, establishing the space he'd need to swing the hatchet, and Pinkie obliged without argument. He took up position a few feet behind, allowing himself range to thrust his hammer. Anything that got past Fred would run straight into twenty pounds of bone-crushing steel.

'COME ON THEN,' Fred roared, standing ready, waiting for Rhonda to bring that wretch in.

It was so close to her that the timing had to be perfect. Fred needed to be in motion even before Rhonda was safely by, for an instant making it seem as though *she* might be his intended target.

The word "No" had almost reached Rhonda's tongue when she felt the air off the blade going past her cheek and within the next breath the hatchet had found the wretch's face, cleaving so deep that it became firmly wedged.

Fred fully expected the black-eyes to fall then, but it remained standing, those gaunt features contorting around either side of the hatchet's edge and they quickly changed from that initial expression of vacant shock to a vicious look of determination.

'Give it,' Fred hissed, tugging the hatchet's handle and on the second pull the wound issued a thick, wet belch as it stubbornly gave up the blade, the sharp release casting an arc of blood onto Pinkie, who was shielding Rhonda behind.

'Fucksakes,' he spat, as if he weren't already covered.

Where the hatchet had been a red gash now divided the wretch's face, a vertical line right down through the very bone. Still, it staggered on somehow, although it wasn't really looking at Fred anymore. Those eyes were turning outwards, almost like a chameleon's, dark blood oozing through the growing split, and with morbid fascination Fred watched as the skull gradually came apart.

'Jesus wept,' he gasped, a phrase his mother had often used and one which sounded strange coming from his own mouth, yet utterly apt in that moment.

Unbelievably, the wretch continued to advance despite the widening gap in the centre of its skull. Viscera clung to either side, a weak glue barely holding it all together until those other black-eyes came rushing from behind to knock it flat, dashing its brain out across the boards.

That flood of hot mess drove Fred back as he tried vainly to spare his boots and the ground he gave was immediately claimed by the pack of black-eyes, springing forth to attack.

They were utterly ferocious, so much so that they inadvertently hindered each other's movements. Unlike true pack animals there was no sense of space, or role in the attack. There were no tactics, and this allowed an overwhelmed Fred to rally. His hatchet sheared the top of one of their heads and in two chops severed the first hand to touch him, but then he was swamped and pinned against the wall, a mouthful of chipped, rotten teeth snapping mere inches from his face.

'ANY HELP?' he cried, still clinging to his sarcastic persona, although distress was obvious in the pitch of his voice. He went to say it again and stopped when those snapping teeth in his view were abruptly supplanted by the head of Pinkie's hammer.

CRUNCH.

Freed of the black-eyes' coils Fred slumped against the wall, catching his breath, while onward Pinkie lunged, thrusting the hammer in a spearing motion to drive the pack into the wider part of the hall. Once there he swung like a lumberjack gone berserk, only connecting with one in two strikes, but the heavy hammer destroyed whatever it met. Bones crunched wetly, skulls exploded and bodies fell, quickly piling up at his feet and as a shaken Fred regained his bearings he was momentarily awestruck by the sight.

To him it recalled the cover from a book he'd read as a child, one depicting a lone barbarian in the jaws of some epic battle. Outnumbered and surrounded that mighty warrior was riding high atop a pile of enemy corpses, his great axe drawn back, destined to claim the head of the nearest oncoming foe.

Fred couldn't remember the story, or even its title, but that oil painted image had once gripped him so firmly that it'd stayed some forty plus years, lodged deep within his subconscious.

Now in this dazed state he saw it come to life before his very eyes as Pinkie delivered its logical conclusion upon the last black-eyes standing.

THWOCK.

A hail of gore from the smashed head pelted Fred's coveralls. He stood there dripping, unable to suppress the big grin on his face.

'My hero,' he chuckled.

After surveying the fallen, ensuring no threat remained Pinkie looked to Fred, grunted an affectionate, 'Cunt.' Then he lowered the weapon, wincing ever so slightly when he noticed the pain of his ribs again.

'Got any more pills?' he asked, stepping over the dead, and that lapse of focus caused him to miss a previously unseen figure breaking from the shadows in his peripheral.

'WATCH IT,' said Rhonda, just a little too late for either man to react, but this black-eyes paid them no interest. In a blink it'd already slipped past both, headed straight for her, the beam of Fred's head torch catching up a second after to reveal a flash of that ghoulish face.

It was Roxy.

The moment of recognition made Rhonda pause, which cost her. Roxy hit her waist like a bullet and together they tumbled across the corridor.

'SHIT,' said Fred.

Riding the momentum, Rhonda managed to come up on top and the siblings proceeded to wrestle with each other's arms in a violent recreation of their childhood playfights. In the midst of it, Rhonda briefly questioned her earlier judgement. She began to wonder if perhaps there *was* something remaining, some reserve of her sister's memory, some vague recognition which had caused her to be targeted over the other two.

Then she looked again into those black, soulless eyes and saw that there was really nothing, not a shred of personality showing through. She realised that it was only a natural, predatory instinct for Roxy to pick out the smallest and unarmed member of their trio. It was the same predatory instinct that wouldn't hesitate to sink those gnashing teeth into the nearest jugular, no matter who it belonged to, and Rhonda could see them inching closer to her own as the struggle continued.

'Hold on luv,' said Fred, moving to help, then he turned at Pinkie's cry.

'UWAZAJ!'

The Polack was looking the other way, toward the spiral staircase and the source of a pounding metallic clatter; a scramble of feet growing louder the higher they climbed.

More black-eyes were coming. A lot more judging by the sounds.

Clearly torn, Fred gave Rhonda a regretful glance before heading off to join his colleague, abandoning her in favour of the more dangerous threat.

'I'm with ya Pinks.'

A utilitarian at heart Rhonda didn't protest or beg him, even if it wound up costing her life. She knew she had better chance of fighting Roxy off than Pinkie did facing that army alone.

If *they* made it up the stairs, nobody would survive.

'Right,' Fred snarled, arriving at Pinkie's side. 'LET'S 'AVE IT THEN.'

The rising clamour of the others approaching seemed to excite Roxy, or to further aggravate, as her thrashing became ever more violent, forcing Rhonda into side mount. The strength surging through that slight body was amazing as it was terrifying. Rhonda felt another buck like that could easily throw her off altogether and in preparation she hooked her feet, spread her weight.

Then something unexpected happened.

In her mindless frenzy Roxy turned over, unwittingly giving up her back and almost disbelieving the luck Rhonda took it fast, wrapping around the way a baby monkey clings to its mother.

A sudden jerk almost threw her off when Roxy braced arms and pressed herself up. Rhonda realised then what Roxy was trying to do. She was trying to stand and judging by the ease with which she moved she was probably going to succeed, even carrying Rhonda's weight on top.

There was a prolonged scraping sound as Roxy drew her knees in, dragging them over the rough floor and peeling a layer of skin to plant her right foot. But when she began to stand, she also did something else. She lifted her head, leaving her neck completely exposed.

Seeing the opportunity Rhonda embraced it, slipping her arm under, closing tight as Roxy raised them both off the floor. Gravity lent the choke power so Rhonda's arm bit deep into Roxy's thin neck. The trachea took the full strain of the ten stone hanging from it, while a deep, reptilian growl resonated up from the empty, shrunken gut.

Even though Roxy continued to struggle Rhonda could feel the fading vibrations of that growl against her forearm, telling her that all she had to do was grit her teeth and hang on.

'Easy,' she whispered, as though soothing a baby. 'Shhh, go to sleep.'

Eventually Roxy did. Her oxygen-deprived brain shut off and she flopped backward, her weight coming down on top of Rhonda, who held that choke a little longer, partly to be certain, partly just to say goodbye.

When it was finally over, she pushed the body off and stood wiping sweat from her cheeks. No, not sweat. These were tears. Having gone to such effort to help Roxy, it nevertheless surprised Rhonda to find just how much she truly cared about her sister. Until then, she'd assumed she was mainly acting out of pride, a sense of duty. But standing there, still gasping from the task, the sight of Roxy's inert body stirred a deep swell of grief, grief for all the life she'd missed, all the time misspent, and Rhonda realised she'd been acting out of love from the start.

At that very moment, more than any other, she was overwhelmed by an urge to break down and weep, and this time she might've submitted if not for the gruff voice calling her back into the present.

'COME ON YA SMACKEADS,' Fred roared, clashing his hatchet off the stair rail, the sound like a ringside bell commencing the next round.

He and Pinkie were posted either side at the top of the staircase, weapons primed, and that footfall was growing louder, the rusted frame visibly trembling from the weight of the mass scrambling up.

'COME ON,' went Fred. 'WHO'S FIRST?'

Rhonda hurried over with the intention of helping. As she arrived the first of the black-eyes reached the top step and was promptly cut down by the two men swinging in opposite time.

The pair immediately moved on to the next in line, cutting it down just as fast. Using the bottleneck to their advantage they almost made it look easy, as if they could've kept going all night. But a glance over the rail showed Rhonda the black-eyes' number and she realised this couldn't last.

Eventually Fred and Pinkie would tire. Eventually the black-eyes would get through. There were just too many of them.

Far too many.

Bodies were fast piling up on the stairs, blocking the way, and though it would seem that was a good thing, those stacked corpses presented another problem. Now the black-eyes no longer had to get by Fred and Pinkie and could instead use their fallen as ledges to climb up.

Anticipating this, Fred left Pinkie's side to block the first breach. He caught the black-eyes when it was halfway over the rail, hacked into its skull and threw it back. The body spun and twisted in the air, pinballing off the bannister until it hit the mob crowding the second bend. The scene briefly resembled some macabre crowdsurf before the body was pitched aside and it plummeted down a further flight, crashed onto empty steps.

At the moment of impact a jarring crunch sounded overhead and the whole staircase shifted slightly, sending the mob reeling, falling into each other. Like animals they swiped and snarled spitefully between themselves while a shower of dust rained from the ceiling, illuminated by shards of fresh light from above.

Moonlight.

Rhonda looked up and saw that the struts supporting the staircase were coming away, taking parts of the rotten ceiling with it, exposing the damaged roof. She realised it probably wouldn't take much for Fred and Pinkie to bring the whole thing down. They'd be sacrificing their escape route, but that had already been lost to the black-eyed legion.

'Hit the rail,' she tried to say and only part of that came out for a body tackled her from behind, the blow stealing her breath as they tumbled together.

This time Rhonda wasn't able to recover. She wasn't able to ride the momentum to come out on top. She was slammed hard against the rail, pinned there and could only cross her arms in defence. Between them she glimpsed the face of her attacker. It was a face she'd never expected to see again.

Roxy's face.

A barrage of ham-fisted blows battered Rhonda's arms, breaking her guard. Then Roxy lunged forward, head-first, teeth snapping like a crocodile.

Quick as a cat Rhonda twisted away so Roxy's bite found the staircase instead. That jaw clamped firmly around the rusted rail, breaking several teeth with a shudder-inducing crunch. Roxy didn't seem to feel it though and only appeared more menacing afterwards as she snarled through a mouthful of jagged, splintered teeth streaming blood.

By now Rhonda's compassion was utterly spent, overruled by ruthless instinct for survival at any cost, and on Roxy's next lunge Rhonda's hands went up again.

This wasn't another defensive tactic, however. This was an attack. Rhonda aimed her thumbs directly at Roxy's eyes and with the aid of Roxy's own impetus they plunged knuckle-deep.

A faint, wet pop preluded an ear-splitting shriek as a surge of warm, bloody vitreous fluid streamed down Rhonda's wrists. Squeamishly she shut her own eyes and continued to push, expecting Roxy to relent and retreat.

But she never did. Instead, Roxy violently thrust her head downward, using the very bone of her eye sockets to dislocate both of Rhonda's intruding thumbs.

SNAP.

It was Rhonda who then withdrew, wincing from the sickening pain. Her hands trembled when she put them back up and she didn't notice the other black-eyes stretching through the railing behind, until its hand had already found her throat.

Dirty, spindly fingers squeezed, crushing Rhonda's windpipe like a soda can. She croaked for air while Roxy blindly lunged in again, only to bash her head off the rail. Like a shark against a diver's cage Roxy thrashed and gnashed in frustrated frenzy, unaware that her intended target lay choking on the floor, just a few feet away.

Rhonda was in real danger now, closer to death than she'd ever been. Those mangled thumbs had left her too weak to fend off the black-eyes throttling her. She couldn't break its grip, no matter how hard she tried, and her vision was going dim, oxygen failing to reach her brain.

From experience she knew it would soon all go dark and probably forever. She couldn't rely on the other two to save her since they were swamped themselves. She could still hear the chops and thuds of their continuing battle as her world dimmed. Then suddenly there was another sound - metal on metal.

Fred and Pinkie were striking the rail.

There went four ear-splitting clangs, the grating screech of metal twisting, followed by a thunderous crash. Simultaneously the pressure loosened on Rhonda's throat as the entire staircase lurched to one side, dropping several feet, and the bannister rail severed that black-eyes' grabbing arm like a guillotine.

As if by the flick of a switch Rhonda sprang back to life and she seized upon that disembodied limb, using it to bat Roxy away. Repeatedly she swiped the arm, but her breath straining through the crushed windpipe couldn't maintain such exertion for long and on the third swing her strength faltered, her grip failed, leaving nothing to keep Roxy at bay.

Roxy sensed it too. Even blind as she was. She'd

felt the way those blows wavered and could hear the high-pitched wheeze of Rhonda's strangled breaths betraying her location. Purposefully, she turned her eyeless gaze toward it and her cheeks, stained with a mixture of blood, vitreous and the previous night's makeup, stretched back into a horrendous grin. It was the mouth of some nightmare creature, drooling blood, and like a creature Roxy came scuttling on all fours.

In terror Rhonda tried to pedal back, yet her muscles wouldn't cooperate. They were utterly spent, taxed of oxygen. This would be it now, she realised, a horrific and ironic death at the hands of the very person she'd been trying to save. The only question remaining was how? Would Roxy bite her throat out? Would she bash her head in? Or would she return the injury done to her eyes?

All Rhonda could do was sit there and wait to find out.

'HEADS,' cried Fred.

There was a faint whistling sound of something travelling through the air, then the hatchet struck Roxy's head, knocking it back as the edge stuck deep in the parting of her hair. She froze, an arm held straight up as if seeking permission to speak in class, and after a beat she slumped back onto her haunches, an arc of blood spraying from the wound like a garden sprinkler.

'SHOT,' Fred cheered, clearly pleased with the aim, although his celebration was short-lived as he immediately became entangled with yet another black-eyes.

'Get off me ya cunt.'

The staircase had collapsed, but not far, and even at the extreme angle it'd come to rest, surviving black-eyes were still clambering up.

All the while Rhonda sat by, exhausted and wheezing, her tearful eyes fixed on Roxy, on the blood jetting out of her head, with just one thought, one wish going round inside her own.

Please be dead this time.
Please be dead this time
Please.

19

Roxy hadn't moved for ten seconds and although in that situation ten seconds felt like a lifetime, Rhonda still couldn't tear her gaze away. She couldn't bring herself to move either. She'd fallen into a state of frozen watchfulness, a symptom of shock partly brought on by the trauma of her struggle with Roxy, partly because she could barely breathe through her crushed trachea.

'Come on girl.'

A great hand engulfed Rhonda's wrist, an almost irresistible force lifting her from the ground.

'*Come on*,' Pinkie barked and he bent, hoisting her onto his shoulder in a fireman's carry. He managed this single-handed, his right still lugging the sledgehammer, yet Rhonda sensed the pain it caused him, heard the strain in his breathing.

The position wasn't helping her own. Not that she'd ever complain. In fact, she couldn't have been more grateful because as Pinkie ferried her away down the hall, she could still see the horror he was taking her from.

First, she saw Fred retrieve his axe from Roxy's skull, saw him cast her body over the side after.

Then she saw how the black-eyes, dozens of them, were climbing one over another, up the wreckage of the staircase to reach their floor.

Most of her view was subsequently blocked by Fred's mass. From then he trailed close, and she only caught intermittent glimpses around him, but those were enough. Each time she saw them the black-eyes' number had increased. Each time she saw them they'd gained on Fred.

Now they were just a few strides behind.

'Through the door,' Fred puffed. 'Don't bust it.'

They were nearing a T-junction where a right turn would lead back to the room in which Rhonda first met them. But Fred had clocked another option and now Pinkie had too.

Past that junction, at the end of the hall, the door stood ajar, and Pinkie turned at the last moment to barge it open with his unburdened shoulder. The world spun before Rhonda's eyes. Then in the next instant she was on the floor of an unfamiliar room, watching the men bolster that door from inside.

'Wedge it,' said Fred and Pinkie propped his sledge under the handle just a fraction before the black-eyes hit.

BOOM.

The whole room seemed to shake from the impact as the first bodies crashed against the door. It sounded as though some giant monster were trying to break in.

Dust fell from the frame and the door flexed slightly, bowing inward. There was an alarming snap of wood and Fred quickly turned to press his back against it, digging his heels, while Pinkie leaned into a deeper stance.

BOOM.

The next wave hit like a truck, but the men held firm, roaring in unified defiance. Fortunately for them each successive crash was lessened by the buffer of the bodies in those first waves. However, pressure was still building. The horde on the other side were now packed tight as commuters on a rush hour tube. Something had to give. Either Fred and Pinkie would eventually be pressed back, or the door would simply explode into matchsticks.

From her seat on the floor Rhonda could only

watch, her failing breath preventing much else. She desperately wanted to help them. She just couldn't move, her oxygen-starved muscles refusing to cooperate.

But her heart was pounding so fast.

Like the gentle breeze that builds to a hurricane, Rhonda felt the early signs of an adrenaline spike creep in as a slight tremble of her knees. The feeling quickly grew to immense proportions, far greater than any rush she'd ever known, spreading throughout her body within two short breaths, the second of which coincided with a short, yet violent convulsion.

Suddenly Rhonda was up on her feet and although first intent had been to assist with the door, something else caught her eye, something on the other side of the room. It was another door, steel, with a button panel beside it.

They were in an elevator lobby.

That steel double door cracked open with surprising ease. Rhonda guessed its lock needed electricity in order to function. She could still feel heavy resistance though, some kind of spring mechanism, and in an effort to open it fully she propped her back against one side while pushing the other with her feet.

Fred noticed what she was up to and said to Pinkie, 'Help her get that fucker open. We can shimmy down on the cables or somethin'.'

Pinkie looked at him, incredulous.

'You must be joking.'

'Any better ideas? Go on, get it open Pinks. I've got the door.'

'I'll hold door,' Pinkie insisted. 'I'm stronger.'

'Like fuck you are,' Fred snapped. 'I can squat two hundred k. I can bench one-fifty an' I weigh one-twenty. I can hold this better 'n you with those busted ribs.'

'Suit yourself,' Pinkie muttered.

Regardless any doubts of Fred's stats he understood time was too short to debate much longer and rushed over to assist Rhonda. Together they opened the doors wide, then he held them while she peered through.

'What do you see?' he asked, his voice echoing about the shaft. 'Can we get down?'

Beyond the threshold Rhonda saw only a yawning abyss, its secrets cloaked in impenetrable darkness. She crouched and felt around, her fingertips recognising the roughness of brickwork, the tackiness of cobweb, then the familiar and welcome coldness of steel.

It was a single bar, roughly an inch thick and spanning a little less than shoulder width. She stretched further and found another bar of the exact same size directly underneath.

An access ladder.

'Yes,' she gasped, her voice a coarse whisper, and without hesitation she swung her legs over, gladly beginning a descent into the unknown. Those broken thumbs proved no hindrance and although her adapted grip of the ladder appeared to put greater strain on her hands and wrists, somehow Rhonda couldn't feel it. A side effect of the adrenaline she assumed.

Seeing her go Pinkie beckoned to Fred, 'Come on.'

'I can't mate,' said Fred, his bulk rocked by the shuddering door.

'Just run for it.'

'Soon as I let go of this door, they'll be on me. I can't get over there in time.'

A Hot Dose of Hell

'Just try,' Pinkie urged again and Fred gave a slight shake of his head. Then he went into his pocket and pitched the van keys.

They hit Pinkie's chest, dropped to the ground and he slid down against the elevator doors to retrieve them.

'I'm not daft, mate,' said Fred. 'I know how this'll turn out. Least if I hang on, you'll have a bit a' time to get away.'

All of a sudden, those keys seemed heavier in Pinkie's palm. He thought to throw them back but didn't. Dire as the situation was, Fred seemed to have accepted it with an air of stoicism. It stood an example of the mythic British resolve Pinkie had heard about yet never witnessed until that very moment.

Out of respect and sense of logic Pinkie had to accept it too, no matter how much he hated it. And after pocketing the keys he gave Fred a long, regretful look, while placing a foot on the first rung of the ladder.

He tested the rung with a portion of his weight, breathing a relieved sigh when it didn't give. Then, still holding the doors, he lowered himself to the third rung. But just before he allowed them to close a final objection found its way to the tip of his tongue.

'Could-'

A bloody hand burst through the dry wall above Fred's left shoulder. Furiously it groped around, a great red spider pouncing for prey.

Fred tilted his neck to avoid the touch and cursed through his teeth. 'Fuck off will ya, Pinks. I can't keep 'em out much longer. Just name your next kid after me eh? An' make sure he doesn't grow up to be a cunt.'

Pinkie gave an earnest nod. He'd keep that promise.

'Nara,' he said.

Fred smiled as if he knew the word and gave a sort of salute with his hatchet.

'You too ya fuckin' commie.'

On release the elevator doors snapped shut, plunging Pinkie into total darkness.

<u>20</u>

Pinkie could only feel the ladder rail in his hands, hear the metallic resonance of Rhonda descending. From its faintness he deduced she was nearing the bottom and he began to climb down at quick pace, dropping two rungs at a time.

'On my way,' he said, to warn her.

Overhead something crashed against those steel doors, followed by a hammering so rapid it quickly became white noise.

The black-eyes must've gotten by Fred.

Pinkie wouldn't mourn him yet though. There would be time once he got out of the place. *If* he got out of the place. Maintaining speed, he continued down, unsure how much further he had to go. Answer arrived within a few moments as his boot met something else in place of the next rung. It was a solid platform, the elevator car.

'Girl? You there?'

A sharp whistle of a whisper came from the darkness, 'I've found something.'

Pinkie left the ladder in search of the voice's origin, carefully picking his feet up to avoid any trip hazards. The toe of his boot struck something soft.

'Hey,' Rhonda rasped.

'Sorry.'

Something clicked, a lock or latch.

'I think I've got a way through,' said Rhonda. 'Help me get this open.'

Pinkie crouched, feeling for her arms. Once he'd found them, he traced down to her wrists, to the handle in her grasp. It had to be some sort of hatch.

'Alright,' he said, taking hold. 'Pull.'

The thing flew open, and the pair toppled. Pinkie fell back against the ladder. Rhonda onto her buttocks. They'd grossly overestimated the hatch's resistance, its weight and used far too much force.

'Come on,' said Rhonda, lowering herself through the open panel, where she dangled briefly before a graceful landing.

The lift suspension shuddered unnervingly when Pinkie dropped in after. He was glad to find light there, a thin shard beaming through a gap in the sliding doors. Rhonda needled her fingers into that gap to pull one side as Pinkie seized the other and the doors parted with a grating sound, the mechanism groaning in complaint after years gone unused.

From all signs the lobby appeared mercifully empty, save another discarded LED lantern. His shoulder firmly bracing the door, Pinkie looked to Rhonda and flicked his head slightly.

'Go.'

Rhonda was set to comply when a loud bang sounded from high above. A fraction later the ceiling seemed to explode and they both dropped to the ground, covering their heads while the doors they'd released snapped shut.

Darkness engulfed them, the commotion giving way to a brief silence where all they could hear was a faint ringing, an after effect of the crash. Then Pinkie felt something dripping and looked up, squinting through the gloom to find one of the black-eyes hovering overhead.

The wretch was hanging head-first through a fresh hole in the elevator ceiling, blood dribbling steadily from its broken skull. It must've fallen from the second floor, a hell of a drop and thankfully enough to kill it.

But before Pinkie or Rhonda had chance to get up another came bursting through, followed by another and another.

Like lemmings the black-eyes came raining down on that elevator. Luckily most died on impact or were so severely injured that they expired a few moments later. Only one survived the fall, just barely. It slithered down through the broken ceiling and flopped onto the elevator floor where it proceeded to paw at Rhonda's leg, its limp, broken arm incapable of much more.

Rhonda shed the unwelcome touch with a merciless stomp. Then during the brief respite that followed she and Pinkie seized the chance to pry the doors apart before any others got through. They were safely in the lobby, on the other side of sealed doors, by the time the next series of crashes occurred.

Eight loud bangs followed by silence.

'Listen,' said Pinkie.

From inside the elevator arose a persistent scratching, the distinct squeak of skin rubbing steel. It told that others were now surviving the fall and that they'd figure their way out of that elevator soon.

'Come on,' said Pinkie, picking up the lantern, hurrying at the sound of further crashes. In his haste he threw the lobby door wide, not thinking about what he could be opening it onto. This was a mistake he immediately came to regret when a female black-eyes pounced through at him, claws-first.

'Look out,' squeaked Rhonda.

Barely in time to save his eyes, Pinkie leaned back like Ali on the ropes and the black-eyes' nails caught his cheek instead, opening a deep gash as she lunged past him.

Pinkie expertly pivoted to track her, in that

moment recognising that her speed far outmatched his own. He quickly brought the lantern up to shield his face, but those nails slashed that hand too, the sting causing him to drop it, leaving his head exposed.

Her follow-up swipe audibly cut the air like a blade, those nails seeking Pinkie's eyes again and in the millisecond between he could do little more than close them and pull a stupid face.

For one terrifying instant Pinkie felt the nails touch his eyelids, yet only just. Then they retreated and he looked to see that Rhonda had joined the fray. She had the black-eyes trapped tight in a rear chokehold, where a sudden, vicious jerk produced a gut-churning pop of dislocating bones.

After that the black-eyes went limp and Rhonda dumped it on the floor in a twisted heap.

'Ch-cheers,' Pinkie stuttered as he retrieved the lantern. Considering Rhonda's size, her injuries, he almost couldn't believe what he'd just witnessed. She'd snapped that black-eyes' neck like a chicken's.

'How did y-'

A rattling sound cut Pinkie off, pulling his attention back to the elevator. Like pale slugs, numerous fingers were oozing through the widening gap between its doors. He guessed the black-eyes were maybe seconds from escape and the pair wasted no more time before fleeing into a long, branching corridor.

'Which way?' said Rhonda, her voice now sounding like she was sucking air through a soggy paper straw. Again she wheezed, 'Which way?'

The light from Pinkie's lantern didn't reach far and there was no telling how many other black-eyes lay in wait on that floor. He judged best course was to follow the straight route. Eventually it would lead to an exit. All hotels, even the old ones, lawfully require at least two in case of fire.

'Just keep going.'

Behind them a chilling, demented scream pierced the air and echoed down the vacant corridors. It heralded another stampede as a flood of bodies came rushing from the elevator. The still-twitching pile of dead atop its busted ceiling provided soft landing for any who followed and as a result these runners had survived the two-storey drop relatively unscathed.

Skinny, lanky limbs and low body mass enabled them to cut the lead fast. Within seconds the front runner came so close that the ends of Rhonda's plait soaked up the blood from his reaching fingertips. She desperately needed to speed up and although she had the capacity to run faster, she couldn't. There was one very large obstacle in her way.

Due to his bulk Pinkie ran slower than Rhonda and his broad frame was too wide for her to overtake in that narrow corridor. Sensing the black-eyes' proximity she knew that soon they'd be upon her, probably within the next few seconds, maybe less if Pinkie faltered or tripped. So she took a risk, pausing to throw out a back kick.

At full speed the lead black-eyes impaled himself on Rhonda's heel. He folded and fell causing the next row to trip and stumble over him. As she ran on Rhonda heard his bones crunching under the feet of the rest of them and she resisted an urge to look back. That kick may have bought her some breathing room, but not enough for that, not nearly enough.

Within a few strides she could already feel the unpleasant tickle of more snatching fingers grazing her spine, their ratty nails snagging the hem of her vest.

Stark Terror

'EXIT,' Pinkie bellowed.

Rhonda saw the moment he said it, a moonlit portal shining in the gloom. They'd both entered that way not an hour ago and each prepared to bound from the upcoming porch steps they knew to be there.

Rushing through into the cool night air Pinkie took the leap first, yet somehow Rhonda landed beside him at the exact same time. In stride they sprinted together until she outpaced him, while behind them many of the black-eyed horde collided through uncoordinated leaps.

This didn't slow the pursuers much, however. Like the tide hammering the rocks below, the next wave just rolled over to take the frontrunners' place. Then when those fallen regained their feet they simply filed in at the back.

The chase was relentless, and Rhonda could see no end to it. Until that exact moment she'd been nurturing a paper-thin hope the black-eyes would be reluctant to leave their lair, that they might shy away from any hint of civilisation, like monsters in the movies. She cursed herself for entertaining such a fantasy. But even if the latter *were* true, from atop that cliff civilisation remained a distant mirage. The only sign existed in the reflection of a nightclub's sky beacon gleaming off Edd's Caravelle.

Behind it, Rhonda saw the grubby white tradesman's van and realised who that belonged to now.

Pinkie ditched the lantern.

'Get in the van,' he puffed, while he sacrificed precious speed to fish Fred's keys from his pocket. His thumb pressed the remote unlock and the van responded with a welcoming blink of its lights, letting him know it was ready.

Rhonda got there first, arriving way ahead of Pinkie. She hopped onto the passenger seat and slammed the door but didn't lock it for his sake. On tenterhooks she watched him through the side mirror, her palm hovering over the lock just in case he didn't make it. It didn't look like he was going to. Those black-eyes were almost at arm's reach and gaining.

By now Pinkie was lagging. His lungs felt as if on fire, unaccustomed as they were to him running after ten years of solely anaerobic output. His mouth and throat were dry as sandpaper and his muscles had begun to rebel with agonising cramps.

Over forty metres of concrete still lay between him and the van and less than two feet of thin air between him and the black-eyes at his back. Within the next few strides he realised he probably wasn't going to make it. Regardless, he grit his teeth and ran on, primed to swing at the first to touch him.

'COME ON,' Rhonda squeaked, her voice as shrill as nails on slate, her fist pounding the cockpit. 'COME ON, COME ON.'

Afraid to so much as blink she continued to watch, urging his every step. But her encouragement stopped short when Pinkie suddenly dropped out of the mirror's view.

'No,' she whispered.

Almost three seconds went by with no sign, no sound, not a cry of pain. Nothing. It was as though the mob had simply absorbed the big man and she was about to lock herself in when she heard the van's back door open. It was too late. The whole vehicle rocked from some fresh burden as she turned to peer through the cage mesh divide, dreading the drooling, black-eyed faces she'd surely find.

But it was Pinkie. He'd dove in and skidded to a

halt on his back amidst a scattering of Fred's tools and the black-eyed mob were pressing through after him, all at once. Thankfully not one possessed the sense to open the adjoining door which created a choke point, buying Pinkie precious seconds to rally.

Without looking he snatched the nearest tool to hand and sat up swinging as hard as he could. Only on connection did he realise what he held - a set of garden shears and their open blades blinded the first black-eyes who reacted violently, lashing out at everything in its proximity. The fellow black-eyes it assailed reacted in kind and like rabid dogs they tore into each other, temporarily forgetting their original target.

While they raged on Rhonda didn't dare speak, for fear any noise from her direction might pull their focus back to Pinkie. But she wanted to say something, she'd had an idea. If only she could warn him, she thought, her fingers closing on the lever.

Although Rhonda had never driven, or even attempted to drive before, she understood how a handbrake worked and through the windscreen she could tell how the hill sloped away toward the harbour. She figured with the weight of the van they would build momentum fast, hopefully fast enough to see them clear of this mob.

Gripping the release, she winced as she squeezed and was startled by the unexpected sound of a motor revving. Not the van, she quickly realised. It was something else.

Pinkie had found Fred's chainsaw.

21

Blood gushed, squirted and sprayed all over the van's interior, flooding the floor around Pinkie's boots.

Two to three at a time the black-eyes were squirming through the door only to be cut down at the neck seconds later, their gurning heads tumbling into the van. Like coconuts they piled up fast at the end nearest Rhonda, who hoarsely cheered through the cage mesh. Never before had such a horrific sight been so welcome to her. Never before had the nerve-shredding buzz of a chainsaw sounded so glorious. And for a moment it seemed as if the problem were virtually solved, as though it could just be a matter of time and will before Pinkie dispatched them all.

Then somehow, the other door got opened.

'LOOK OUT,' Rhonda tried to scream, not as if it would've made any difference. The black-eyes were already in and Pinkie was already fully aware of his situation.

Holding the saw out in defence, he backed away until his shoulder blades met the mesh, leaving nowhere else to go. That was when one of the black-eyes split from the pack to impale itself on the saw, simultaneously smothering the chain, clogging it with its own guts, killing the engine.

In the saw's absence the sudden silence felt deafening and throughout his dying gasps that black-eyes wore a bloody rictus grin which could've easily been taken for one of triumph, as if he knew full well what he'd done, as if this were a conscious act of self-sacrifice.

'Fucking pizda,' Pinkie snarled, furiously yanking the starter chord. Repeatedly he tried, to no avail. He couldn't even pull the saw free and the dead weight on the end quickly became too much to bear. He had to let it go.

Blood splashed as the half-cut black-eyes collapsed in an awkward heap, the saw striking the floor with a loud clang to shake Rhonda into action. Thinking fast, she dropped the handbrake and slid over it into the driver's seat.

Instantly the vehicle started to roll, gathering speed along the sharp decline of the hill. Approaching 20mph they pulled away from the black-eyes chasing the van. At 30mph these pursuers were mere blips in the distance, but there was still those in the back with Pinkie.

When the van set off the initial jolt of momentum had thrown these other passengers off balance and bought Pinkie a brief reprieve. Standing with his back firmly against the cage mesh he hadn't stumbled or fell as they had, and he'd used the opportunity to take up the shears once more.

Those wet blades now glimmered rapidly in his steely grasp as he turned, thrusting them at the oncoming mass.

SNIK, SNIK - A black-eyes squealed for the loss of three fingers.

SNIK, SNIK - Another had its windpipe cut.

SNIK, SNIK.

Rhonda could hear Pinkie pruning away behind her, though she didn't dare look around. She had her own situation to worry about. The van was still gathering on its descent of the winding hill, the speedometer reading over 40mph, even with the engine off.

'HANG ON,' she rasped, her hands gripping the wheel white-knuckle-tight, the backs of them riddled with veins like she'd never seen before.

Or had she?

Not on herself perhaps...

But there was no time to dwell over that. All too fast the bright lights of the harbourside had gone from twinkling stars to blazing suns and at any moment the van would hit the main strip where droves of carefree revellers were drunkenly spilling from bar to bar. The cattle market, as many called it, could soon resemble an abattoir if Rhonda failed to act correctly.

At risk of those runners catching up she knew she'd have to slow down and through a frantic process of elimination, she found the foot brake. But by then she'd somehow stopped caring, stopped worrying altogether. Another sensation was creeping over her, something new.

Something alien.

On the other side of the cage mesh Pinkie turned his shears toward the next comer, a gangly, long-haired scarecrow in a piss-smelling camo jacket. Mindlessly this scarecrow charged, arms outstretched, practically gifting its neck to Pinkie, who held the blades wide like a hungry mouth awaiting food.

In the fraction before contact, those pumped muscles primed to squeeze, to cut that head clean off. Then at the last instant a swerve of the van spoiled the aim and Pinkie missed, snipping nothing but thin air.

'Chryste,' he cursed.

That overreach left Pinkie off balance, open for quick hands to grab his forearms, his waist, and like constrictors they coiled tight, digging in with dirty, ragged fingernails.

They were all over him now, smothering his body so he barely had the space to breathe. He felt a sharp sting from dull teeth piercing his ear, another far worse as one sank its jaws deep into his calf.

This would be a particularly horrible death, he knew, for it would not be quick. It would be a vicious and prolonged mauling. Helpless to escape, he grit his teeth in anticipation yet was still struggling furiously when like a backhand from God, another swerve cast them all to the side of the van.

Pinkie bumped hard, so hard he dented the panel. They were all then flung against the opposite side, those severed heads bouncing about them. Four live bodies and five dead were now rattling around that compartment, like bugs in a tin can at the mercy of a sadistic child.

It fast became apparent this was Rhonda's steering, or lack of, causing the van to veer so violently and with tremendous effort Pinkie fought his way free from a tangle of groping limbs to bark through the cage mesh at the back of her head.

'WHAT YOU DOING GIRL?'

Rhonda didn't answer and Pinkie winced, flinching from nails which raked his face before another bump in the road sent the assailant flying back.

Pinkie held on though, clinging to the cage for dear life while his fingers, half skinned from being forced through the too-small holes, bled profusely onto the driver's headrest.

'HEY,' he snarled. 'WHAT YOU DOING?'

On that Rhonda's hands abandoned the wheel, then her body whipped around with simian aggression. She slammed both palms against the cage as if in retaliation and just as Pinkie noticed the shiny blackness of her eyeballs, she sank her teeth into one of his protruding fingers.

Pinkie cried out, a primal scream of rage and despair. The van was clocking nearly fifty now and in a matter of seconds the black-eyes would be all over him again.

Death was coming one way or another. He only hoped it would be in the inevitable crash, not at the hands of the black-eyes, and thought his modest wish answered when the van took flight off a steep speed bump preceding the harbour.

At the apex of the jump, in the tiny ticks between seconds before gravity reclaimed them, he had just enough time to utter a single word, one which for him summed up the whole situation.

'Kurwa.'

The van landed with a bang, left front tyre exploding. Then it grazed a parked taxicab, crushing that vehicle's right side, and tipped, all the way over.

Everything came down on top of Pinkie, bodies, tools, severed heads, burying him completely, his cries drowned by the ear-splitting scrape of steel on concrete as the vehicle proceeded to skid along on its side.

For more than thirty metres the van maintained its momentum, with sparks crackling underneath threatening fire, but never catching alight. Up ahead the Saturday night crowd parted like the red sea and only after jumping a curb and bursting through a pub's front windows did the van finally come to rest.

Those shattered panes gave way to a wall of noise, female screams, male shouts and more broken glass mingling underneath the thudding dance music. Previously coveted tables loaded with pricey drinks were immediately abandoned. The three-deep queue at the bar scattered and the highly competitive game of pool taking place at the back would never reach a conclusive result, its twenty quid stakes left sitting on the cushion.

'GET BACK,' someone shouted.

'TERRORISTS,' screamed another and panic flooded the room, sending a wave of bodies surging toward the exit farthest from the van.

Glass smashed intermittently as drinks were knocked or dropped. Tables and stools got upturned in a clatter, tripping many who ran. Several people were trampled or crushed against walls adjacent to the exit doors. But the music kept right on playing for the DJ had fled his post and like some unfortunate others, now lay bleeding and unconscious upon the wet bar floor.

While his bones were crushed under the feet of hundreds his friends in the security team were nowhere to be seen, nor the landlord or barstaff, who'd sought refuge in the cellar.

Only the pool players had stayed put. They were a team of scaffolders, each built like light heavyweights, and for them engaging with the situation felt more natural than fleeing it.

Of the four, two were ex-marines and three were heavily into MMA. Doug, Tony and Bill had all been attending the same class for years. Their boss Pete always said he had no time for that stuff nowadays. But in the service, he'd been known as quite the fighter and due to the physicality of their trade he still looked it too.

'C'mon lads,' he said, assuming his natural role as leader.

'With you,' said Doug and brandishing their cues the four proceeded toward the van with caution, glass crunching beneath every step. Amongst the pools of spilled drink and ice a blanket of glistening shards coated the dance floor ahead, their size increasing nearer the broken windows and the van itself.

Strangely, no noise was coming from the vehicle. There were no cries for help, not a murmur, and the engine wasn't running. But even from a distance the men could detect something moving inside the rear compartment, something, or somethings, heavy enough to make it shake slightly.

At Pete's signal the group split into two pairs, spreading out across the dance floor and they converged on the van while the shaking continued in random, frantic bursts.

Doug and Tony quickly set to work shifting tables and stools, clearing a route to the van's rear doors. Pete and Bill squatted to check the cockpit.

'Anyone in there?' said Pete.

Blood covered much of the cracked windscreen, making it difficult to view the inside under the dim lighting. A few thrusts from the end of a pool cue soon cleared a hole.

'It's a bird,' Bill said, leaning in.

'Let's get her out then,' said Pete. He wasn't waiting for paramedics - he could smell gas.

'Hurry it,' he added, prompting Bill to reach through the hole. 'There's a chance this thing might go up, mate.'

Inside the cockpit Rhonda lay prone, her bloodied face resting on the pub's wood floor through the broken side window. Although she remained silent Bill could see her chest moving with each breath as he stretched for her.

'Gotcha,' he said, seizing the strap of her top. A fraction later Rhonda's hand found his and he tried to assure her.

'Don't worry,' he began to say. Then when he saw her hideous black eyes, the web of veins streaking her skin, those words died in his throat.

'You got her?' asked Pete, receiving no reply.

The expression on Rhonda's face turned malign just as Bill felt an immense pressure in his hand. He immediately tried to withdraw, but Rhonda held firm and used her other hand to isolate his index finger.

'Don't,' Bill said, sensing the intent, though not fully believing it until she'd already bent that finger ninety degrees the wrong way. The moment his nail scratched the back of his wrist he let out a gasp of shock and when the pain registered, he started to pull away violently, bracing his foot against the van's hood for leverage.

'What the fuck?' said Pete, who dropped his pool cue to help, wrapping both arms around Bill's waist.

'GET HER OFF ME,' Bill cried. 'GET HER OFF.'

Together they heaved, yet they failed to free Bill's hand and only succeeded in dragging Rhonda through the smashed windscreen. Glass scored her scalp and shoulders on the way out and she fell atop the men in a bloody heap, never letting go of Bill.

He cried out at the sight of her face looming close, then like a steel trap her teeth clamped around his nose, distorting the scream. Doug and Tony reappeared just in time to see her tear it clean off.

'JESUS,' said Doug and on reflex he struck Rhonda with the pool cue, snapping it across her head.

CRACK!

Rhonda slumped back against the van, seemingly unconscious. Less than a second later she sprang back to life and lunged for the defenceless Bill. The man had no chance to recover before she plunged two fingers deep into his exposed nasal cavity, so deep that when she curled them, she scratched the roof of his mouth.

A Hot Dose of Hell

Helpless and choking, Bill vomited up Rhonda's arm, some of it blowing back onto Pete as he squirmed his way out from under them both. Tony took his turn to break a cue on Rhonda's head, and Doug was about to follow with a right straight when they were jumped from behind by three more black-eyes.

Four police arrived outside the pub within the next minute and were immediately taken out by the large pack of black-eyes charging down the hill. Some passers-by tried to intervene on those officers' behalf. They wound up either dead or bleeding on the pavement beside them.

Shattered glass signalled more chaos spilling from the pub out into the street, with Pete, Tony and Doug fending off their surprise attackers, only to be mobbed by more. It fast looked like a riot, like a scene from the worst days of football hooliganism, as have-a-go-heroes armed with beer bottles, takeaway signs and other makeshift weapons rushed to join the fray.

But for some there were no clear sides and through the confusion many non-black-eyes were soon fighting amongst themselves. In short order a team of riot police were mobilised and when several were felled, by black-eyes and hooligans alike, an armed response team formed up behind them.

The traditional eight o'clock happy hour saw gunshots echo about Scarmouth harbour and volleys of lead perforating flesh. It only took a single stray round, a bullet travelling through and through a target's body, to spark a fire with all that spilled liquor and gasoline.

Flames spread quickly across the bar floor to the van's fuel tank, causing an explosion which spat glass out into the street. This was followed closely by a series of smaller explosions from the pressurised beer kegs in the cellar.

At the sergeant's command the police fell back to safe range as spectators crowded behind them and firemen took their place in front.

There were no black-eyes left standing, yet the blaze burned on into dawn. All the while a pair of drones hovered quietly overhead, watching, recording.

22

At the heart of Scarmouth, atop a three-storey commercial building, above a defunct travel agency and call centre, sat a luxury apartment encompassing the entire floor.

Inside, its spacious living room lay sparse, the blank walls only partially lit by the soft glow from a cluster of monitor screens at its centre. These stood arranged in a ring formation, beaming into each other so that the light kept largely within that circle.

Everything else was darkness. Every window and skylight had been blacked out with spray paint thick enough to block the rising sun and all the cracks around the door had been taped and soundproofed, as well as the hardwood floor and plaster walls.

Inside that ring of light, that LCD Stonehenge, three figures worked back-to-back on office chairs facing four screens each. Busily and silently these expert hands manipulated fiddly controls, while those screens showed the fire and wreckage at Scarmouth harbour from multiple angles and various distances.

On through the early hours the trio continued, watching, documenting everything around the incident, only pausing when a shadow from outside that circle stepped forth into the light and spoke.

'That's a wrap folks,' said Hancock, his managerial blue suit showing green in the artificial glare, and he gave a brief clap of approval for a job well done.

Relieved, Patel swivelled his chair from the drone controls to meet the back of Poole's head, the fuzzy rolls of Morgan's sweaty neck. Both colleagues were still watching their own monitors, engrossed, although it was abundantly clear the experiment had reached a conclusion and not just because Hancock said so.

All the subjects were long down, the fire inside the pub nearly out.

'He said, we're du-uun,' Patel whined in singsong, his impatience obvious. For their part in all this had been fulfilled and since he worked on price, not by the hour he saw zero benefit to lingering. That would only increase chance of crossing paths with the field team. None of them wanted that. Those guys were scary.

'Come on,' said Hancock, 'pack it up.'

'I'm just waiting for them to clear the scene,' said Morgan, suspiciously monotone. 'You know me. I like to be thorough.'

Thorough wasn't a word anyone would've applied to Morgan, unless describing his dedication to consuming tubes of Pringles. Already three empties protruded from the tiny wastebin at his feet, a by-product of just a single night's work.

On the central screen a heaving, dog-paw-tattooed cleavage betrayed his true motive; Morgan was using his drone to get some downblouse shots on various members of the crowd.

Hancock tutted in disapproval. 'I trust you're no longer transmitting.'

'Course not,' said Morgan. 'I cut the feed. I'm just having a bit of fun.'

'Dirty man,' said Poole, although he couldn't help glancing over. His primary function had been to hack into the town's CCTV, which didn't afford any freedom to mess about like that. Sure, he could risk moving one of their cameras by a few degrees or zooming in a little, but any more would tip the real operator it was being controlled by someone outside and likely trigger a security alert.

As a result, Poole had spent most of his shift squinting at grainy figures in the distance, rapidly pushing buttons to enlarge the image or search for better angles.

Static units planted about the Victoria hadn't offered much of interest either. They were motion activated and when they weren't offline, they'd shown mostly rats and bugs. Fleeting glimpses of shuffling druggies and towards the end, a few seconds of mob surges did little to counter the mind-numbing hours that preceded.

If there was one thing Poole had learned from this, his first assignment, it was that next time he'd want to pilot a drone.

'I'm setting the pick-up point now,' said Patel. 'Sending you the coordinates, Morgan.'

Morgan grunted an affirmative then the cleavage rapidly plummeted out of frame as the drone pulled away, straight up into the sky. At forty feet high he was struck by the perspective and thought from there the loitering crowd resembled some kind of growth on the land, like time-lapse footage of a fungus growing and spreading.

Maybe Attenborough has a point, he thought, switching back to thermal camera, through which people appeared more like germs or infections inside the buildings they occupied.

But what he'd observed taking place within the damp walls of the Victoria hadn't looked like that at all. It hadn't looked like anything other than the primal carnage it was and this train of thought brought Morgan to something troubling, like a sudden realisation he'd left the gas on at home.

'Hey, what about the *Rexstacy*? There was still tons

of it scattered on the floor at the Victoria.'

'Not your concern,' said Hancock.

'Righto,' Morgan nodded, those chins multiplying. Instinct told him not to press the subject, so he took a deep breath, moved the conversation on. 'And that's that, another assignment done.'

Speaking over his shoulder he asked his colleagues: 'Sooo what were *your* highlights then guys? Lowlights?'

Poole's answer came knee-jerk quick. 'I really didn't like seeing that fat thug kill the seagull.'

'As opposed to everything else?' said Patel, squinting in disbelief. 'Wow. Not even the stuff on the stairway? *That* was savage.'

Poole shrugged, swinging his chair slightly.

'Hey, you know me, I'm an animal lover. How about you Morgan?'

Morgan's delayed response was a sharp hiss as he quickly steered his drone from an unanticipated obstacle, in the form of a church spire. Rotors skimmed the guttering, briefly throwing the tiny aircraft off-course and when he recovered the face of a scowling gargoyle flashed by, almost subliminally.

A ghost of that image seemed to linger on-screen thereafter, haunting the aerial view of Scarmouth's streets. But that was only Hancock's reflection.

'Careful,' he warned. 'Those aren't cheap. Plus any damage will be deducted from your fee.'

Again, Morgan nodded, sheepish, and he refrained from answering Poole's question. Poole didn't repeat, instead taking advantage of the break to broach another subject, one which had been niggling him for several hours now.

'Y'know in all seriousness, I wish we could've seen what happened inside that van.'

At this Hancock's arched brow twitched like the leg of an agitated spider.

'Are you referring to the *gymnast?'* he asked; it was the name they'd given Rhonda following her manoeuvre with the pipework, back at the Victoria. Although they knew her real name and a whole lot more thanks to mobile phone tracking and social media.

'She lost control,' said Morgan, voice thick with mischief. 'Didn't have her eyes on the road, did she? Bloody women drivers.'

Patel snorted laughter while Poole's mouth tightened.

'*You* might find this funny, but I'm a hundred percent she didn't take any of the formula. And Morgan, please stop calling it *Rexstacy.* It sounds like the title to some kind of dinosaur-themed porn film.'

Morgan forced a chuckle. 'Hey, it was our *john called John* came up with it.'

'No, the hooker called it that,' said Poole, then something caught his eye, and he excitedly wagged a finger at one of his screens.

'Look, look,' he urged. 'Why don't you send the field ops to ask *him* about what happened?'

'Whoa,' said Patel, glancing over, and Hancock tracked their focus to see paramedics loading a gurney into the back of an ambulance.

The patient riding that trolley was the one who'd been in the van with Rhonda, the only non-infected male they'd failed to identify.

"Hammer" they called him, for his use of the sledge.

'*He* made it?' Patel gasped. 'But how?'

'We know which hospital they'll take him to,' said Poole, looking at Hancock. 'We could send somebody to interview him there.'

Caught off-guard Hancock hesitated to speak. In truth he wasn't at all pleased by the discovery, nor did he wish to do anything about it. Random outliers like Rhonda Caine typically undermined studies, leading researchers down blind rabbit holes, setting projects back by months, even years.

If details of the girl's unexplained infection were to reach the board, they'd have him run yet another field test, further delaying the next phase and crushing any chances of that juicy bonus he'd been promised.

Hancock couldn't have that. He wouldn't have that.

'*Firstly*,' he stressed, an oily hand making the politician's thumb, 'there's no way for the formula's effects to be transmitted. It *has* to be administered. The gymnast simply *must've* tried some at the Victoria. We just missed it. *Perhaps* when we were watching something else.'

Hush descended in wake of the implied blame and Hancock gladly let it hang for several moments, his gaze fixed on Poole throughout. This fast became uncomfortable for the newbie, who held the most tenuous, most replaceable position.

With a chill he remembered Patel's warning prior to the assignment. 'In this outfit,' he'd said, 'rocking the boat is a guaranteed route to unemployment, or worse. Best to keep your head down, keep the tone light. The thoughtful ones don't last long.'

'You're right, Mr Hancock,' said Poole in robotic monotone, the sense of an agreement given reluctantly, of submission, and as the hollow words left his mouth, he could hear it himself, so went further to compensate.

'You're absolutely right, there was a gap there, w-when we were watching the activists on the ground floor.'

'Yeah true,' said Patel and Morgan enthusiastically grunted along, nodding like a dog.

'Yes, yes there was.'

This forced consensus seemed to pacify Hancock, but he still stared at Poole, just to make him uncomfortable, to make him squirm. Poole looked away first.

'Ooh wait,' said Morgan, changing subject. '*That* was my highlight…when the Rob Zombie lookalike bounced that guy's head like a basketball.'

'*Slam dunked* it like *Space Jam*,' Patel chuckled, eager to help shift the mood back. However, his comment was met with a cowed silence from Poole and an irritated snort from Hancock to chill the atmosphere once again.

Patel cleared his throat.

'I'm approaching destination,' he said, more soberly.

'Carry on,' said Hancock.

From the five possible pick-up points, which had all been strategically selected based on access and distance, Patel was aiming for the open top floor of a multi-storey car park. The building stood only seven hundred yards from the pub massacre scene and when he banked toward it the drone's thermal camera caught sight of a transit van climbing the ramp to that floor.

Right away Patel could tell this was the field team. Apart from illegal immigrants crossing the channel tunnel, under no other circumstances would you find six men packed in the back of a windowless van like that.

Hot in there, he thought, noting how vague the heat signatures were, how they all melded into each other to form one big, pulsating blob.

As the van reached the top floor he casually circled to say 'Hello', before landing the drone in the centre of an outlined parking space.

'Touchdown.'

Moments later a gloved hand came into view on-screen, scooping the device up.

'Falcon one has been tethered,' said Patel. 'Repeat, Falcon one has been teth-

'I'm going to wake the others,' said Hancock, suddenly weary, and he crossed to the bedroom, knocked the closed door, twisted a dimmer switch to bring the main lights up.

'Assignment over folks. Come on people. It's clear out time.'

It'd been seven hours since changeover occurred, and Hancock thought it adequate rest for the second surveillance team. He genuinely expected them to be up if not ready, but there was no audible response from the other side of that door, giving him cause for concern.

He knocked again.

'Wake up B-teamers,' chuckled Morgan. 'You missed the best part of the show by the way.'

Still no answer came and during the wait Hancock saw a flash of the ill-fated Daedalus team. Those poor souls had all taken their own lives partway through an assignment, guilt and fear no doubt the overriding reasons.

It was why Hancock now had to supervise in person and why this team had all been psyche evaluated prior to acceptance, but Hancock put little stock in such tests. As the wait drew on his fear grew, fear that he'd find a similar scene in the room beyond; another batch of very clean, orderly suicides all

A Hot Dose of Hell

tucked up in the beds of a sterile room.

Hancock had little doubt a second such occurrence would hinder his career. At the very least it'd be an embarrassment, one hard to live down. His relief at having avoided that was the sole reason he beamed so broadly when the door finally creaked open to reveal a dishevelled looking Herman.

'Morning boss,' said Herman, as he donned specs and blinked through them, the size of those bleary eyes dramatically reduced by thick lenses.

'Any news about my bonus?'

Out of the whole team this assignment had demanded the most from Herman, leaving him physically and emotionally exhausted. His short sleep, when it finally came, had been troubled by dreams of that addict's knife in his face, of that prostitute's casual cruelty, her words echoing in his head.

I thought that was why you pulled up. I thought you wanted to do a bit more than expose yourself, gettit?

Being a tech-op Herman had never experienced such a traumatic situation first-hand and although the thrill of that success initially brought him to laughter, the giddy sensation had faded fast, giving way to an intense anxiety he feared he might never overcome.

In hindsight he couldn't quite fathom how they'd talked him into the task, why he'd agreed to go along. They hadn't really explained, or perhaps even anticipated the risk on his part. The least they could do now he felt, was imburse him for future therapy bills.

And why not? It was all just taxpayers' money anyway.

'Your pay is under review,' said Hancock, speaking

quietly so as not to be heard by the team behind him, or the others stirring from their cots.

Herman's haunted gaze fell to the floor.

'I see.'

'Listen,' Hancock purred as he placed a hand on Herman's shoulder and in turn Herman summoned the effort to look up once more, his eyelids flickering nervously almost as if affected by the glare from Hancock's disingenuous smile.

'We don't underestimate the importance of what you achieved,' said Hancock, which was actually true. The field team, who were all ex-police and armed forces still carried that air. Had one of them stood in as "The Seller" it would've raised suspicion; the scum would've smelled the authority on the man and likely stayed away.

That hooker and her pimp certainly wouldn't have dared attempt a robbery and even though such a turn of events had been unplanned it was no less welcome, since it cut down the time and risk of making multiple sales.

Profit from those was never the goal. Only circulating the formula was, among the right kind of people of course.

'The payment is under review,' Hancock repeated, leaning in, 'because they're creating a standard rate for a dual role such as that, a rate you'd be entitled to in future assignments. Trust me, I'll ensure you receive ample reward for your work.'

Herman nodded once, inhaling deeply and for a moment it seemed he could go either way, as if he might blow up or breakdown. His next words were a trembling whisper, threatening the latter.

'It was just...hard,' he said. 'That guy put a knife in my face, and he *touched* me. You should've smelled him. He absolutely stank. I had to change clothes just because I'd been *near* him.'

'I can imagine,' said Hancock, whispering back to show empathy, giving a nod to portray understanding, compassion; techniques learned from a communication coach at a behavioural seminar the previous summer.

'Would you be glad to know he's dead now, Herman?'

A flicker of surprise registered on Herman's face at the question itself, as well as the information contained.

'What about the girl?' he asked. 'The prostitute?'
'Dead too.'

Herman absorbed that knowledge with a deep sigh, feeling strange about it, unsure of his emotions. He'd never been directly involved in anyone's death before. For him death, violence had always remained at a distance, a step removed, something viewed on a screen, and while the weight of it sank in, he couldn't help blinking, as though something had just invaded his eye.

'Okay?' said Hancock, his gaze searching Herman's bookish features and this scrutiny made Herman uncomfortable, self-conscious. He quickly moved the conversation on.

'How long from initial dose?' he asked, and Hancock checked his watch, a gleaming platinum Rolex.

'Approximately twenty hours.'
'Is that the longest?'

Hancock ducked the question. Then he literally pivoted, a hand gliding up Herman's back to give him the slightest nudge.

'You know, I understand it's been quite the

experience and with my personal thanks I'm happy for you to take the rest of today off, starting now.'

As further prompt he gave Herman's shoulder a parting pat, yet Herman hesitated to move, unsure whether he'd heard that right.

Confirmation arrived swiftly by way of Patel.

'See ya Herman,' he chirped, shortly echoed by Morgan and Poole. All three were now busy disconnecting cables, breaking down their workstations.

'Couldn't have done it without you mate,' added Poole and Herman received the compliment with an appreciative nod, taking the cue to wheel out his suitcase.

He muttered a goodbye of his own on the way to the door, all the while his conflicting feelings about the experience were becoming clearer, purer.

Above all, he was glad for it to be over, to be going home to his cat after three days away. But even though Roxy and her accomplice had ripped him off, threatened him, he couldn't ignore or suppress a sense of guilt at their passing.

This wasn't the level of guilt you might expect however, more how an average person might feel after they accidentally tread on a snail. The kind of guilt which arrives in a wave and fades just a few strides on.

In Herman's case it'd passed by the time he reached the small parking lot at the building's rear, overshadowed by sudden concern for the state of his car.

'Bastards,' he whined, surveying the scene. 'Dirty bastards.'

Overnight the trash had been completely ransacked by vermin, leaving a carpet of waste and scraps covering most of the asphalt. Some even sprinkled the array of vehicles there; high-end all, each belonging to members of Herman's team.

From where he stood Herman's car lay out of sight, parked a row behind, and he hastily set off in that direction, tiptoeing through the trash, occasionally lifting his case to spare its wheels from the filth.

Along the way he came across a dead pigeon, tiny chest torn open, most likely by a cat he assumed. The exposed innards looked like worms, red and stringy and as he circumvented these remains an intimidatingly large gull eyed him from its perch upon a toppled wheelie bin.

Herman didn't look close enough to notice the blood dripping from this gull's beak. He barely afforded a second glance, yet couldn't shake the uncanny sense it was assessing him, sizing him up.

'Haven't got any food,' he explained, as if to keep the gull pacified and he wheeled his case around Morgan's Audi to find his own car draped in trash, spattered with guano.

'Shit.'

That heavily modified Merc was Herman's pride and joy. Seeing it in such a state brought his blood to a boil. Prior to this, he'd naturally tuned out the squabble of gulls in the background, but now suddenly he became very aware of it, the jarring sound feeling eerily reminiscent to playground mockery endured decades before.

'Assholes,' he said, a curse repeated when he swept a takeaway box off his bonnet, peeled wet newspaper from the windscreen.

'Literal flying assholes, that's all you are.'

The Merc started with a roar and Herman revved aggressively in attempt to scare the gull on the bin.

Much to his annoyance this failed to have any effect and he pulled off at speed, still feeling the burn of that bird's impassive gaze long after it'd fallen from his rear-view mirror.

'Flyin' asshole.'

Herman wasn't paying attention and just before the next junction he had to brake sharply, screeching to a halt so that the vehicle's nose only just crossed the line.

He quickly realised how needless that was when he saw how empty the road lay in either direction. From there he went a quarter mile without seeing another car or pedestrian. Not a single straggler or slapper doing the walk of shame.

For all Herman knew this may have been typical for Sunday in Scarmouth, but to a Londoner like him it resembled a post-apocalyptic scene of stillness, a frame straight out of Mad Max, save the scavenging gulls crowding every bin.

Those damn birds were crowding other areas too. At a red light, he noticed a gaggle of them in a shop doorway attacking an unattended sleeping bag.

Probably some tramp's, he thought.

Probably food left inside.

Yet he failed to notice how the bag was moving of its own volition, seeming to react, to recoil from each peck. Only when it sprouted an arm did Herman realise there was a man inside and that it was him the gulls were going for.

'Jesus.'

Relentlessly, those sharp beaks stabbed at the bag; the shudder-inducing tap of bone audible even from where Herman sat. He couldn't quite believe what he was seeing. Notorious and maligned as they are, he'd never witnessed seagulls behaving in such a way before, never seen them attack a *person* with so much ferocity, such determination. It was only ever to steal chips or takeaway food, and any injuries were purely incidental.

But the way they were going at this tramp, it seemed as if *he* was food to them and no matter how much the man wriggled, how violently he kicked, they kept coming.

Peck-peck. Peck-peck.

All the while dark stains were appearing in multiple spots on the bag, and these were growing, spreading, merging by the second.

'HELP,' went the tramp, the tail of his cry a high-pitched shriek. 'GET EM ORRRF.'

The very instant the light turned green Herman revved so hard the rear wheels spun. Then he tore away, focus returning to the two-lane road ahead.

Once he'd put a few hundred yards between himself and those bloodthirsty gulls he snapped his phone into the dashboard holder to make a loudspeaker call.

'Come on, come on.'

Patel's voice answered on the third ring.

'Miss me already?'

'Patel listen,' panted Herman, adrenaline racing through his system, jumbling his speech. He had a clear point to make, a grim and terrifying theory based on the scene he'd just witnessed, only what came out was:

'The seagulls, they're acting weird. I've just seen them attacking a tramp.'

The other end fell silent.

'Patel?'

The phone's tiny speaker issued a crackle of static as the sky darkened; Herman had entered a tunnel.

'Patel?'

In the distance Herman could see natural light and sped toward it, desperate to reconnect on the other side. As soon as he emerged, he resumed his call of, 'Patel? Patel?' but there was still no reply. They'd lost connection completely.

'Fucksake, come on.'

For just a moment Herman took his eyes off the road to redial, then like a magnet his hand returned to the wheel upon a sudden impact in front. Shaken, he glanced up in time to see a flash of grey, white disappear, leaving streaks of blood and circular cracks in the windscreen glass.

Before Herman could take action the glass was struck again. Only this time he clearly saw the offending missile, saw its feathered wings spread wide, which prevented him spotting the six-car pile-up ahead.

'GET OFF,' Herman snarled and he hit the brakes, just a fraction too late to keep from ploughing into a stationary wreck.

BANG.

At over forty miles an hour the vehicles collided, sending the wreck rolling into the hard shoulder while Herman's Merc crawled to a gradual stop on the wrong side of the road.

Herman struggled to raise his head off the airbag, his nose and brow stinging where his specs had been embedded by the impact. Tinnitus rang hard through both ears like an alarm clock for his mind. Still, he could hear loud music coming from one of the other cars and someone screaming nearby, cries of pain.

Another voice called a name, over and over while a horn emitted a flat, constant honk.

Like a balloon Herman's airbag suddenly popped,

startling him, and as it deflated it revealed the seagull pressed to the windscreen, its beak now poking through a hole in the glass.

Herman first thought it dead until that beak moved, thrusting at his face, so close he could smell its rank breath.

Peck-peck.

Groggily Herman's head fell back, and he slowly raised a trembling hand, his muscles frustratingly sluggish, uncooperative. Meanwhile the bird kept coming, kept pushing, determined to somehow squeeze itself through that two-inch hole, no matter how much damage it suffered in the process, those white feathers turning red.

Rapid hail sounded overhead as more of its kind landed on the car's roof and Herman felt the suspension shift from the burden.

There had to be legions of them up there, he thought, with more still descending onto the car's rear and hood. A steady percussion of little flat feet. Some were soon peering in the windows, looking at him the same way as the gull on the bin, beaks intermittently tapping the glass, probing for weakness. They'd find it soon enough.

At last, Herman's hand reached the wheel, but only managed to fall upon it, utterly spent. There was no chance he could restart the engine. His other arm wouldn't move at all, and that beak was coming closer, closer, the hole in the glass getting wider and wider.

Peck-peck.

'No,' Herman croaked, voice hindered by something catching in his throat, the coppery tang of his own blood, and with his next breath he noticed a sharp pain streaking his chest.

Peck-peck.

That curved beak lay only inches away now and Herman had nothing left to fend it off. His body had grown cold, and he detected a wetness running down his neck.

It wasn't sweat.

Herman was dying and staring down that seagull's grotesque maw the very last thing he saw confirmed his unspoken fear, what he'd been trying to warn Patel about.

The gull's eyes weren't yellow as they should've been.

They were black.